A Latte Difficulty

The CafFUNated Mysteries

Book One A Caffeine Conundrum
Book Two A Cuppa Trouble

A Latte Difficulty

Book Three in the CafFUNated Mysteries

By

Angela Ruth Strong

Dedication

To my mom whose laughter is like sugar.
It makes life sweeter.

Acknowledgments

I got to go to a Christian writer's conference last month with no agenda but to hang out with the people I love in the writing world. We ate Tex-Mex and sandwiches on donuts and overpriced steak at an awards banquet. We dressed up like we were going to prom and walked down the River Walk and tried to break into the rooftop pool after hours. We prayed in the prayer room and encouraged beginning writers and plotted new novels. We lined up for Starbucks coffee A LOT and chatted until two in the morning.

So here's to my editor, my agent, my critique partners, my author and publicist friends, my readers, and my family who have laughed and cried with me along this journey. I thank God for you, and I can't wait to see what else the Author of Life has in store, because this life I'm living now was once nothing more than a dream. Know that if you are reading this, you are a beautiful part of my dream, and I hope I can be a part of yours.

Chapter One

"Black is a good color for coffee, not bridesmaid dresses."

Tandy Brandt turned away from the bride-to-be in order to hide her smile while grinding more nutty-scented coffee beans. She knew Marissa Alexander, a reformed Midwest beauty queen, would never use black as a wedding color, which made it all the more fun to suggest. "Black will be my wedding color," she declared.

"Ugh." Marissa pulled yet another wedding magazine out from under the counter at their shop, Caffeine Conundrum. For the last five months, she'd spent every free moment obsessing about her upcoming wedding.

Their shop was finally starting to clear out after a morning of pouring iced coffee and sweet tea. Customers trickled through the exit to the street for a parade that would kick off the weeklong Americana Festival leading to Independence Day.

Besides Greg St. James and Connor Thomas, who were at the shop to assist their girlfriends, only Randon, the local hipster millionaire, remained at a table, waiting for his order.

"Greg," Marissa addressed Tandy's childhood sweetheart with a huge sigh. "Please tell me you won't let Tandy make me wear a black dress when you two get married."

"Can we talk about this after there's an actual engagement?" Greg suggested, though it was hard to take him seriously when he was dressed like Abraham Lincoln. He tugged his fake beard low enough to sip from a straw then grimaced. "Though I can tell you that if I let Tandy dress me like this to hand out coupons during the parade for your Red, White, and Brew booth at the fair, then I'm not going to have much say in wedding planning."

Things were getting more serious between them, but there was no rush. Especially since Tandy would never want to overshadow Marissa's time as the bride-to-be.

Tandy grinned over her shoulder from where she filled the espresso machine with fresh grounds. "I didn't really think you'd wear that costume, Greg. I suggested it as a joke."

Greg stood taller and straightened the lapel on his long black suit jacket. "Oh, I don't joke about our 16th president. He's the reason I decided to become a lawyer in the first place."

Connor hid a smile by sipping from his mug. "You wish you were wearing a shirt like mine, don't you?" He puffed up his chest to better display the image of Captain America's shield screen-printed on the front of his t-shirt.

"So badly." Greg replaced his beard with a snap of elastic.

Marissa waved away her fiancé's interference. "Don't listen to him, Greg. You look fabulous and should really get some pictures of yourself in costume."

Tandy combined two shots of espresso with steamed coconut milk. "He's already been in your photobooth, Marissa."

Connor crossed his arms and leaned against the counter to face Greg. "I'd think after what happened to President Lincoln at Ford's Theatre, you'd want to avoid Booths."

"Not cool, Captain. Not cool."

While Connor was taking the Lincoln jokes too far, Marissa was taking the photobooth thing too far. Just because she'd gotten a good deal on renting the booth for her wedding reception in the fall by advertising it in their shop during Americana Week, that didn't mean she had to force everyone to use it.

Tandy grinned at her friends and left them to their banter so she could deliver Randon's latte. He'd ordered a hot beverage despite the fact the temperature was already into the 80s. The guy had also grown a full beard. Not the best way to keep cool during the summer.

She set his mug on the stainless-steel table with a clink. "Aren't you going outside for the parade?"

He didn't glance up from his laptop. "Negative."

For a know-it-all, he'd been unusually quiet today. Probably designing another phone app. One of these days she'd get him to make her one for their business where customers could pre-order drinks.

"Working on something important?" she asked.

"Always." This time he did glance up but only to make sure she wasn't looking at his computer screen when he angled it away from her.

Fine. If he didn't want to talk, she wouldn't waste her time. She rolled her eyes and turned back toward her friends, but they'd all disappeared.

A light flashed from inside the photobooth set up next to the stairs leading to the tea loft. Had all three of them crammed inside? Marissa's laughter spilled out. Yep.

Tandy changed directions and pulled back the photobooth curtain to get a peek. Marissa sat in the middle of the bench, wearing the Statue of Liberty crown and holding Lady Liberty's torch. She'd somehow gotten Connor to put on sunglasses and hold a sign on a stick that read "All American Dude." Greg, of course, was already in costume.

Grinning, Tandy tugged a little flag from a jar on the prop table and squeezed in to sit on Greg's lap.

The group grunted and shifted to make room for her while the camera snapped shots at the most awkward moments then flashed their images on the screen. The whole booth shook with Marissa's laughter.

Greg wrapped an arm around Tandy's waist to keep her from sliding to the floor. "This really isn't very presidential behavior."

Marissa wiped at her eyes. "But it's so fun. Aren't you glad we're renting this photobooth for our wedding, Connor?"

Connor shook his head but couldn't keep from smiling. "As fun as this is, we should probably head out to the parade or we'll miss the float I built for The Farmstead."

Tandy clicked her tongue. "I hate to tell you this, Marissa, but Randon isn't planning to leave the shop. We're not going to be able to close down."

Marissa frowned and pulled back the curtain to see for herself. "I'd kick him out, but I'm hoping we can get him to build us an app one of these days."

"Me too." Tandy arched an eyebrow. "Plus, I'm a little scared of him. Do you remember when he mentioned the Ohio Power outage like he had something to do with it?"

"I remember." Connor slid his glasses to the top of his head, messing up his messy do. "I've also been wondering if he's had anything to do with the new computer virus that everyone's talking about."

Marissa looked around the tiny space in confusion. "What virus?"

Greg stroked his beard. "That could be how he's making his millions."

Marissa turned to Tandy, eyebrows pinched. "He's making money off a virus?"

Connor wrapped an arm around her shoulders. "No.

Though if you don't know about the virus, you might be spending a little too much time planning our wedding."

Marissa held her hands wide, knocking Tandy in the face with her torch. "I only have three more months before the big day. I have to make sure nothing goes wrong."

"I know, I know." Connor humored her with a grin. "If you want to know about the virus, it's a form of ransomware. You've heard of ransomware, haven't you?"

"I've heard of a ransom."

"It's like that." Connor snapped and pointed. "Hackers hold all the information on your computer for ransom unless you pay them a fee to return it. It can really affect big businesses. Like Ohio Power for example."

Her eyes widened. "You think Randon is a hacker?"

Tandy lifted a shoulder. This wouldn't be the first time she'd suspected him of a crime. "When I took him coffee, he did turn his computer away from me so I couldn't see what was on his screen."

"Then we certainly shouldn't leave him alone." Greg cleared his throat. "We could watch the parade from the windows."

Tandy twisted to grin at him. "You just don't want to go outside in your costume."

"I don't blame you." Connor shifted his weight to stand without knocking anyone else off the bench. "But if I stay inside, the crowd on the sidewalk will block my view of my parents' float." He ducked out of the booth to give the rest of them room to move.

Tandy smoothed Greg's fuzzy beard. "And you're supposed to hand out our coupons."

Greg sighed and scooted her off his lap onto the bench next to Marissa so he could stand as well. "You're right. Both Abe and I are men of our word."

Tandy grinned up at him. "Thank you." He was normally as polished as Cary Grant, which made his ridiculous costume that much more endearing. "I'd come with you if I could, but one of us has to stay here to ensure Randon doesn't hack our laptop and hold Marissa's precious wedding plans for ransom."

Marissa shooed her away. "They're my wedding plans. I'll keep them safe. Plus, Greg needs you."

Greg nodded solemnly. "I do."

Tandy let herself be pulled away. She'd leave Marissa to her obsessive wedding planning.

Marissa waved goodbye then smiled at her image in the photobooth's computer screen. She'd earned herself more free time to plan her wedding, though, honestly, she'd been planning since she was a seven-year-old flower girl.

The bell over the door rang repeatedly, joining in with the music from the marching band outside and announcing her friends' exit. She didn't envy them at all. While they were going out into the crowds and heat, she got to stay in the cool and the quiet. Not to mention, having the whole photobooth to herself.

She removed Lady Liberty's crown from her head and set down the torch, as well. The next time she was in this booth, she'd be wearing a wedding dress, and all the photobooth strips would be taken home by guests as mementos of her big day. She twisted her long, blonde hair up to imagine how she might want to style it. Though Connor liked her hair down. She released it to cascade over her shoulders.

Should she make a strip of photos for Connor? She could

hold out the engagement ring for a closeup on one then blow him a kiss in another. Or she could spell out the word LOVE with her hands by forming one letter in each of the four photos taken. That would be cute.

She practiced her poses then reached for the button to start the countdown.

"Give me the file." A deep voice boomed through the room.

She froze in place. A shiver slid down her spine. Who was talking?

She leaned forward and pulled the curtain back a few inches. Across the shop, a man stood with his back to her in jeans and a white t-shirt, holding a gun pointed at Randon.

Marissa covered her mouth to keep from gasping aloud, but that didn't stop her heart from quivering.

Randon glared up at him. "How'd you find me?"

He knew the man? He knew what file the man wanted? Then why didn't he hand it over so he wouldn't get killed?

"I traced your computer location. What? You thought you'd be safe in this crowd?"

Randon snapped his laptop shut.

Marissa wanted to scream, *No, Randon! Your stupid apps are not worth dying for!* But then she might also get killed. Was there any way she could save them both?

She fumbled through her jean pockets then apron in search of her phone. All empty except for one of her "Save the Date" cards she'd been planning to give to Tandy. She must have left her cell with her magazines. If she didn't do something fast, she might not even make it to her own wedding.

"You won't get away with this," Randon growled.

The man laughed. It was a low and menacing sound that

would haunt Marissa's nightmares.

What else could she remember about this guy? Jeans and a white t-shirt weren't that memorable. If he killed Randon, how would she ever be able to describe him to Sheriff Griffin?

From the back, she could see the perpetrator had dark skin, but that wasn't unusual in the summer. What else?

There wasn't much hair on his head. He was either bald or had a buzz cut. And he seemed to be in pretty good shape. She'd guess six foot and 180 pounds—a little leaner than Connor. She needed more.

He lifted the gun. Hopefully it was only to make a threat that Randon would take very, very seriously. "Ironically, this crowd is what will allow me to get away with whatever I want. I could shoot you, and nobody would hear it over the bang of those drums."

As if on cue, a heavy drumbeat broke through the white noise of festivity.

Marissa tugged the curtain open a little farther to see the people on the street. Every back was turned her way. If she ran and screamed for help, she'd never make it. She could be shot and killed within feet of her friends as they obliviously sang Yankee Doodle, laughed at Shriners in little cars, and caught candy.

Randon lifted his hands as if being arrested by the cops. "How do I know that if I give you what you want, you'll let me go?"

That was such a good question. But not worth the risk of refusing to obey.

The gunman shook his head. Ooh, he had a mark on his neck. Like a tattoo.

Marissa narrowed her eyes to decipher its shape. She leaned sideways to get a more direct view. Her elbow bumped the front of the booth.

Had the gunman heard the thud over the sounds from outside? Her heart jumped to her throat as she waited. The man didn't even move. Whew, that was a close…

A flash lit up the photobooth.

Oh no. She'd bumped the button.

The gunman turned. His jaw hardened.

"Run, Marissa," Randon yelled as he splashed the contents of his coffee mug over the man's white shirt.

The gunman turned to retaliate.

Marissa charged up the staircase. It was closer than the front door, and that way she wouldn't have to pass the guy with the gun.

Her feet scrambled. Her arms pumped. Her pulse pounded louder and faster than the drums outside. She dared to look over her shoulder to see if she needed to duck bullets.

The man brought the butt of his gun down against Randon's head. Randon crumpled. The gunman jumped over his body and bolted toward the stairs.

Tingles shot down Marissa's arms and legs. She couldn't run fast enough. Feeling the pressure as if swimming upstream, she dodged ornate tables and chairs to reach the metal exit door.

She burst into the warmth of sunshine on the roof and the jovial tunes of a marching band below. It felt like breaking the surface when drowning—igniting a surge of hope mixed with the fear of being sucked back under.

She spun and faced off with the man who'd cleared the stairs and was close enough that she could make out not only his light green eyes but the symbol on his neck. Then with every millisecond stretched into a lifetime, she scooped the doorstop off the ground, slammed the door in his face, and jabbed the tiny triangle underneath the door.

The door rattled against his weight but held. Thank goodness they still had the doorstop from the last time Tandy had forgotten to take her crumpets out of the oven and they'd had to ventilate the building. Because of it, she'd survived. Though she didn't know if she could say the same for Randon.

Chapter Two

TANDY WAVED AT SUSAN ON THE float designed to resemble one of Joseph Cross's steamboats with two stories of white railing, two black smokestacks, and a giant red paddlewheel. It looked authentic, as did Susan's costume from the turn of the century. Her pink hair? Not so much.

But Randon would appreciate her hairstyle, as he did everything about her. Why hadn't he come outside to watch the parade if he knew his girlfriend was going to be in it?

Tandy glanced over her shoulder to see if he was even looking out the window. He wasn't sitting at his table anymore. Where'd he go?

"Tandy!" Someone called her name, though it was hard to hear over the music that blared from the parade. First the marching band, then the calliope music piped through speakers on the float.

She looked up and down the sidewalk. No faces turned her way. Even Greg was busy, handing out the flyers they'd made for the shop. Maybe she'd imagined it.

Connor tapped her shoulder. "Here comes my float," he yelled over the noise.

She nodded her acknowledgement of the green tractor that pulled a flatbed trailer. On the trailer sat a little red barn surrounded by bales of hay. The hay served as a fence to hold in actual farm animals.

He cupped his hands around his mouth like a megaphone. "Mom is taking the farm animals to the park to offer a petting zoo. I think that's really why Marissa didn't come out here. She's afraid of the goats."

Tandy nodded. She'd heard all about how the goats had eaten Marissa's favorite polka dot Converse.

"Tandy!" There it was again.

She frowned and looked around. Everyone else seemed to be watching kids toss candy from a float advertising the local church's Vacation Bible School. If she'd been watching, she would have been prepared for the piece that smacked her on the top of the head.

"Ow." She rubbed at the sting. "One of those kids must be a little league pitcher."

Connor squatted next to her then stood, holding Marissa's red patent leather flip flops. "You didn't get hit with candy. You got hit with one of these."

Tandy blinked. How did the kids get her business partner's shoes on their float? Hadn't Marissa been wearing those earlier?

"Tandy!" There it was again.

She looked up. Marissa waved like a maniac from the roof. She must have thrown the shoes to get Tandy's attention.

Tandy pointed Connor toward his fiancée. They both looked up to find Marissa motioning them toward the door of the shop. She was yelling something too, but a guy on the next float had a microphone on which he overrode her words with his recitation of the Declaration of Independence.

Tandy did her best to decipher. "It looks like Marissa wants us to watch the parade with her from the roof."

"That would actually be a good spot."

"And she'd be safer from farm animals."

Connor waved at Marissa as he took steps toward the entrance. "Are you coming, Tandy, or are you going to stay down here with Greg?"

Greg stood halfway down the sidewalk, fanning himself with the flyers. His suit and fake beard had to be hot in this burning sunshine. "I'll stay with—"

The door to the shop burst open. A man careened through, knocking Connor into her. Tandy grabbed a lamppost to stay upright, but Connor continued toward the ground, landing hard.

The guy in a white t-shirt shoved his way through the crowd. Such a jerk. And what had he even been doing in their shop? Did it have something to do with Marissa's mime show?

Tandy frowned through the window and caught sight of Randon's striped tank top crumpled on the floor with him in it. "Oh no."

Connor jumped to his feet and charged after the guy.

At least Tandy knew Marissa was okay.

Greg made his way toward her, glancing over his shoulder at Connor bolting through the crowd. "What's going on?"

Tandy's heart shuddered. "Someone attacked Randon in the shop. Go find Sheriff Griffin. I'm going to check on Marissa."

Greg whipped off his hat and beard, handing them to her along with the flyers before taking off down the street.

Tandy pushed through the door of her shop, leaving the festivities behind. She dropped everything in her hands onto a nearby table and grabbed the phone out of her back pocket to call for an ambulance. Randon lay as though lifeless, but she could see his belly rise and fall with every breath. He was alive.

The door to the roof clanked open in the loft above, and blinding light shone through. Marissa's silhouette appeared in the opening. "Tandy get up here with your phone. I can see which way the bad guy is going from this vantage point. I can direct Griffin."

Tandy jabbed at her phone and took the stairs two at a time.

Griffin answered in the middle of the first ring. "Tandy, Greg told me Randon was attacked in your shop. Are you okay?"

"Yes, but Randon's not." She raced through the door onto the roof and joined Marissa at the edge. With all the people below, she couldn't tell who she was supposed to be looking for. All she'd seen on the street was the back of a white t-shirt, which was what most of the men down there were wearing. "I'm going to hand the phone to Marissa. We're on the roof, and she can see which way Randon's attacker is going."

Hopefully Marissa got a better look at the guy.

Marissa scrambled for the phone, almost dropping it over the edge with her jitters. Her eyes stayed glued to the bald guy in the white shirt like she was playing the shell game. She couldn't let him get away with it.

"He's heading down the parade route. Fifth and Main Street."

A siren blared through the noise below. Red lights flashed on the white motorcycle where Griffin had previously cut off traffic.

The cop's voice sounded muffled, like he was speaking through an earpiece on his bike helmet. "Greg said Connor is chasing him. Is Connor still on him?"

Marissa watched as the perp darted across a corner and Connor kept going. Her heart skipped a beat with relief. As brave as Connor was, she didn't want him taking down a gunman on his own. "No. The bad guy turned down Fifth."

Griffin's motorcycle joined the parade, zipping past floats. The sea of spectators parted for him. "Which way?"

"The same way the parade circles." Though the parade had continued down to Fourth Street before turning, the gunman was still on the parade route, still surrounded by civilians. "Careful, he has a gun."

Tandy gasped. "He has a gun?"

Marissa covered the mouthpiece. "Yes. That's why I ran up here. Randon saved my life by dumping coffee on him." She uncovered the mouthpiece to guide Griffin again. "He's wearing a white shirt with coffee splashed on it. He's bald with a big tattoo on his neck. Tan. Green eyes. A little smaller than Connor."

Griffin's motorcycle sped toward Fifth Street.

"Turn right, and you'll see him. He's at the end of the block."

The man in white jogged to the corner, turned, and disappeared around a building and out of sight.

Griffin's motorcycle turned down the open street. "I don't see him, Marissa."

Blood pumped through her veins like she was the one in hot pursuit. "I can't see him now either. But you're so close. Turn left on Park Place, and you'll have him."

The marching band led the parade through the intersection in front of Griffin. Even from this distance she could still feel the boom of the drums reverberate through her chest.

"What's that? I can't hear you."

"You have him," she yelled. "You have him."

He had to. Before the gunman disappeared for good.

Griffin swung a leg off his motorcycle and charged

downstream against the flow of the parade. Then he too vanished from view behind the wall of a building.

Tandy clutched her arm. "Does he have him?"

Griffin's breath puffed loudly in her ear. She pictured him running after the bad guy, gun in hand, helmet still on his head.

"Do you have him?" she asked.

"I see a guy with a tattoo on his neck. But he's not wearing a shirt."

Marissa gritted her teeth. Had the gunman taken off his shirt, or had he gotten away? "What's the tattoo look like?"

"It's a dollar sign. No. Wait. It looks like a dollar sign, but with the letter B instead of an S."

Marissa rose onto the tiptoes of her bare feet. "Is he bald?"

"Yes."

"That's him." Because what were the chances another bald guy with such a tattoo was in their tiny town on the exact same street at the exact same time? The only neck tattoo she'd ever seen in town was the image of three crosses, and it belonged to the youth pastor.

"I'll arrest him, but you'll have to I.D. him."

"Yes." She wanted him behind bars.

"Stop. Grace Springs PD. You're under arrest."

Marissa pulled Tandy closer, gripping her arm in return.

"What? What's happening?" Tandy asked.

Marissa blew out her breath, lowered the phone, and clicked it to speaker. They both listened to Griffin recite the Miranda warning.

She handed the phone back to its rightful owner, fingers still trembling. "At least he can't hurt anyone else now."

Tandy ended the call and stuffed the phone in her pocket. "Are you hurt?"

Marissa shook her head. "Did you see Randon when you came in? Is he…is he…?"

"He's alive."

Thank you, Jesus. She wasn't the hipster's biggest fan, and he'd probably done something shady to get himself into this situation, but he'd also risked his life to save hers. He wasn't all bad.

More sirens blared. They looked down to see an ambulance pulling up like the grand finale to the parade. Connor or Greg must have called them.

Two EMTs climbed out, laden down with equipment. Passersby slowed to watch. A pink-haired southern belle emerged from the crowd, looking as confused as Marissa had felt. "Susan," she said.

Tandy closed her eyes. "First her uncle, now this."

"I better brew some tea."

They made their way back inside, through the loft, down to the coffee bar. While the EMTs approached Randon swiftly and efficiently, Susan gasped upon entry. She flung herself on Randon's unconscious body, her full skirt puffing around her. Sobs racked her torso and the big floppy hat on her head fell to the floor.

Marissa swallowed the lump in her throat that formed when she pictured herself in Susan's shoes. Had that been Connor lying on the ground, she'd be a mess.

One of the EMTs pulled Susan away so they could continue checking Randon's vitals. Tandy took the man's place, an arm around Susan's shoulder.

"Oh, honey." Marissa poured steaming water from the kettle over an infuser of chamomile then crossed the room to offer it to the grieving girlfriend. "It could have been so much worse. Randon could have been shot."

"Shot?" Susan acted like she didn't even see the tea

offered, which was surprising with how wide her eyes had gotten.

Tandy pressed her lips together and tilted her head. "I don't think you're helping, Marissa."

Marissa put herself in Susan's shoes again. Yeah, telling her that the man she loved had almost been shot might not come across as soothing. "Oh, he was so brave. When the bad guy realized I was here, he turned the gun on me. Randon splashed him with coffee so I could get away."

More tears rained from Susan's dark eyes. "He sacrificed his life for yours?"

"No." Tandy stepped in. "Randon is going to live. He's in good hands now."

Ah...*those* would probably have been the right words to say.

More EMTs rolled in a gurney.

Susan pressed the back of a hand to her mouth to hold in the sobs.

The EMT who'd held her earlier stood to face them. "He's stable, but he's not responding. We're going to get him to the hospital where they can better treat him. Would you like a ride, miss?"

Susan nodded but stayed in place as if afraid of what the hospital might hold.

Marissa set the tea down so she could take her hand. She passed the poor girl off to the emergency workers. "Don't worry. Sheriff Griffin arrested the guy who did this, and I'm going to ID him. He's going to jail for a long, long time."

Susan broke down again, and the EMT had to put an arm around her to usher her out.

Tandy shook her head. "I can't imagine."

"I don't have to. I was there." Marissa picked up the cup of chamomile she'd offered Susan and sipped for herself. Her insides were still too jittery to think straight, and the soothing liquid might help calm her nerves.

Connor pushed through the door, Marissa's red flip flops in his hands. He didn't even take time to let them go before wrapping her in his arms. It was a good thing she'd finished the tea already, otherwise the perp wouldn't be the only one with caffeine on his clothing.

"I shouldn't have left you in here alone with the door unlocked."

She hugged him back, appreciating his protective side. "I'm okay now."

He gripped her shoulders along with her shoes that he must have picked up outside and held her at arm's length. He studied her with a flicker of fear in his gray eyes. "But what if something had happened to you?"

The bell over the door rang, announcing Greg's return. "What did happen?"

That was a question she had an answer for. "The gunman wanted a file from Randon. Randon said no and closed his computer."

She pointed to Randon's table as evidence. Except there was no computer. Maybe it was a different table.

Marissa scanned the surrounding tables. All empty.

Greg looked with her. "There's no computer."

Her heart dropped. "The gunman must have taken it with him. Griffin will have seized it in the arrest."

The bell over the door rang again. Griffin stepped inside and crossed his arms. "I caught a guy, but I'm not sure it's the right guy."

Marissa took her shoes from Connor, dropped them to the floor, and slid her toes through the slots. She needed to find firm footing to have this conversation. "He has the tattoo with the B and the lines running through it?"

Greg stroked his chin as if he was still wearing the Abe Lincoln beard. "A bitcoin tattoo?" Whatever that meant.

"Yes." Griffin nodded. "I'd thought that's what that was."

Connor leaned toward her ear to answer her question before she even asked. "A bitcoin is cyber money that's transacted online. It's how hackers are paid off for returning information they stole through viruses."

"Oh..." The guy had to be involved with Randon then. "If he had the tattoo, then why don't you think he's the right guy?"

"No evidence." Griffin huffed. "No shirt. No gun."

"No laptop?" asked Tandy.

Griffin lowered his eyebrows. "No laptop."

Connor put an arm around Marissa's shoulders. "Then who is he? And why is he here? I've never seen a guy with a tattoo like that in town before."

Griffin rubbed a hand over his head. "He's Cash Hudson, a former Marine come to town for the pancake breakfast to honor veterans."

Tandy arched an eyebrow at her boyfriend.

Greg grimaced. "Then he probably owns guns even if he didn't have one on him when you caught him."

"We'll be scouring the area, but if we don't find anything..." Griffin shrugged.

Marissa cringed. "Then there's nothing to go on but my word that he's the one who attacked Randon."

Chapter Three

After giving her statement, Marissa left the shop with Sheriff Griffin so she could go to the police department and identify Cash Hudson. As small as their town was, Griffin served as both sheriff and police chief. It wasn't long ago that he'd been a fresh-faced deputy who she still remembered as the little boy she used to babysit, but with all the crime that had recently come to their community, he'd been forced to mature beyond his years.

Unfortunately, Marissa still didn't feel completely safe having him protect her as she faced the guy who'd tried to kill her. If only Tandy hadn't had to stay at the shop and Connor hadn't had to go help his mom with the shoe-chewing farm animals.

"Cash won't be able to see me, will he?" she asked. Would he recognize her if he did? She'd been running with her back to him. All he'd likely recognize was her long, blonde hair. If not for her upcoming wedding, she'd be tempted to chop it off as a disguise.

"No. He'll be on the mirrored side of a one-way mirror."

Marissa bit her lip. Had Randon said her name in front of him at the coffee shop? "Will he know my name? Will it be in the newspaper or anything?"

Griffin parked in front of the two-story brick building and opened the door for her like a limo driver. "I don't know if it will be reported, but since you are the blonde owner of Caffeine Conundrum, it wouldn't be hard to figure out."

Chills shivered down Marissa's spine despite the

embrace of warm sunshine as she stepped onto the sidewalk. "If you caught the right guy and I identify him, he'll stay in jail until his trial, right?"

"I doubt Judge McMinn would grant bail with one of his alleged victims in the hospital."

That was comforting, at least. "Here's hoping you caught the right guy."

"I caught the guy you told me to." Griffin led her inside the musty scented building and had her wait by Kristin at the front desk while he checked in with his new deputy.

Marissa focused on breathing slowly in an attempt to calm her nerves. She'd had her life threatened before, but she'd never been alone in her troubles. She closed her eyes and prayed for courage, justice, and a quick recovery for Randon.

The tapping sound of Kristin's acrylic nails against the desk interrupted her thoughts. She peeked up to find the bleached blonde receptionist leaning forward over her desk as if impatient for the latest gossip. "Your wedding coming up?"

There had been an attempt on Marissa's life, and this was the latest gossip? "Yeah. Dress fitting tomorrow."

"You're so lucky. Connor is the most eligible bachelor out there. Or he was, I should say."

Marissa sighed. She was lucky to still be alive for the upcoming ceremony. "Yeah."

Kristin continued to stare, which was not helping Marissa's edginess. "I heard Randon Evans is in a coma."

Marissa twisted her fingers together. She'd stop by the hospital after this to check on him. "Hopefully not for long. Then he can help identify the guy who was…"

A bald head appeared in the hallway.

Marissa's heart rate lurched. She stumbled backwards

and gripped a chair for balance. Adrenaline surged through her like a triple shot espresso. She grabbed a stapler off the desk to use in self-defense.

Why was the gunman out here? Shouldn't he at least be handcuffed? Had he hurt Griffin and gotten away?

The man's head turned. Brown eyes met hers. Brown, not green. Though just as penetrating.

This man set a hat on his head. It resembled the one worn by Smokey the Bear but with a gold star on the front. The collar to his uniform hid his neck, but it was the kind of uniform worn by law enforcement.

She was safe.

Kristin tugged her stapler free from Marissa's grip and returned it to her desk. Some weapon. "Meet Deputy Adrian Romero."

Marissa clutched her fingers together again. Hopefully nobody had noticed her jumpiness.

Deputy Romero strode forward and reached for her hand.

Oh, yeah. She should shake. She squeezed his rough palm tightly in hopes that he couldn't feel her tremble. "You must be new here," she said.

She hadn't seen him around town that she could remember. Or maybe she had, and she simply didn't remember because she hadn't had a reason to fear bald men until now.

"I transferred in." That told her nothing. Where did he transfer from? Did his dark skin come from his heritage? Did he own green contact lenses?

She shook the crazy thought out of her head to trail after him down a hallway. She assumed he wanted her to follow from the curt tilt of his head, though he didn't actually say so. He waited at a door for her to enter first.

She eyed him again then peeked into a dim, dusty room with little furniture. Of course, had it been decorated for high tea, she wouldn't have even noticed. All her attention focused through a window into another room where half a dozen men milled about.

Her gaze zeroed in on a black neck tattoo. It was the same one she'd seen before.

The guy with the tattoo leaned against a wall and rubbed his head like he didn't have a care in the world. If this was the guy Griffin claimed to have caught shirtless, someone had since given him another shirt.

How could he be so nonchalant after attempting murder? Was it part of his military training? Or was he a psychopath?

She saw the deputy enter the other room before she even realized he'd left her alone. He lined up the men. They were all bald and had dark skin, though their heights and weight varied. Only one of them had the tattoo.

Footsteps tapped behind her.

She whirled and grabbed a mop from the corner.

Griffin stood there, thumbs hooked on his belt. "I know this place is a little dirty, but try to focus, Marissa."

At least she hadn't whacked the sheriff over the head. She set her makeshift weapon down before Griffin realized she was prepared to use it like a bo staff. "Sorry."

Griffin planted himself next to her and gazed into the other room. "Do you recognize any of these men?"

Without a word, Deputy Romero pointed for the men to line up along the far wall.

Marissa studied them all. "Is number three the guy you caught downtown? Cash Hudson?"

Griffin crossed his arms. "Is he the man who came after you?"

"I recognize his tattoo." Was there a possibility she could

ID the wrong man? Then it would be all her fault that a killer was set free and an innocent man was sent to jail. "But I can't really see the color of his eyes from here."

Griffin leaned over a slim microphone in the wall that she hadn't noticed before. "Number one, please step toward the mirror."

The first guy crossed the room to come face to face with her. He had facial hair that could not possibly have grown in the span of an hour.

"Not him."

"Number two, step forward," Griffin barked.

The first guy traded places with a second. This one had green eyes, but his ears stuck out. And he had a pointy chin. He didn't look nearly as menacing as the man who'd turned a gun on her.

"No."

"Number three?"

The man with the neck tattoo stepped forward, his green eyes rolling as if his presence here was ridiculous. But then he lowered his gaze toward the glass like he was looking straight at her and mocking her authority as a witness.

Her skin burned in righteous indignation—fear manifested in anger.

The man crossed his light green eyes then snickered at his own sense of humor.

The contents of her stomach roiled at the idea he could make light of attempted murder. She might be sick. "That's him."

Griffin nodded. "Number three, say the following phrase: Give me the files." That was one of the phrases she'd overheard from the photobooth.

The sharp angles of the man's face hardened for an instant, but then he lifted his chin as if to gaze down his nose in challenge. "Give me the files," he said in a monotone of boredom.

Griffin looked at her. "Does that sound like him?"

"I'm pretty sure." She wanted to say yes. Even if the guy wasn't the gunman, he should be imprisoned for his arrogance alone. "Have him say something else. Like, 'I'm guilty of pistol-whipping a man and chasing a woman with a gun, but, despite her reputation for clumsiness, she was still faster than me.'"

Griffin cocked his head and blinked slowly. "Or…" He turned back to the microphone. "Say: I traced your computer location."

The man rubbed his pointy cheekbone. "I didn't even know you could do that."

What a liar. Did he really think being difficult would make him less of a suspect?

"Say it," Griffin barked.

The suspect shrugged. "I traced your IP address."

Griffin hadn't said "IP address." Marissa looked at Griffin to see if the slip could be used as evidence. Griffin smirked with success. They both knew they had the right guy. Now they had to prove it.

Tandy pulled her hot hair off her neck and twisted it into a ponytail on the top of her head. Working without Marissa was twice as hard, though it seemed like customers had cared more about hearing what happened to Randon than about ordering a drink. She was so ready to flip their "open" sign to "closed."

The bell chimed over the door, signaling the entrance of another customer, and she did her best not to groan. She needed to go home and pick up Cocoa for his competition in the Star-Spangled Pet Competition. Never before had she willingly dressed her Pomeranian in people clothes, but moving to the small town was starting to have an effect on her.

"Tandy, are you okay?" asked Billie, the older Asian woman who ran the antique store from across the street.

Tension drained from Tandy's shoulders. She didn't mind a visit from the lady she considered a mentor. "I was watching the parade when Randon was attacked, but they caught him. Marissa is identifying him at the police station now."

Billie held a hand over her heart. "Thank you, Jesus."

Joseph Cross stood next to her, putting the suit in suitor. Had Tandy not known the silver-haired tycoon from past experience, she would have assumed his getup had to be a costume much like Greg's. But no. The man was always prepared in case paparazzi needed to snap his photo for the cover of GQ. How was he not drenched in sweat?

The gentleman cleared his throat. "Do we know why Randon was attacked?"

Tandy wiped a cloth over the counter. If these guys weren't going to order drinks, she could clean up now. "Randon wouldn't give him a file he wanted. The gunman ended up taking his whole computer."

Cross stroked his well-trimmed whiskers. "Hmm…"

Tandy stopped her wiping to study him closer. "What do you know?"

"You can tell her, dear." Billie rubbed his back. "It could help this case."

Tandy's eyes widened. How could the businessman possibly be involved?

He grimaced. "About a month ago, a hacker installed

ransomware into my company computers."

Tandy stood up straighter. This couldn't be a coincidence.

"I paid the fee to get it back because I needed to access information to keep business running, but I hired an investigator to try to track down the hacker."

Tandy's heartbeat screeched to a stop. The crime could have been happening right there in Caffeine Conundrum. Had she seen Cross's investigator? Had he pumped her for information without her realizing it? If she'd been asked directly about who she would suspect of the crime, she would have pointed a finger at Randon as the only one in the area who was capable. And he also had the history of taking down Ohio Power. Was that why he'd been attacked? "What did your investigator find?"

"Nothing concrete yet. Though I suspect if a lot of local businesses were hit by this cybercrime, and someone else discovered Randon was involved, they might retaliate by targeting him directly."

It made sense. Except for one thing. "The man who attacked Randon isn't local. And he's not a business owner. He's a military veteran."

Cross stuffed his hands in his pockets. "Then the attacker has experience in tactical maneuvers and might have been hired for the job."

Tandy blew out her breath. "A hitman?" That meant whoever hired him was still on the loose.

Cross nodded. "Hopefully my consultant will dig up some proof, so the prosecutor has a motive to pin on the attacker."

That would only help if Cross went to the police. "Does Griffin know about this at all?"

Cross laughed like she'd told a joke.

Billie patted his back again. "No need to be impolite, dear. It's a valid question."

"Sorry." Cross took a deep breath. "Griffin isn't the stealthiest investigator, and I didn't want Randon to be tipped off that I'm onto him."

Tandy quirked her lips. Cross didn't have to worry about Randon being tipped off anymore.

Billie jumped in. "Of course, we're worried about him."

"Of course." Cross's eyes darted away.

"No matter what he's done, we don't want him to be injured." Billie might not be speaking for the both of them, but hopefully Cross let her soft heart make him a better person.

Billie's influence had already made Tandy a better person. She waited for Cross to look at her again. "Randon risked his life to save Marissa. She might not be alive if not for him." The thought threatened to squeeze her throat shut.

Billie gasped.

Cross nodded in acknowledgement. "Well then, I'm thankful for that."

"Poor Marissa. That had to be terrifying." Billie adjusted her red-framed glasses and looked up at her beau as if expecting to see him tear up alongside her.

Tandy eyed the older man one more time. He didn't seem any more remorseful than when they'd first entered, but he wouldn't have been the one to hire Cash Hudson, would he?

Chapter Four

TANDY READJUSTED THE STAR-SPANGLED BANDANA around her fluffy little dog's neck and adjusted the sunglasses on his snout. Too bad Greg had work to do to make up for helping them at the parade earlier and wouldn't be able to see Cocoa in costume. She'd better take a picture of him now while she could before her dog figured out how to escape the getup. She pulled out her phone and squatted to frame the white park gazebo in the background.

"I see someone has changed her mind about dressing animals up in people clothes. You might start to fit in our small town after all."

Tandy glanced over her shoulder to find Connor with his black lab, Ranger. Or should she say, Connor and Wyatt Earp? His dog had on a cowboy costume, complete with hat, chaps, and sheriff's badge. If one looked at him from the front, he appeared to be a person with a dog face.

She clicked her tongue in mock disapproval. Though now that she was seeing how seriously pet owners took this competition, she was the one who didn't stand a chance at winning a trophy. "Cocoa looks like Joe Cool. As for Ranger, I'm not even sure what his costume has to do with Independence Day."

Connor pointed to the sheriff's badge. "He's star-spangled."

"With that lone star, the only one in competition with him is Griffin."

Connor crossed his arms. "Ranger could beat Griffin at

sniffing out clues with one of his fake costume arms tied behind his back."

A throat cleared. Tandy spotted Griffin and Marissa strolling up behind Connor before he turned around.

"Nice to know you appreciate all this hard work I do to keep our town safe, Thomas."

Connor laughed at himself and their good-natured rivalry before turning serious. "You know I do. Especially when it involves arresting the man who pulled a gun on my fiancée. Did you identify him, hon?"

Marissa's smile didn't light up her face in its usual way. "Yes. I hope that's enough to send him to jail for good."

Connor wrapped an arm around her shoulders, and Ranger licked her toes. She wasn't alone in this, and she quite possibly wasn't the only witness they had anymore either.

"Sheriff." Tandy picked up Cocoa's sunglasses from where he'd knocked them into the grass. She'd worry about them later. "Joseph Cross came into my shop earlier and mentioned that his company had recently been attacked by ransomware. He assumed Randon was involved and hired a private investigator. He thinks that perhaps someone else might have hired Cash Hudson as a hitman for revenge."

Griffin looped his thumbs on his belt and narrowed his eyes. "Why didn't Cross come to me? That's kind of suspicious."

Oh, boy. Tandy didn't want Griffin wasting his time investigating Cross, but she also didn't want to give the real reason Cross hadn't gone to their local law enforcement. The Sheriff was starting to earn respect in town, and the truth could affect his confidence. "Uh…"

A microphone screeched with feedback. Mayor Kensington tapped on it from his position in the gazebo. "Welcome to the nineteenth annual Star-Spangled Pet

Costume Competition!"

The crowd cheered. Dogs barked. Griffin continued to wait for an answer to his question.

The mayor cleared his throat. "I'd like to begin by inviting all our cute contestants up on stage."

Tandy never imagined she'd be so happy to have Cocoa in a costume contest. She dropped to one knee to stick Cocoa's glasses back on him. "Gotta go. We can talk about this later."

Griffin shook his head. "Is this really your priority?"

Tandy stood and let Cocoa prance ahead of her proudly, tongue hanging out of his mouth. "If we win, it's good publicity for Caffeine Conundrum. And we're probably going to need all the good publicity we can get with the number of crimes that have been taking place there."

Marissa clapped as they passed her. "Go, Cocoa."

Connor followed behind with Ranger.

"Go, Ranger!" Marissa cheered.

Tandy clicked her tongue as Marissa fell in step behind them. "You can't cheer for both of us, Marissa. You need to cheer for the dog that will benefit our business."

Marissa walked her to the gazebo steps, though with that dazed expression, she wasn't focused on the competition. "You really think someone hired Cash Hudson as a hitman? That's so scary."

Tandy took a deep breath and climbed the steps. Nervous energy buzzed through her, and it wasn't from stage fright. "I don't know, but if so, at least he's behind bars."

Marissa remained on the grass, but Connor climbed up after Tandy to join six other dogs in costume. He'd been right about Cocoa's costume not being able to compete. There was a large white dog actually painted with red stripes and blue stars, a chihuahua wearing a shiny flag like a cape, a wiener dog in a hot dog costume, a pug in a sequined tie, a Husky dressed like Uncle Sam, and a cocker spaniel in a red, white, and blue tutu.

The owner of the ballerina contestant looked Tandy in the eye as she took her place next to him. He appeared to be in his mid-40s with the appearance of someone who used to be attractive before living a hard life, but it was his intense eye contact that made Tandy do a double take. There was nothing extraordinary about the shape or color of his eyes. They were narrow and blue-gray with feathery eyebrows that lightened enough on the outside that they seemed to disappear. But he watched life around him as if he hadn't yet remembered he was Jason Bourne.

"Hi," she greeted, hoping he'd take his intense scrutiny elsewhere.

"Hi," he said with some kind of an accent. Maybe he wasn't Jason but a spy from another country.

He looked at her a little bit longer like he expected her to say something else, then he focused his attention on Mayor Kensington. Tandy turned toward the Mayor, as well.

"When I call your dog's name, please step forward, turn in a circle, and take a bow."

Tandy watched the first couple of contestants do their thing. The white dog circled too quickly, wrapping up his owner with the leash. The chihuahua yapped at the audience instead of turning. If the contest were judged on performance as well as costume, Cocoa might have a chance.

She looked down at him, sitting tall by her feet. Unfortunately, his sunglasses sat on the ground by his paws. Should she put them back on now or wait until it was their turn?

"And heeere's Sheila!" Mayor Kensington announced like they were on a game show.

The dog in the tutu tugged to pull her owner forward. Sheila was kind of an unexpected name for a dog. Especially for a dog belonging to a government operative.

Shelia turned in a perfect circle. The guy tipped forward in a bow. The crowd applauded.

As he stood, his keys slipped from his pocket and clanged to the ground. He didn't seem to notice over the noise, but Sheila did. She retrieved them and nudged his hand to give them back. The crowd went wild.

Tandy smirked. That seemed a little too rehearsed.

Too bad she and Cocoa hadn't come up with something else to add to their performance. Oh, darn. She hadn't even put his sunglasses back on yet.

Dropping into a squat, she readjusted Cocoa's costume. "You ready, buddy?"

He licked her hand.

Mayor Kensington motioned her way. "Here we have Cocoa!"

Tandy stood and went through the motions. The crowd cheered but not as loudly as they had for Sheila. Where was Marissa's cheerleading experience when Tandy needed it?

She returned to her spot and found Marissa at the back of the audience, not even looking their way when Connor stepped forward with Ranger. Rather, her arms gesticulated wildly as she spoke with Griffin. Was there a new development in the case or was Marissa simply upset over something silly like wedding flowers?

Connor returned to his spot, though he looked over his shoulder at Marissa, probably wondering the same thing. He finally glanced at Tandy, concern dampening his gaze.

"I wish I could read lips," she said.

"I can read lips," the man next to her volunteered with his Eastern European take on English, though if he could read lips, perhaps his accent was actually from being deaf. Had he also read her lips?

Tandy arched her eyebrows. Could she trust the guy? Might as well test him out while Mayor Kensington made a big deal of thanking their sponsors.

She pointed at Marissa and the Sheriff. "What are they saying?"

The guy eyed her, his expression cloudy as if maybe she was the one who couldn't be trusted for spying on a police officer. But rather than question her intentions aloud, he looked across the crowd to Marissa.

Connor leaned around Tandy so the man could see his lips when he asked a question of his own. "Is she okay?"

The man didn't seem to realize Connor was speaking to him, but his dog nudged his hand to let him know. The man looked down to find the dog looking at Connor. He followed the dog's gaze.

Connor repeated his question. "Is she okay?"

The man glanced out at Marissa again. "I think she's okay. But she's upset to find out about an attempted murder at the hospital."

Tandy gasped. She turned bulging eyes on Connor to see if they were thinking the same thing.

Connor lifted his chin, like he was ready for a fight.

The man eyed them both. "Do you guys know who she's talking about? She seems to think it was random."

"Not random." Tandy's heart hammered. "Randon."

Connor charged off the end of the stage, Ranger leaping next to him.

Tandy followed, pounding down the stairs. If there was someone out there still trying to kill Randon, then Marissa wouldn't be safe either.

"And now the results..." The booming voice over the

loudspeaker broke off at their commotion. "Well, uh, it looks like two of our contestants are dropping out."

Tandy would be getting publicity from the contest, but it wasn't going to be the good kind. Not that a costume contest compared to Randon's life. But if the deaf dude had read Marissa's lips correctly, she'd said *attempted* murder. Which meant Randon was still alive. For now.

"This means..." Mayor Kensington proclaimed. "The winner is Sheila!"

Tandy scooped Cocoa into her arms so she could keep up with Connor and his larger dog's strides. She looked back to see Sheila's crowning moment only to find the dog's owner staring after them as if wanting to read more lips and find out what was going on.

She waved him towards Mayor Kensington. If he didn't know who Randon was, there was no reason for him to get involved. He'd be better off enjoying the Americana Festival, while the rest of them focused on finding a killer. Unless the guy was really CIA or something.

Marissa frantically scanned their surroundings. "Did your deputy release Cash Hudson?" she demanded.

Who else would have tried to murder Randon? If there was a second killer out there, she still wouldn't be safe even with Cash in jail.

"Of course he didn't release Cash," Griffin argued.

"Did you ask him? Did you double check? The guy was creepily quiet at your station."

"Creepily?"

Why was Griffin arguing with her? There was a murderer out there, and his job was to catch them, which would mean ruling out who he could.

If Cash wasn't ruled out, he could be anywhere. He could be at the Americana Festival with them. He could be watching her. He could be the guy walking around in the bald eagle costume.

She narrowed her eyes at the eagle, ready to run if he took a step in her direction.

Griffin huffed. "You think Deputy Romero is in on this now?"

Marissa glared at the eagle. "You never know. That's why you need to ask."

"Fine." Griffin pinched the walkie-talkie receiver attached to his lapel. "Griffin to Romero. Over."

The eagle flapped a wing and headed her way.

Marissa pivoted on the ball of her foot and ran straight into a solid chest. The man grabbed her upper arms and held her in place.

Oh no. The eagle had an accomplice.

She took a deep breath, ready to scream *fire!* That's what she'd always heard you were supposed to scream instead of *help* when you were getting attacked. Because people would look for fire.

But her inhale carried with it the scent of sawdust. She knew that smell. Her eyes shot up to Connor's chiseled features and her muscles sagged with her exhale.

Ranger's tongue slathered a wet patch along her calf.

She felt safer with him there, but Connor's mom had been working on Ranger's costume for a year. "Why are you not on stage?"

Tandy jogged up beside them, her little dog chillin' in her arms. "We heard about Randon. Did they catch the killer?"

Marissa glanced over her shoulder at the bald eagle. He'd taken off the mascot head to reveal himself to be Troy, her ex from the fire department. That's why he'd waved. Good thing she hadn't yelled "fire!" Probably could have gotten her into real trouble.

At least now his wife and baby had shown up to distract him. Otherwise she'd be stuck explaining that she'd mistaken him for a hitman. His wife sent her a dirty look as if she knew.

Anyway… "I think the deputy let Cash out of jail. There was something I didn't like about that guy."

Connor hugged her close. "What didn't you like about him, hon?"

Griffin joined their circle. "He's creepily quiet."

Tandy pursed her lips. "Creepily?"

"Yes. It's a word." Marissa pushed away from Connor's chest to face the sheriff. "Did you find out if he released Cash?"

Griffin crossed his arms. "He didn't."

"Or so he says."

Griffin rolled his eyes sideways to look at Connor and Tandy. "What I want to know is how you two heard about Randon."

Marissa frowned at her friends. That was a good question.

Tandy pointed to the stage where the winning pet owner held a trophy overhead in victory. The guy's dog looked a little like Lady from Lady and the Tramp except she was wearing a tutu. As much as Marissa liked tutus, she wouldn't have picked the costume over Ranger's sheriff's ensemble or even Cocoa's crooked shades.

"He reads lips," Tandy said. "We asked him to read yours."

Marissa blinked. Speaking of creepily…

"Yeah. Well." Griffin shot a curious but quick glance at

the contest winner. "I've got to get to the hospital."

Marissa grabbed Connor's hand and pulled him after the sheriff. She needed to know what Griffin found out. Needed to know if she should still be worried someone might also come after her.

"We're going too."

Griffin turned around and marched right back to face her. "As much as I would love your opinions on which suspect is the creepiest…"

Tandy stepped between them. "We're going to the hospital to support Susan."

"That's right." Marissa nodded. It was both a good excuse as well as an important role. "She has nobody else."

Marissa had tried to put herself in Susan's shoes earlier, but now she didn't even want to. She didn't want to feel the emotions of having her boyfriend almost killed twice in one day. The important thing was that Randon was still alive. And they were going to help keep him that way.

Chapter Five

Tandy eyed the hospital. Memories of her own near-death experience at Valentine's constricted her lungs, but she forced herself to breathe slowly and think about the current situation. The one where she wasn't in any danger.

"Tandy," Connor called from behind.

She glanced over her shoulder. She wanted to get this over with, and she didn't like that he was slowing down the process. "What?"

He nodded toward her death grip on Cocoa. "I don't think you're supposed to take dogs inside the hospital."

She looked down at the pup and registered his soft fur beneath her touch like a security blanket. He looked up at her with innocent and trusting eyes. If only all people were as honest as dogs.

Connor walked Ranger forward and held out a hand for her leash. "I'll watch these guys out here."

Tandy pouted for a moment. Of all the places where dogs should be allowed, hospitals should be at the top of the list. Animals were healing. "Okay. Thanks." She nuzzled Cocoa one last time before setting him down.

Marissa had already made it to the glass doors but was peering around like she thought the killer could jump out any minute. Of the two of them, Marissa was the one who had been chased by a man with a gun earlier. She was the one who had the right to be fearful. Tandy would choose to be strong for her. And for Susan.

They found Randon's pink-haired girlfriend seated in the

tiny waiting room across from Sheriff Griffin. She had changed from her Little Bo Peep dress into a pair of jeans and a red shirt that clashed with her hair. She wasn't as emotional as the last time Tandy had seen her, but she clenched a tissue and stared at the floor as if she had no more tears to shed.

Griffin looked up at the sound of their footsteps, met Tandy's gaze, and motioned them to join Susan. Tandy took a spot on her far side on what might have been considered a sofa. She put an arm around Susan's slumped shoulders, expecting Marissa to do the same, but Marissa hesitated, looking toward the hallway that lead to the ICU.

"Is someone watching Randon?"

Griffin flicked her a hard gaze. A challenge. "Deputy Romero."

"Is that safe?"

Susan looked up then, eyes so puffy she almost resembled a goldfish. Or a "pinkfish," if there was such a thing. "Why wouldn't that be safe?"

Tandy closed her eyes. They were supposed to be helping here, not making things worse.

The Sheriff cleared his throat. "Randon is in good hands now, Marissa. Please sit down so Susan can tell us what happened."

Marissa glanced down the hallway once more. "You're going to question the nurses too, right? If it wasn't Romero, then—"

"Yes, I'm going to question the nurses..." Griffin's words came out clipped. "...while you stay with Susan, since you came here to comfort her."

Tandy nodded toward the seat on the other side of Susan. Marissa's concern about following procedure correctly was keeping them from getting started, and it could very well get them tossed out. Though Marissa's fear about the new deputy was making Tandy curious. Exactly how creepy was he?

Marissa bit her lip but then quickly sank beside Susan and gripped her hand. "I'm so sorry, Susan. I want to get this killer as badly as you do."

Susan trembled underneath Tandy's touch. She sniffed. "Thank you."

"Now, Susan." Officer Griffin pulled out a stylus to use for writing on his phone screen. "I know this is hard, but I have to ask you some questions."

She covered her face for a moment then sat up bravely. "I'll try to remember as best I can."

"That's all I can ask. Let's start by having you tell me what happened in your own words."

The story came out choppy and shaky. Sometimes too quiet to discern. But it basically sounded something like, "I went to get a snack to eat from the vending machine, and when I came back there was a pillow over Randon's face. I checked his pulse and screamed, and the doctors were able to resuscitate him, but they are unsure of how the loss of air has affected his brain."

Tandy covered her mouth. So though Randon was technically alive, he could have severe brain damage. She swallowed. "Do you think you scared off the killer, or do you think they left believing their job was done?"

Susan shook her head, eyes shining. "Either way, it's awful. What if he never wakes up? Or what if he wakes up and he's...he's...not the same?"

Tandy hugged the young woman, which said a lot since Tandy wasn't a hugger. But she would never wish such pain on anyone. Randon had been brilliant. A millionaire...

Her eyes narrowed. "Does he have a will? Could someone be after his money?"

People in their 20s like Randon usually didn't have wills. Especially if he didn't have any heirs. But could he have an institute or a charity that would get his estate if he passed? Maybe even a fund that would benefit Cash. Like a scholarship for injured veterans. She'd have to look into it.

Susan shook her head. "I don't know. You really think someone would do that?"

Tandy shrugged. She'd seen people do some pretty awful things in life. Including Randon. But she wouldn't mention to Susan that the young woman's own boss thought Randon was responsible for the ransomware attack at Cross Enterprises.

"It's possible," said Griffin. "It's also possible someone was out for revenge because they thought he'd been scamming companies with ransomware."

Tandy dropped her head backwards. So much for being discreet and respectful.

"What?" Susan glanced from Griffin to Marissa.

Griffin tilted his head in challenge. "You don't know anything about the virus?"

Okay, now he was speculating. Playing good cop/bad cop by himself.

Susan's knuckles turned white enough to match the tissues she clenched. "Randon would never do something like that. I mean, he could. But he wouldn't."

"Hm..." Griffin scribbled away. "You work for Cross Enterprises, do you not?"

"I do. You know I do. But what does that have to do with—"

"Their recent ransomware attack? Don't tell me you don't know about that."

"Yes, but..."

"But it's just a coincidence that you work there and your

boyfriend, as you stated, has the ability to con companies out of big bucks?"

Susan's mouth fell open. Her eyes looked from Marissa to Tandy, as innocent and trusting as Cocoa's had been.

Tandy sighed. She'd been in Susan's place, not so long ago. Accused of a crime she knew nothing about. It wasn't fun. Especially when Griffin could be checking hospital surveillance videos and meeting with Cross's private eye to figure out what had already been discovered, rather than harassing the victim's girlfriend. Even if Susan did know something about Randon's dirty deeds, that wasn't the crime they were investigating.

"Susan," she smoothed the woman's cotton candy hair away from her damp forehead. "Griffin is looking for motives for attempted murder. Is there anyone you can think of who had issues with Randon? Anyone who might want him dead? This will help put the criminal in jail and give Randon the best chance to recover."

"I...uh..." Susan stammered. "There's a lot of people who don't like Randon."

Tandy scrunched her face at the bluntness of such a truth. If Susan knew how many people didn't like Randon, what did she see in him? His money? Or did she see something nobody else did? They were both a little on the edgy/artsy side.

Tandy might doubt Susan's sincerity if she hadn't seen how Randon had wooed her. And it wasn't like Susan was taking advantage of his wealth. She worked for a living and rented an apartment above Opal's garage.

Susan shook her head. "But I can't think of anyone who would kill him."

Marissa patted Susan's hand. It was a good thing she and Tandy were here with the way Griffin was interrogating her. Obviously, the whole ransomware thing had been just as big a shock to Susan as it had been to Marissa.

"Griffin, why don't you give Susan a little break and see what the nurses know."

"Romero is questioning the nurses."

Of course, he was. The perfect way for him to hide evidence. "You probably should too."

Griffin narrowed his eyes. "I'll see what he's found out and check security footage." He pulled a card from his breast pocket and held it out. "Susan, if you think of anything else, I want you to call me immediately."

Susan took the card but avoided eye contact as if ashamed for what her boyfriend might have done to bring this on himself. "I will."

Griffin rose and headed down the hallway, his shoes squeaking.

Susan wiped her eyes and took a deep breath. "Is Randon really responsible for the ransomware?"

Tandy lifted a shoulder. "Cross hired an investigator to look into it."

With as many mysteries as Marissa and Tandy had solved, it was a little offensive that Cross hadn't asked them to look into it. But they could now. Especially if the investigation involved someone hiring Cash Hudson.

"Really?' Susan blinked back more tears. "Mr. Cross didn't tell me."

"I don't think he wanted to tip Randon off."

Susan slumped in her seat. "If Randon was responsible

for the virus, do you think he could have used me to get to Cross? Do you think he took my password number to log into the system?"

Marissa leaned back to make a face at Tandy behind Susan's back. That could very well be what happened. Because she'd never seen Randon be nice to anyone before Susan, it could have all been an act. In which case, if Susan had found out, she would also be a suspect. She could have been the one to try to smother Randon. But the security cameras would reveal such a scenario for sure.

Tandy scratched her head. "I don't know, Susan. But let's not worry about that right now. Griffin is looking at security footage, so that should give us some clues."

Marissa nodded. Good answer. No need to jump to conclusions when there was evidence waiting to be reviewed.

Griffin's dress shoes squeaked quicker and louder on his way back down the hall. That was fast. He must have found something.

He appeared in the doorway, arms wide like a gladiator stepping into the coliseum. He looked towards the entrance, chin lifted, then in Oscar-winning fashion, he turned his face slowly their way.

Marissa's stomach roiled in anticipation. This was it. He was going to tell them the identity of the killer.

"The security footage…"

Yes? Who did it reveal? Marissa scooted to the edge of her seat.

"…Has been wiped clean."

Marissa should have known. She shot to her feet and pointed. "It's the creepy guy. You left him alone back there."

"What creepy guy?" Susan held her arms wide. "How did this happen, Sheriff? You have a deputy back there watching out for Randon, don't you?"

Tandy snorted. "Marissa thinks the deputy is the creepy guy."

Griffin rubbed his temples. "It wasn't the creepy guy. I mean, it wasn't Romero."

Marissa stomped her foot. Simply because Griffin was in law enforcement didn't mean he should automatically trust other officers. "How do you know?"

"Because." He stared her down though he wasn't that scary. He should try growing a little stubble on his baby face to look more like a cop. "There *is* footage of Romero questioning employees in front of Randon's room the whole time we've been here."

Huh. There went that theory. Unless the deputy had snuck in earlier and erased the footage. Which was possible. At this point, anything was possible. "Did he find any leads from the nurses?"

"No." Griffin shook his head. "They'd been in the middle of changing shifts and distracted at the time of the crime."

"Or so your deputy says."

The front door of the hospital whooshed open. Connor stood there, flanked by Cocoa in his bandana and Ranger on the other side in his sheriff's costume. "What's going on?"

He must have been watching through the window and seen Marissa leap up.

Griffin eyed him. "The security footage from the second attempt on Randon's life has been deleted."

Connor's eyes bulged. "Meaning you have no suspects, and there's a murderer running around free on our streets."

"Or." Marissa held up a finger. "The killer is in this hospital right now, pretending to be an officer of the law."

Connor glanced past her then shot her his signature warning look. She hated that look. Because it was always right.

Marissa twisted to find Deputy Romero standing in the hallway. His beady eyes lasered in on her. Did he know she was accusing him of murder? And how did he get there without making a sound? Connor would have to admit it was pretty creepy.

"Who is pretending to be an officer of the law?" the deputy asked.

Marissa might as well share her concerns. She opened her mouth.

"Ranger," Tandy blurted, drawing everyone's attention. She pointed to the dog in the doorway. "Ranger is wearing a sheriff's costume. He's impersonating an officer."

Marissa shifted her weight to one side and planted a hand on her hip. How far were her friends going to take this charade? And did they really think the creeper was innocent? Just because she had no proof…

"Though." Connor nodded her way. "Until Griffin finds the killer, it would be good if you took Ranger home at night, Marissa. He may not be an actual sheriff, but he is a great watchdog. And I'd feel a lot better, knowing you aren't alone."

Chapter Six

MARISSA SAT ON HER SOFA IN golden light of early morning, sipped her buttery popcorn tea, and stared into Ranger's solemn eyes. Either the deputy had been scared of making a move with a dog in her house, which most likely was Connor's intention even though he said he didn't think the guy seemed creepy, *or* the deputy wasn't going to attack her at all.

She'd made it through the night unharmed. But now it was time to go to work, and she didn't know what to do with Connor's dog.

Did she take Ranger with her to Caffeine Conundrum? There was a puppy corner, so that was an option. But she had a wedding dress fitting at noon, which she couldn't take a dog to. Would Tandy mind watching him at the shop?

She'd reschedule, except that would involve inconveniencing her mother...or being blamed for inconveniencing her mother. Not that Mom had any goals in life other than to dress up Marissa and show her off.

She scratched behind Ranger's fuzzy ears. "I can leave you here, can't I? Connor leaves you at home all the time."

Ranger smacked his tail against the floor twice in response.

"You're not going to chew up my shoes like a goat, are you?"

Thwack. Thwack.

She'd close her closet just in case.

"I know Connor is worried about another attempt on my

life, but with Mom meeting me at the wedding planner's, I'm more worried about my dress fitting."

Her snow-white gown taunted her from the window rod where she'd hung it so she wouldn't forget it on her way out the door. The beading on the bodice would make it difficult to take out seams if needed in the fitting. She'd probably do well to lay off the scones and creamer until her big day.

"I've gained a few pounds from all the baking I've been doing, and the dress has gotten a little tight."

Ranger didn't even flinch at her admission.

"Good dog." She patted his head. If only her mom was as nonjudgmental.

She stood and took her teacup into the kitchen. She might have to follow up her cuppa with an espresso chaser once she got to the shop. She hadn't even started work, and she was already tired. At least she could count on this day being less drama-filled than yesterday.

Her phone buzzed on the counter. Tandy's name flashed across the screen. Maybe Marissa should knock on wood.

She swiped the smooth screen to connect the call. "Everything all right, Tandy?"

"Cross came in with his investigator. He wants to ask you some questions about what happened with Randon."

Marissa grimaced. She didn't want to relive the incident, but if it would help put the deputy behind bars, she would. "Okay." Her mind spun with memories.

The harsh voice. The glint of light off the gun. Randon yelling for her to run.

Her belly did a dive roll. "I'm on my way."

She wanted to get her part over with so Griffin could arrest whoever tried to kill Randon the second time. With a resigned exhale, she grabbed her keys and hurried out the door.

Tandy handed Trenton Dirkes a large white mug. For some reason she'd expected him to look more like Magnum P.I., and she was trying not to be too critical of his bowtie and stocky build. Having a brainy side would benefit the puzzle-solving aspect of putting clues together. And though he was short, he walked with his arms held wide like a G.I. Joe action figure, so he was probably fit enough to chase down a perp when needed.

"Did you find any evidence it was Randon who had planted the virus at Cross Enterprises?" she asked him.

He sipped his beverage, nodded in approval at the drink, then peered up like he hadn't even heard her. "Did you see Randon in here yesterday before you left for the parade?"

"Uh…yeah." She'd already mentioned that to Cross right in front of Trenton. Why was he repeating his questions and ignoring hers? With the line of customers forming, she didn't have time to explain a second time.

She nodded at the guy in line behind Trenton. The skinny, middle-aged guy who dressed in baggy clothes like a skater and owned a tutu-wearing dog named Sheila. She smiled. "Hi."

This time his intent gaze at her lips made sense. "Hi." The slightly elongated vowel sounds made sense too.

"What can I get you?"

"Can you make a Mexican Mocha?"

"Sure." She turned to grind beans into the portafilter basket. "Congratulations," she said before remembering she needed to face him when she spoke. She tamped the grinds down, hooked them into the espresso machine, and turned on the water before looking over her shoulder. "Congratulations on winning the trophy yesterday."

His serious expression cracked into a smile. "Thank you. Sheila loves putting on a show." He nodded toward Puppy Corner where his cocker spaniel and Cocoa took turns sniffing each other.

Trenton set his mug down on the counter. "Did Randon seem upset at all before he was attacked?"

"No." Tandy glanced back at the P.I. This obviously wasn't the best time for her to be questioned, but at least she could respond to him while turned away to make coffee. She grabbed chocolate milk out of the mini fridge and poured it into the metal pitcher to steam as she thought back to her last interactions with Randon. "He'd been too busy to brag about himself, which was weird."

She mixed all the ingredients in a mug for her customer and turned to find him watching Trenton.

He looked to her. "Randon? Is that who is in the hospital? I thought your friend said 'random' yesterday, not 'Randon.'"

"Randon." She pronounced clearly. "He was attacked here during the parade, and police are investigating." She set the mug in front of him. "That's five bucks."

He unfolded his leather wallet and pulled out a five-dollar bill.

She plucked it from his hand so she could move to the next customer. "Thanks."

"Thank you." He sipped. "Could I get more syrup and some actual cinnamon to sprinkle on top?"

Tandy arched her eyebrows. Nobody had ever complained about her coffee before. Maybe he just liked things sweet. "Okay…"

She pivoted to grab the bottle and spice jar. She'd barely placed the syrup on the counter before he swiped it up and flipped it in the air. Oh no. He was a male version of Marissa, and Tandy was going to have another big mess to clean up.

Except he caught the bottle. Then he slipped it behind his neck to catch with the other hand, grabbed the cinnamon, and juggled the two for a moment. This all lead to him pouring another splash of syrup and topping the foam with cinnamon sprinkles.

Tandy's lips parted as she watched the show.

Trenton ignored the act like he was used to jugglers entertaining during investigations. "Does Randon usually brag about himself?"

The guy swirled the bottle around his head then rolled it down his arm. Apparently, his dog wasn't the only one who put on a show.

Tandy laughed and clapped. The customers in line behind the guy joined her applause.

Trenton continued straight-faced. "What do you think of Randon's girlfriend?"

The guy flipped the syrup bottle behind his back and spun around to catch it.

The bell over the door jingled. Marissa bustled in, eyes roving the crowd then landing on the performance taking place.

The guy repeatedly tossed the cinnamon in the air, circling the syrup bottle over and under it like a jump rope.

Marissa dodged tables and patrons. "What's going on?"

Tandy motioned to the juggler since that was the best explanation she could come up with.

Trenton folded his hands on the bar. "Do you think Randon might have used his girlfriend to get to Cross?"

Tandy would have enjoyed the act more if Trenton wasn't dripping with questions like Chinese water torture. At least Marissa was here now to help Tandy catch up.

Marissa stepped closer to the counter. Then with a "whoop" she was gone. Had she slipped?

The juggler wobbled. The jar landed securely in his hand. But despite his impressive balancing skills, he disappeared too.

The line of customers stared at a spot on the floor on the other side of the counter.

Trenton straightened his tie. "Does Randon have any enemies?"

Tandy shook her head in frustration then circled the bar to make sure she wouldn't be dealing with a second day of ambulance rides to the hospital.

Both Marissa and their customer sat on the floor, rubbing their heads.

Tandy cringed. "You two okay?"

Marissa picked up her purse off the floor and adjusted the sheer gold pleats of her skirt. "I think I slipped on cinnamon."

Tandy pointed at her high-heeled strappy sandals. "You're also wearing those."

Marissa rolled over to her knees to try to push herself up on wobbly legs like a baby giraffe. "I have my dress fitting today, and I wanted to see how the sandals looked with my wedding gown."

The guy on the floor looked back and forth between them, probably trying to keep up with their conversation. "I'm sorry."

Tandy reached an arm down to help him up. "It's not your fault. My business partner likes to make an entrance. That's Marissa, and I'm Tandy."

The man pushed off the ground with his other hand so Tandy barely had to pull. He let go to scoop the jar and bottle off the floor. "I'm Zam. It's short for my last name,

Zamorano."

"Nice to meet you, Zam. That was quite the show you put on. I'd love to keep chatting, but I've got more drinks to serve."

Marissa held her hands out for balance then brushed herself off. "I'll help. Though at noon I have to go..." She looked around. "Oh crud. I forgot my dress."

Trenton had turned to lean against the bar as he sipped his coffee. "You're Marissa? You witnessed the attack on Randon?"

Tandy rubbed her face. Marissa wasn't going to be much help with making drinks when the private eye was playing twenty questions. "Marissa, why don't you take Mr. Dirkes upstairs to the tea loft?"

Marissa looked from Trenton to the growing line of customers. "But you've got—"

"Please."

Marissa ushered the guy away, and Tandy was finally able to think.

Mayor Kensington stepped up to the counter and rubbed his bald spot. "I have a meeting in ten minutes. Think you can make me a LiberTea in time?"

Tandy took a deep breath. It was good to have customers, but she preferred how much more smoothly her service went when they weren't asking a million questions about a recent attempted murder or rolling on the floor in cinnamon. "I'll do my best."

Zam stood at the end of the bar, watching in his attentive way. "What's in a LiberTea?"

Tandy jabbed at the iPad to ring up her sale. "It's half black tea, half lemonade, a drop of honey and a sprinkle of basil."

"I got it," he said.

Tandy took the mayor's debit card to swipe in the card reader. "It's okay. I'll…"

Zam flipped open the lid on the ice machine then ice cubes flew in the air over Tandy's head to land in the plastic cup he held. Tea trickled. Honey plunked. Zam spun away with the pitcher of lemonade and returned with a basil sprig to the sound of applause before Tandy even finished her transaction.

The mayor took his cup and lifted it like he was going to make a toast. "Best service I've ever gotten. Thanks, Tandy."

Tandy shrugged since the service had nothing to do with her. When the mayor turned to leave, she mouthed "thank you" to Zam.

They continued like that through the rest of the early morning rush. The guy didn't know his drinks, so she had to tell him how to prepare each one, but he did so with panache. Once the line died down, she settled back with her own smooth cup o' Joe to watch him clean the same way he'd poured.

When he looked up from snapping the dishrag into place, she asked, "Where'd you learn to do that?"

He pointed out the window. "I used to own the bar down the street."

"Oh…" That made sense. "You don't own it anymore?"

He lifted a shoulder. "I became a Christian and felt like God has something different for me."

Tandy had also come to Grace Springs because God had something different for her. "I'm a Christian too."

The uncertainty in Zam's eyes cleared. Perhaps peace at knowing she could relate. "It's nice to find a place where I fit in again."

Tandy nodded. "You didn't only fit in, you are very much appreciated. My partner…" Tandy glanced up toward the loft then waved away the rest of her sentence. Zam had just started to feel like he fit in. She didn't want to scare him off.

His eyebrows drew together. "She dresses for a fashion show, knocks people over, then abandons you to do all the work?"

"Sometimes." Tandy grinned so he knew she was joking. "Actually, she does all the baking. But what I was going to say is that she witnessed an attempted murder here yesterday. So she's part of an investigation."

Zam crossed his arms and narrowed his eyes in speculation. "Randon Evans?"

Marissa dropped her head backwards. "For the last time, I have no idea if Randon Evans used Susan to get access to Mr. Cross's computer system."

Was this private investigator charging by the hour? That way he could get nowhere and get rich at the same time. Meanwhile, Tandy was running everything downstairs. At least, by the sounds of it, business had quieted down. Though that usually didn't happen until eleven or so…

Marissa lifted her wrist to get a good look at her diamond watch. It was past eleven. And she still had to run home for her wedding dress. Stupid, stupid, stupid.

"Mr. Dirkes, the only part of this investigation I can be any help with is convicting Cash Hudson, and he's already been arrested." She pressed her chair back and stood. "If you're wanting to know about Randon's relationship with Susan, you're really going to have to talk to her. You can probably find her at the hospital. As for me, I have a wedding to plan, a business to run, and festival events to oversee."

The man stood as well. Perhaps his atrocious bowtie was also a symbol of good breeding, and not just bad fashion sense. "Thank you for your time, Miss Alexander. I'll be in touch if I have any more questions."

Or if he wanted to repeat all his questions again…

Marissa shook away the negative attitude. She wouldn't be feeling this way if he'd been as forthcoming with the questions she'd asked him. But apparently he had some kind of confidentiality clause with Cross Enterprises. And it wasn't like she could help out on the computer hacker side of things. She had trouble enough remembering the password for her phone.

"Best of luck on your investigation." She shook out her skirt and headed toward the stairs, but before she took a step, one last question snagged her back. She pivoted on the toe of her sandals and stuck one hand on her hip. "If you do discover that Randon planted the virus in Mr. Cross's computer system, what can you do about it? Can you press charges if he's in a coma?"

"That." Mr. Dirkes folded his fleshy hands. "And we can file a lawsuit against his estate."

Marissa scrunched her nose. If Randon came to, she'd hate to be the one to break the news to him that his estate had to pay thousands of dollars in damages and that he was probably going to jail. Such a penalty made sense, but it was hard to think about when he was still wounded from saving her life. Would Susan stick by him?

Marissa blew out her breath, headed down the stairs, and smacked straight into that same guy who'd fallen on her earlier. Goodness. He was even clumsier than she was. Crazy that Tandy let him toss glass around in their shop.

She caught herself on his arms. "Sorry."

He held onto her arms and looked into her eyes. Wow.

Penetrating gaze.

She bugged her eyes at Tandy who seemed awfully relaxed at a table with her motorcycle boots kicked up on a chair. Did she not think this man's behavior strange?

The man let go and stepped away so she could pass. "I'm sorry. I didn't hear you coming. Usually my hearing dog lets me know when people are around, but she's in the puppy pen at the moment."

Hearing dog? That fuzzy looking dog with the floppy ears taking a nap with Cocoa was a hearing dog. Which meant Zam couldn't hear. That's why he didn't react very quickly when she skidded across the floor into his shins earlier. He wasn't clumsy, but she'd need to be extra careful around him.

She shook her head, her dangly earrings brushing against her neck. "It's all right. I'm just in a hurry." She trotted forward past Tandy. "You don't mind if I leave early for my fitting, do you? I need to run home for my dress."

Tandy motioned to the empty room. "Zam and I can handle it, but if you feel guilty for leaving early, you can always repay me by letting me wear a black bridesmaid dress."

"Black?" asked Zam. "Black is for funerals."

"You tell her, Zam." Marissa laughed and pushed through the door.

Tandy was fine. Better than fine. Whereas Marissa needed to hurry.

She glanced at her watch again. Not only was time ticking by, threatening to make her late, but the timepiece was silver. Mom would never approve of a silver watch with the gold skirt she was wearing.

She drove with one hand, while taking off the watch and blowing out her breath. She could do this. It was only a dress fitting. If only Tandy could get her bridesmaid dress fitted at the same time to be moral support, but then they would have had to close the shop.

Marissa's phone buzzed from its place in the console. She used to answer every time Mom called, but she'd finally learned to set boundaries. If it was important, Mom would follow up with a text. Otherwise she'd wait to see her at As You Wish Weddings.

Marissa pulled into her driveway and clip-clopped down the sidewalk and up the steps to the front porch of her renovated craftsman style cottage. There was her dress, still hanging in the bay window.

She shoved the key in the lock, ready to grab the gown and hold it high overhead on the way back to her car to keep it from getting dirty. She probably should have put the protective case over it, but she liked admiring its beauty and dreaming about walking down the aisle toward Connor.

Yes. That's what she needed to think about when overwhelmed by wedding planning sessions with Mom. Connor. She smiled softly, shoved the door open, then gasped in shock.

Splotches of red blood stood out boldly against the shiny white wedding dress.

Red. Blood.

Chapter Seven

FEAR CLAWED ITS WAY UP MARISSA'S spine. Did she want to know where that blood came from? Dare she look around further like the stupid girl who always got herself killed in horror movies? Or should she run away shrieking?

She tightened her grip on the doorknob, ready to slam it shut on any knife-wielding psychos. But the living room remained eerily quiet.

She held her breath and let her eyes travel from one hiding place to the next. No shadows in the kitchen. No movement behind the couch. No feet underneath the curtains on the far wall. But wait. There was a dark smear on the curtain at about waist height. More blood?

Her senses sharpened as if her gaze were the luminol CSI agents used to find blood at crime scenes. Blood on the carpet. Blood on the bookshelves. Though there probably wasn't enough for her house to be a murder scene.

Something pattered against the wood floor down the hallway.

Marissa jumped. Her heart lurched. She opened her mouth to scream.

A black blur rounded the corner and planted itself in her path. Ranger. Connor's dog.

She was safe, but she screamed anyway.

Her pulse continued to thrum, as well.

Had someone broken into her house and Ranger attacked, spraying blood in the process?

The visual was more than she could handle. "Come on,

Ranger. Come here, boy."

The dog bounded forward, and as soon as he made it through the front door, she slammed it. Her safe haven was no longer safe.

She raced him down the stairs back to her Jeep Cherokee. Opening the driver's side, she motioned him in then checked over her shoulder before following.

What was that verse in the Bible about the wicked fleeing though no one pursues but the righteous were as bold as a lion? She did not feel bold. She felt like there was a lion in wait for her.

Ranger turned in two circles before sitting tall on her leather seats. He did all of that before her shaking fingers were able to dial Griffin.

The sheriff answered on the first ring. "What's wrong, Marissa?"

"There's blood in my house." Was there really? It felt so surreal.

Pause. "Are you bleeding?"

"No." Her eyes darted from the front door to the back gate to the rearview mirror. She pressed the lock button for her car doors. "I came home and found blood spatters everywhere. I was afraid to go in."

"I'm on my way. Where are you now?"

She twisted to check her blind spots. All clear for the moment. "I'm locked in my car. Should I stay here? Should I drive away?"

"I'm in the neighborhood. Stay right there but don't hang up. Are you alone?"

Marissa reached to rub the top of Ranger's sleek head. "Ranger is with me. Connor wanted his dog to stay at my house last night. I think maybe he caught someone trying to break in."

"That's a possibility. Is Ranger okay?"

Marissa ran her hand over the black lab's back and down his sides. He leaned in and licked her cheek, leaving behind the scent of beef jerky. "I think so. He seems normal."

"That's good. I'm glad Connor thought to send him home with you. Maybe we'll get some DNA and be able to nail this perp."

Marissa grimaced. She was okay. And though she'd rather not be hiding out in her car with her stained wedding gown in the house, she was glad whoever wanted Randon dead had tried to hurt her, because now the police would have DNA evidence that could lead to his arrest.

Could it be Deputy Romero? He probably would have covered his tracks better.

"Where is your deputy?" she asked, just in case.

"He's patrolling the car show. With our history of car thieves in the area, we wanted to make sure everyone was safe."

Marissa rolled her eyes. Carjackings were so last Valentine's Day.

Meanwhile, her future was being destroyed. "My wedding dress has blood on it."

"Okay…" Quiet. "I'm going to let you call Connor about that after I get there. You doin' okay?"

She'd have to call Connor *and* her mom. Marissa dropped her head back, wishing she was safe enough to close her eyes and grieve over the drama her mother was about to put her through for a ruined wedding dress. Instead she checked her perimeter for creepers like Deputy Romero. "I'm fine. Are you close?"

"Turning onto your street now."

Marissa twisted to watch the cop car roll silently down their street, lights flashing. Did Griffin think he was sneaking up on someone? Like the bad guy was still in her house, oblivious to the fact that she'd come and gone, taking the dog with her? As ludicrous as the idea sounded, a rush of relief flooded up from her toes as Griffin neared.

"I see you. I'm calling Connor now."

Marissa disconnected and clicked on her contact list while watching the sheriff draw his gun and circle the house. Not a curtain rustled.

The phone rang in her ear.

"Marissa?" Connor's deep voice could barely be heard over the din of background noise. "I'm at the car show, and I think I need a 1948 Ford F-1 pickup as my wedding gift."

Marissa frowned at the phone. Connor already had a truck, and it was a lot newer than that. "Do you mind marrying a woman who has blood all over her wedding gown?"

A truck door slammed. The background noise faded. "I'm not following."

Marissa replayed the sentence in her head. The creepy factor of her situation made Deputy Romero seem normal. She'd try again. "It's a good thing you let me take Ranger overnight. Someone snuck in, and he caught them."

"What?" An engine revved. "Are you okay?"

"Yeah. I saw the blood and called the sheriff. Ranger and I are sitting in my car right now waiting to see if Griffin finds anyone."

"Oh." Connor blew out his breath.

Marissa tilted her head. Connor seemed extremely calm for the news she'd given him.

"You didn't actually see someone break in?" he asked.

Marissa narrowed her eyes. "Were you hoping I'd be a witness to two crimes? Because the one is more than enough."

"No. No. Definitely not. I just…" Connor paused. "What

kind of blood did you find?"

Marissa shook her head in confusion then focused on Griffin sneaking underneath her windows back to the front porch. "What do you mean 'what kind'? It was all over the place like Bob Ross dipped his paintbrush in red paint and decided to make happy little blood spatters."

"That sounds like…"

"What?" Marissa bit her lip. This had happened before?

Connor chuckled. "Oh, honey."

"What?" Why was he laughing?

"Check Ranger's tail."

Marissa eyed the dog. How did the blood in her home have anything to do with Ranger's tail? She dropped her gaze to his tail. It looked thick and black like normal. "What am I looking for?"

"Blood on the tip."

Like he'd chased his tail and caught it instead of a perp? That sounded highly unlikely. In all the cute dog videos Marissa had seen online, none of them actually caught their own tail. But, just in case, she reached over and circled her fingers around Ranger's appendage then ran them along the sleek fur to the tip. Something crusty caught on her skin.

"Ew…"

She lifted the end of Ranger's tail despite his attempt to wag it away. She never would have found the dull, matted spot if she weren't looking for it, but there it was.

"I should have warned you." Connor's voice attempted to soothe her nerves over the phone line. "Ranger gets Happy Tail Syndrome sometimes. He'll be wagging so hard that his tail thwacks something and ruptures the skin. Then he keeps wagging and gets blood everywhere. I'll come pick him up to wrap his tail in a bandage."

This was a thing? And this dog was going to move into

her house after she married Connor? She'd be dealing with blood spatter indefinitely.

She would have to try wrapping Ranger's tail in bubble wrap. He was supposed to be there to protect her, not ruin her wedding plans. "Happy Tail Syndrome is a horrible name for the bloodbath I'm going to have to clean."

"I'll help you." Connor chuckled again. "Is Griffin still at your house?"

Marissa looked out the windshield with a sulk. She watched Griffin bust through her front door like he was taking down a cartel. Should she tell him now about Ranger's ailment or let him finish his search?

Griffin held his gun in front of him as he scanned her living room. She'd wait. It wasn't like she needed to hurry to her fitting now. Not with a dress covered in blood.

"Your dress is covered in blood!"

The wedding planner Mom hired sure was a master of the obvious. Marissa would love to make a blonde joke about her, but their hair colors were identical. Not to mention their height, weight, and turned up noses. The only difference was that the owner of As You Wish Weddings wore silver shoes to match her silver watch.

Mom floated over, looking all Christie Brinkley-ish. "Marissa, what did you do this time?"

Marissa turned to hang the dress on the front of a full-length oval mirror with scrollwork trim in the bedazzled studio. Funny how this kind of excess used to seem normal to her. As did Mom's contempt. "Connor's dog had Happy Tail Syndrome."

Moria gasped. The woman even sounded like her.

"Connor saw your dress?"

Mom crossed her arms and tapped the pointy toe of her designer heels.

"No." Not that Connor seeing her dress was Marissa's biggest concern at the moment. "Connor wanted Ranger to sleep over at my house to protect me because I'm a witness to the attempted murder of Randon Evans."

Mom looked away in disapproval. "Of course you are."

What did that mean?

The wedding planner placed a hand on Marissa's wrist. It was probably supposed to feel comforting, but it only felt cold. The woman even shivered a little. If she was that chilly, why didn't she turn down the air conditioning or put on a sweater? "Don't worry. I've removed worse dress stains. Stay right here."

Moria strode from the room, leaving Marissa to face Mom alone.

As Mom didn't seem to care about the threat on her life, Marissa busied herself by retrieving the latest wedding magazine from her handbag. "I'll show you the bridesmaid dresses I've decided on."

Mom took a seat on a brocade chaise lounge, crossed her legs, and laced her fingers together over the top knee. "You still refuse to have my brother's daughters be part of the ceremony? They're very affluent, you know."

Affluent was one word for the twins. "The only reason they'd want to be in my wedding would be in hope of me falling off the stage so they could make fun of me on social media like they did at the Miss Ohio pageant."

"Simply don't fall off this time."

Mom made it sound so easy. "I'm not going to have a stage since the wedding is on Connor's farm, and I'd hate to make Alex and Andrea travel all the way from Chicago only to be disappointed."

Mom wrinkled her nose like she could smell the cows in the barn. "Still set on the farm idea, are you?"

Marissa flipped through her magazine to change the subject. Not that Mom was going to approve of the dresses when she didn't approve of the venue. "There." She pointed to the halter dress with full, knee-length skirt.

Mom barely glanced at the page before directing all the force of her scorn Marissa's way. "It's black."

Marissa shook her head. She should have known to explain first. Even she scorned the idea of black bridesmaid dresses. "I want to order it in teal. I'm thinking teal dresses will really make the sunflowers pop."

"Sunflowers? That's so provincial. You haven't already spoken with Flower Girls yet, have you? Where is Moria when I need her?"

"Sunflowers will be bright and—"

"You really think that goth business partner of yours is going to want to carry something bright, let alone wear teal?" Mom stood and fanned her face. "Moria?"

Marissa rolled her eyes when Mom wasn't looking. She'd known this was going to be tough, but there was no reason to bring her business partner into it. "Tandy's not goth. More like…"

"Urban pirate," Moria finished for her, heels clicking against the shiny teak flooring.

Marissa's lips twitched at the image. "I was going to say biker babe."

"I can see that too." Moria nodded then knelt in front of the dress with a bottle of hydrogen peroxide and a Q-tip. "Sorry that took so long. I had to track down our first aid kit."

Mom pressed her lips together. "Well, this *is* an emergency. Not to mention the fact that Marissa wants to use sunflowers. Have you discussed her flower options with her yet?"

Moria dipped her cotton swab then dabbed at the dress. "Per your instructions, I have not had any private conversations with Marissa."

Marissa stood taller. She narrowed her eyes at Mom. Whose wedding was this? "Per your instructions?"

Mom smoothed her French twist. "I am the one paying for the event."

Really? *Mom* was paying? "You haven't paid for a thing since you won Miss Ohio thirty years ago."

"Marissa," Mom hissed.

They stared at each other.

What? Was Marissa supposed to apologize? It was true. Mom majored in marketing, but since meeting Marissa's father she had only used that degree to go shopping. If she'd stayed home to make Marissa her first priority, that would have been one thing, but Marissa had pretty much been raised by her grandmother.

"It's working." Moria continued dabbing at the dress as if she wasn't in the middle of a standoff.

"That's good," Mom said. "Because there's no way I'd pay for another dress now."

Marissa pressed her lips together though her eyebrows arched rebelliously. Tandy and her urban pirate ways were rubbing off on her.

Mom turned her head to glare out of the corner of her eye. "Don't you dare go to your father about this behind my back."

Marissa held her hands wide. Mom made it sound like that was something Marissa had done in the past. Okay, she'd tried once in junior high when Mom wouldn't support her playing the tuba, but that was her last attempt. Not because

Marissa's parents were united, but because Dad was scared of his wife. "I'm not asking you or anyone to buy me a new dress."

Mom planted a hand on her hip. "But sunflowers? This isn't Kansas."

"If only I was marrying a guy whose family owned a farm where he could grow sunflowers for me, then you wouldn't have to pay for them at all." Marissa crossed her arms. "Oh wait. I am."

Mom lifted her chin. "A wedding is supposed to be a bonding time for mother and daughter, but it sounds like you don't even need me here."

Moria shot to her feet with that. "Mrs. Alexander, sunflowers can be a very beautiful selection. You could mix them with white roses for the bride to add some class, and…"

"Class?" Marissa stared down the woman who could be her own evil twin. The wedding planner was even bonding with Marissa's mom over fixing her. Like Marissa was their project. Is this how Marissa used to act before she'd met Tandy and turned her back on pageanting? "You don't think I have enough class?"

Moria's sapphire eyes widened. "I didn't mean it that way."

Mom blinked in boredom. "Well, you should."

Moria held up her hands to smooth things over but paused as if not sure in which direction to start. "By class I don't mean stylish excellence. You have style. What I mean is sophistication. We don't want anything to embarrass you on your big day. I'm only thinking of you the way your mother was when she suggested the tea length dress so you don't trip over the train."

Marissa's spine stiffened. She turned slowly to face her mother who'd twisted her lips into a disapproving grimace.

"You told me I should get tea length because I like tea."

Mom patted her hair. "That's one reason."

Heat rose from Marissa's chest like a furnace, warming her cheeks, her forehead, the tips of her ears. While she'd refused to let her cousins be in her wedding because of the way they'd made fun of her, they weren't nearly as bad as her mom. So why was she letting the woman ridicule her this way? Just so she'd pay for the reception? She'd rather elope than let Mom poison one more moment of her life.

She shook her head slowly. This was it.

Mom's gaze snagged on her movement. Hardened. Narrowed in warning.

Moria looked around as if desperately trying to find a distraction from conflict, but there wasn't any part of Marissa's dream wedding that wouldn't conflict with Mom's plans.

The front door swung open, pouring in sunlight. It took a moment for Marissa's eyes to adjust to the brightness enough to make out Connor's huge grin. "Hey, hon. I don't want to interrupt. I'm only here to pick up Ranger."

Moria clapped at the sight of him like he was the distraction she'd been praying for. She stepped forward to shake hands. "You must be the groom. Connor, right? I'm Moria Evans, the wedding planner."

Evans? Marissa tilted her head to get a closer look at the woman. She'd never connected Moria's last name with Randon before. The wedding planner didn't look much like the other Evans in town.

Connor shook hands then looked between the three women. "Are you sure you're not related to the Alexanders? You look like you could all be sisters. Or Charlie's Angels or something."

Marissa did a double take to question her boyfriend with

lowered eyebrows. While the three of them may look alike, Marissa was the only crime fighter of the group. And the way these women tried to plan her wedding was the most recent crime.

Mom chuckled. "Trying to get on my good side, eh, Connor?"

Did Mom have a good side? Marissa had only seen her manipulative side.

"Nah. Like I said, I'm here to…" His gaze landed on the dress hanging in front of the mirror. "Oh, is that your dress, 'Rissa? I don't see any blood on it. Were you able to get it out?"

Moria squealed and rushed to block Connor's view with her body.

Mom gave Marissa another look as if it was her fault Connor had seen her dress. "Connor, it's bad luck to see your bride's dress before the wedding."

"Sorry." Connor turned and held his hand up like a blinder to the side of his face. It was sweet and adorable, but Marissa didn't want him to cater to her mother's whims any more than she wanted to.

"It's okay, Connor." Marissa reached for his hand, pulled it down, and laced her fingers with his. "I'm not wearing that dress anyway."

Mom huffed. "Marissa, I told you I'm not paying for another one."

"I know." Marissa pulled Connor toward the door, feeling more free than she'd felt in a long time. "I don't want your money, and I don't want you planning my wedding."

Mom gave her signature huff. "You expect Connor here to pay for a new dress and wedding planner?"

Connor froze, except for his gaze which locked onto hers. They probably should have talked about this first. Hopefully he understood.

"Nope." She apologized with her eyes. "I'll do it myself. We've already got the farm and flowers. All I have to do is find a new dress."

"With this time frame, you'll have to get a dress off..." Moria covered her mouth in horror, preventing whatever it was she wanted to say. She finally whispered the rest of the comment. "Off the rack."

"Sure." Having her first gown custom made had become a bit of a nightmare. So why not? Moria probably only cared because it would cut into her commission.

Connor squeezed her hand. "I'd like you to step outside with me for a moment."

Marissa squeezed back. "We might as well leave. There's nothing more for me here."

"Marissa." Mom stood regally and clutched her purse to her chest as if she held the winning ticket. "If you walk out that door, there's no coming back. You'll never get your dream wedding."

"My dream wedding or your dream wedding, Mom?"

Mom slung her purse over one shoulder and strode out. Connor watched her leave. The door thudded shut and his eyes met Marissa's once again, twitchy with concern.

Without missing a beat, Moria grabbed a binder, flipped it open, and offered them a peek. "I don't know what your budget is, but if you can't afford the package your parents signed up for, there are still other options. I have the date open, and..."

Connor held up a hand to stop her. "We're going to have to get back with you."

"Yes, yes of course." Moria set the binder on a glass counter and retrieved a lacy business card from its holder. "But you'll need to do so quickly. This is wedding season, you know. I won't stay available if you don't pay the remaining balance for my services."

Marissa's heart sank. She tossed it a figurative life preserver. If she could plan a grand opening for her tea house, then she could certainly plan a wedding, as well. They just might have to let some things go. Like the photobooth.

Connor snagged the business card, nodded politely, then ushered Marissa out the double doors into the alcove entrance along Main Street. He wiped a hand along his slick forehead, though Marissa couldn't be sure his sweat was from the steamy temperatures or the stress of the curveball she'd thrown him. "What happened in there?" he asked.

Mom's Lexus rolled by. She didn't look up.

Marissa's stomach cramped. "I found out that Mom wanted me to get a short dress so I didn't trip in it and embarrass her."

Connor's touch tickled as he brushed hair away from her face. A sweet gesture, and one that made her want to elope even more, though he likely did it to give himself a moment to process. "Do you *want* to trip?"

She jutted her chin forward. "No, I don't want to trip."

A corner of Connor's mouth curved up. "If you do, I'll catch you."

Marissa's shoulders sagged in relief. This was the kind of relationship she'd been looking for her whole life. This was what had helped her realize her relationship with her mom was not healthy. "And if I fire the wedding planner, will you also help me plan the wedding?"

His arms wrapped around her waist so he could sway with her like he would on their first wedding dance. "I'll even make sure my dog doesn't splatter blood all over your next dress."

"Ahh... You whisper the best sweet nothings." She

smiled up at him.

He kissed her nose.

"But first I'll have to find another dress." She could do that in three months, right? "At least Tandy has her dress picked out, and…" Tandy's dress. Marissa had shown Mom the picture but forgot to place the order. "Hold on one second."

She kicked off her heels so she could run her errand quicker, pushed open the door, and padded against the cool, smooth wooden planks. Where was that catalog again?

"We'll get you out of there, Cash."

Moria's voice stopped Marissa in her tracks. She looked up from the glossy magazines to find the wedding planner pacing in a back office, phone to her ear. Could she be talking to Cash Hudson? And by getting him out of there, did she mean jail?

Marissa's heart hammered in her chest, threatening to drown out Moria's next words.

"Nobody has questioned my relationship to Randon so far, but if they realize we're dating, that might give the prosecutor an even stronger motive to pin on you."

Marissa gasped and took a step backwards. She had to get out of there. Because her wedding planner's boyfriend had her scared for her life.

Chapter Eight

Marissa spun and lunged for the door. A brocade upholstered bench got in her way. It caught her shin, tipping her forward. She dropped the catalog to catch herself on the bench.

Her rear landed on the bench's padding, but the momentum pushed her over the side. Her bare feet stayed up in the air, legs held by the bench, the slip underneath her sheer pleated skirt flared like a tutu.

"Marissa." Moria rushed over, setting her phone on the glass counter as she passed. She paused at the bench as if unsure how to help her bride-to-be up off the floor in a ladylike fashion. Though, if she was in cahoots with Cash, she could actually be looking for a way to use the position against her. Perhaps kill her, then blame it on Marissa's clumsiness. She wouldn't be the first criminal to try out such an evil plan. "Are you okay?"

Marissa propped herself up on her elbows so she'd be prepared if Moria tried to stab her with a feather pen or smother her with a garment bag. If Moria didn't make any moves, should she reveal that she overheard the woman's phone conversation or play dumb?

"I'm fine." In the past, Marissa had gotten herself into trouble by trying to solve these things herself. With her wedding coming up, she really needed to stay out of trouble. She'd play dumb so she could take this info to Griffin and let him interrogate the wedding planner.

"I...uh..." She looked around for any excuse as for why

she might have been running around the shop without looking where she was going. The catalog lay open by her side. "I ran back inside to place the order for my bridesmaid dresses. Tandy likes that black one in a size six. Except—"

The front door swung open.

Marissa exhaled in relief at the sight of her fiancé. It was good to not be alone with the girlfriend of the guy who'd wanted to kill her. Except Connor stared at her like she'd announced she wanted to skydive for her wedding entrance. He should be used to her falling over things by now.

"I didn't see the bench," she explained.

"It happens." A small smile softened Connor's concern. "I just wanted to let you know that when I got Ranger out of your car, I put your shoes inside. If you're okay, I'm gonna run—"

"Wait." Connor couldn't leave her alone with a suspect. She rolled over and pushed up. "Don't leave me."

A wrinkle formed between Connor's sandy eyebrows. That had sounded weird, hadn't it? She glanced at Moria whose blue eyes had turned steely. Had she guessed the reason Marissa wanted to get away?

"I..." Marissa jerked upright and smoothed her skirt. "I want to kiss you goodbye."

Connor's smile split wider. He pushed the door fully open and waved her through in front of him with a small bow.

Oh good. He was playing along.

Moria crossed her arms. "Come back when you can, Marissa. I'll get Tandy's dress ordered, and we'll discuss other wedding planning options." That probably wasn't all Moria wanted to talk about.

"Sure." This is when Marissa's fake smile from her pageant days came in handy. She beamed her brightest then bounced out the door, heart hammering the same way it had when she had to pirouette in stilettos on stage during the ballgown portion of competition.

Connor followed to her Jeep.

She fumbled through her purse, not sure which she should grab first—her phone to call Griffin or her keys to drive to the police station. She turned to tell Connor her dilemma.

He wrapped his arms around her back and pulled her close. Oh yeah. He thought they were going to kiss.

"Connor," she hissed to keep him from silencing her with his lips.

He paused an inch away, that wrinkle returning to mar his brow. "What?"

She gripped his biceps to squeeze like stress balls, only they didn't squish in her grip. Wow. All his construction work was going to pay off in more ways than one when they got married. She squeezed again.

He gripped her waist and pulled her far enough away to draw her attention up to his face. "What's going on?"

She peeked over his shoulder at the storefront. Moria peered out the window, watching them. "When I went back into the shop, I heard my wedding planner talking to Cash Hudson. Not only are they dating, but if she's related to Randon, she stands to inherit his fortune."

Connor's eyes widened. "She's related to Randon?"

"Her last name *is* Evans."

Connor twisted to look over his shoulder.

"Don't look."

He faced her again. "I only wanted to see if she looks like Randon."

Marissa shook her head. With Randon's dark hair and olive skin, she never would have guessed the two were related. "She doesn't."

Connor narrowed his eyes. "Marriage then? Ex-wife? We don't know much about Randon before he moved here. Perhaps this doesn't have anything at all to do with an inheritance and everything to do with jealousy. Cash didn't like the kind of relationship his girlfriend had with her ex."

Marissa bit her lip. As wealthy as Randon was, it was hard to believe money wasn't involved. "Either one is a valid motive."

"I'm glad she doesn't have to be your wedding planner anymore." Connor reached behind her to pull open her door. "Now let's get you to the police station before there's another attempt on your life."

"I'm going to get this even if it kills me." Tandy growled in frustration from behind the coffee shop bar.

"It's not going to kill you. It's a napkin." Zam demonstrated once again, flipping the folded napkin in the air like a frisbee, catching it on the side of his bent elbow, popping it into the air again to catch on the back of his hand, then turning his hand over to guide the napkin to the table with his knuckles.

Tandy twisted her wrist to twirl the napkin up, but it rocketed forward against Zam's chest. "You make it look so easy."

"It gets easier the more you do it." He retrieved the napkin from where it had clung to his t-shirt like a dryer sheet. "Lead with the crease. The weight will guide it."

She took the napkin, angled the crease, and flicked. Up it went. "Oh…oh…" She bent her elbow then bent her knees to get under the napkin. It wasn't pretty, but it was the first time she'd caught the flimsy piece of paper. She grinned triumphantly, afraid to move. "I got it."

Zam pumped a fist in the air.

The front door swung open, ringing the bell. Was Tandy ready to try out her new skill on customers?

Oh, it was only Marissa. Though that might be better.

"Hey, watch my new trick." Tandy grabbed the napkin, spun it in the air, and caught it on her elbow again. She didn't even have to squat this time.

Marissa stopped on the other side of the bar, watching. She continued watching as if she thought there might be more. "Is that in case I spill tea on your elbow again?"

Tandy grinned at Zam. Had he read Marissa's lips? If so, he might have questions.

Rather than react, he simply demonstrated the full trick, placing the napkin in front of Marissa like a waiter would do before serving her drink.

Marissa did her staring thing again. Wow. Tough crowd.

"Isn't that cool?" Tandy prodded.

"It makes a little more sense than just the elbow thing. I could have used some napkins earlier when Ranger flicked blood all over my wedding dress."

Tandy covered her mouth. "Oh no."

Marissa waved her worry away. How was she so chill about having a bloody wedding dress?

"It's fine. I'm getting a new dress. And I'm firing my wedding planner. You know what that woman did?"

Tandy pursed her lips in thought. "Did she suggest you don't wear heels in case you trip?"

Marissa huffed. "Besides that?"

Tandy scrolled through her mental list of wedding preparations. Food. Cake. Decorations. "Did she—?"

"I'll tell you." Marissa planted her hand on a hip. "She's

dating the guy who tried to kill Randon."

Tandy's jaw dropped. Cash had a local girlfriend? Who happened to be planning Marissa's wedding?

"Randon?" Zam repeated. That was one word he'd caught onto quickly.

Marissa nodded. "And it gets better. Her last name is Evans."

Tandy leaned forward. Were all small towns like living in a soap opera, or had she stumbled onto the set for Days of Our Lives? "I didn't know Randon had any family here. How are they related?"

Marissa lifted a shoulder. "I have no idea, but I stopped at the police station and filled Griffin in. He's going to investigate."

He wasn't the only one. Tandy grabbed her laptop out from underneath the counter. This is where her previous career as a journalist came in handy. "Remember when he was attracted to you? Do you think that's because you look like his ex-wife?"

Marissa gasped. "No…"

Zam's eyebrows leaped toward his receding hairline. If the poor guy simply wanted to juggle drinkware, he'd obviously picked the wrong coffee shop.

Both he and Marissa circled the bar to join Tandy on either side of the computer monitor. She typed in the name Moria Evans. A wedding shop popped up.

Marissa pointed. "Type in Randon and Moria Evans."

Tandy clicked her tongue, but typed it in. If the two had once been married, what did that mean? "Could Moria have hired Cash?" She pressed enter.

Headline: DNA Reveals Self-Made Millionaire to Have Secret Twin

Tandy's jaw dropped. The millionaire would be Randon.

Could Moria be his secret twin? She scrolled down.

Marissa pointed. "Moria is Randon's twin."

How did they not know this? Since the article had been released publicly, it wasn't a secret anymore.

"When was this published?" asked Zam.

Tandy scrolled back up. "Last summer." She looked at Tandy. "When did Randon move here?"

Marissa bit her lip. "I think I first saw him in the dunk tank at last year's Americana Festival. It was a big deal because he was paying a thousand dollars to anybody who could dunk him."

"That's one way to make a splash," Zam deadpanned.

Tandy had always wondered what brought Randon to the area. "Did Moria live here before then? Do you think he moved here to reconnect with her?"

Marissa wandered back to the other side of the counter and sank onto a stool. Her heels had to be hurting her feet. It was amazing she'd lasted this long. "If he moved here for Moria, it's crazy that we've never seen them together."

Zam watched their lips carefully. Tandy would have to consider learning sign language if he was going to keep hanging out and teaching her tricks. But for now, she'd look at him to make sure he didn't feel excluded by his handicap. "When was As You Wish Weddings opened?"

"Are you asking Zam?"

Tandy flicked a frown at Marissa. "No. I'm asking you." She turned back toward Zam. "I'm looking at Zam so he can read my lips and keep up with this insane conversation."

"Oh." Marissa turned her stool to face Zam, as well. "I don't think the wedding business is that old. Mom raved about it being the best thing to come to Grace Springs since the sternwheeler cruises."

Tandy arched an eyebrow. "What about our shop?"

Marissa wrinkled her nose. "I'm pretty sure she specifically didn't mention us on purpose."

Tandy sighed. "I'm sorry, Marissa."

Marissa waved a hand. "I'm used to it. Just look up the grand opening for the wedding shop. I'm curious."

Tandy typed and clicked. A huge headline announced As You Wish Weddings. The date underneath read August of the previous year.

"Holy cappuccino, Batman." Tandy stared, fearing the direction her thoughts were taking her.

"What?" Marissa demanded.

Zam shrugged as if there was no other explanation. "Randon moved here to be with his sister in July, she miraculously had enough money to open a beautiful new shop in August, then they were never seen in public or mentioned each other again."

Marissa covered her mouth. "Could Moria have scammed him? Could she have hired a doctor to lie or fudged the online results?"

Tandy pressed her palms against her cheeks. "Maybe Cash wasn't hired to kill Randon as revenge for his ransomware. Maybe Cash wanted to keep Randon quiet because Moria had scammed him."

Marissa leaned forward. "Where are Randon's parents? Couldn't they confirm this?"

Tandy clicked back to the first article. "It says the babies were adopted by different families when their mother died in childbirth, and they didn't know about each other until they both happened to take DNA tests to see if they could find any relatives. They then both changed their names to their birth parents' name."

"Wow." Zam held up three fingers on either side of his mouth to look like the letter W and opened his mouth into an

O shape. Literally spelling out WOW.

Marissa scrunched her nose. "If she's not really his sister, she took advantage of an orphan."

Oh man. Tandy's mind kept rolling with the possible implications. "Do you think he found out about the scam but was too embarrassed to tell anyone?"

Zam crossed his arms. "Do you think he has a real twin sister out there somewhere?"

"Whether she's really his twin or not..." Tandy looked back and forth between the other two. Though Zam wouldn't have to read her lips to know where their deductive reasoning had taken her. "...Moria is considered to be his only living relative and thus the heir to his fortune."

Chapter Nine

MARISSA LIMPED AFTER TANDY TO HER Volkswagen Beetle. Zam, their new unofficial employee, offered to watch the shop so they could go tell Griffin what they'd discovered, but Marissa's feet were killing her. It was a good thing she'd tried out these shoes before the big day so she knew they would never last through a night of swing dancing. And they certainly wouldn't allow her to run away should anybody else come after her.

She thought of the new deputy's beady eyes and shivered. "Can we stop at my house so I can change shoes before we go to the police station?"

Tandy dropped behind the wheel and gave an amused shake of her head. "Would you just agree to wear cowgirl boots with your dress and be done with it?"

Marissa sank into the passenger seat and kicked off her heels. She wasn't that desperate. Yet. "I will consider it."

Tandy strapped on her seatbelt and started the engine. "If I stop by your house, are you going to change your whole outfit or only your shoes?"

Marissa sulked. She'd bought this skirt to match the shoes. Maybe they could come up with a compromise. "If I can't find shoes that match, then—"

"Your gold flip-flops with the bows."

This was the worst part of having a best friend. Tandy was close enough to call her on her stuff. Except... "I bought those for the honeymoon."

Tandy pulled onto Main Street and headed in the

direction of both Marissa's house and the police station. There was no commitment yet on taking her home. "You also bought those heels for your wedding. You can wear a pair of shoes more than once."

"I think I packed them in my suitcase already."

"Then unpack them. You've got a whole summer before you leave."

"It would probably take longer to unpack than it would for me to change."

"I know how long it takes you to change." Tandy pulled to a stop at the corner. This is where she would either turn to go to the police station or head straight toward Marissa's. "Do you agree to changing shoes only?"

Marissa grunted. She should put on something really hideous to try to embarrass Tandy and make her regret this request. Except Marissa had dressed ridiculously before, and she was the only one embarrassed. Despite being comfortable. "Fine."

Tandy rolled forward. "Is Ranger still at your house?"

"No. But there's still blood all over that I need to clean up." If only they had a local crime scene cleaner like that woman she'd read about in Virginia. It would be especially handy in her situation since Gabby St. Claire was also famous for solving mysteries.

"You know this kind of thing only happens to you, right?" Tandy asked.

"I know." Not even Gabby St. Claire would have had to clean up blood from a dog's happy tail. Marissa leaned her head on the passenger seat. "I witnessed an attempted murder and got chased by the hitman. My fiancé's dog whipped blood around my house like Van Gogh gone wild. Then my wedding planner turned out to be the hitman's girlfriend."

Tandy slowed and turned onto her street. "If he did it for his girlfriend, then he's not a hitman. And she must be the one who tried to smother Randon at the hospital. They are both attempted murderers."

Marissa grimaced. "Yet my mom would rather have her for a daughter."

"That says more about your mom than about you." Tandy sniffed and pulled to the curb. "But you've had your fill of drama for the day. Go change your shoes, and we'll solve this case."

Marissa unbuckled and scooped up the beautiful strappy sandals she would never wear again. "I really wish you'd let me change so I could look good when solving a mystery."

Tandy looked at her watch. "You've got two minutes, then I leave without you."

"Ugh." Marissa climbed out and swung the door shut. Who changed shoes in two minutes? She'd have to completely ignore the mess inside.

She jogged toward the steps, took them two at a time, then froze.

A switchblade held a note to the door.

STAY OFF THE WITNESS STAND

Fear gripped her belly in its fist. She took a step backward and looked around for anybody who could be watching.

No Cash. No Moria. Only Tandy stared in impatience from inside her Bug.

She rolled down the passenger window and leaned toward it. "You've got one minute left, Marissa. Hurry or I'll go speak to Griffin without you."

Marissa wasn't going inside her house alone, and she certainly wasn't going to touch the door before the police dusted it for fingerprints. She glanced around the neighborhood for any movement she might have missed. A lace curtain fell into place two doors down. Was Opal watching her again?

"Uh, Tandy? I'm not going to the station with you."

Tandy held her arms wide and shook her head. "Why not?"

"I think Griffin is going to want to come here." She pointed at her door.

Tandy squinted to see from the road. Then she slowly lifted her phone to her ear. Marissa joined her in the car to await Griffin's arrival.

Within minutes he was at her curb again. He climbed out, hitched up his pants, and slammed the door. "This better be a real crime this time, Marissa. No more crying wolf," he called, but his voice trailed off as he sauntered closer to her front door.

Tandy smirked. "I think he means crying black lab."

Marissa bit her lip. "I wish I *was* crying wolf. Because if our suspicions are right, my wedding planner threatened my life."

Compassion softened Tandy's eyes. "That's pretty scary. Though you could take her."

Marissa popped her door open but didn't climb out until she sent her friend a sardonic look. "I got taken out by the bench in her shop."

Tandy shook her head and followed. "Is your clumsiness all an act to make killers feel overconfident?"

"I wish." With all the killers that had come after her in the past, it was incredible she'd survived this long. Hopefully she'd survive the latest threat.

Tandy made herself as comfortable as she could in the molded plastic chairs at the police station. She would rather be practicing more pouring tricks with Zam, but because of Marissa's past of wild accusations, she was really needed here to back up the story about Moria Evans. Not to mention calming her friend's nerves as they waited for Griffin to question the wedding planner.

Marissa angled her body away from the desk at the back of the room where Deputy Romero sat, working on his computer. "Is he looking at me?" she whispered.

Tandy slid her eyes sideways. The bald guy didn't smile much, but she didn't find him as creepy as Marissa did. "Why would he be looking at you?"

"Because I don't trust him. So, my presence will make him feel guilty over whatever he's hiding."

Tandy pressed her lips together to keep from laughing. Obviously, Marissa had reasons to be afraid, but this seemed to be taking it a bit too far. "If that's the case, I would think he's probably going to try to avoid you."

Marissa leaned forward. "Maybe that's why he doesn't talk much."

Tandy nodded like she was going along with the conspiracy theory. "Which makes you feel all the more suspicious."

Marissa's dark eyes widened. "Exactly," she enunciated slowly.

A door down the hallway squeaked opened.

Marissa sat up straighter.

Tandy crossed her legs and leaned back. Once Moria was taken to jail for collusion, they'd be safe to return to their normal lives. And hopefully Randon would be free to recover. Could it be that Moria had taken him for so much money that he'd felt pressured into using ransomware software?

Heels clicked against cement flooring. Not the kind of heels Griffin wore, but more like high heels. Shouldn't the woman wearing high heels be ushered back to the holding cell?

Moria strode out from the hallway, looking ready for the runway in a pink suit with shorts instead of pants. She saw them and paused with a hip popped out to one side. "Marissa, you can consider our contract terminated. I've already ordered your bridesmaid's dress, but other than that, I want nothing to do with you."

Marissa cocked her head. "You mean you're free to go back to work? You're not going to prison?"

"Of course not."

Griffin emerged from the hallway and paused because Moria was in his way. Had he bungled this one? Had he been sucked in by Moria's charms?

"Griffin..." Tandy implored, motioning with an arm toward their only suspect.

Griffin shook his head. "Miss Evans has a solid alibi. Ever since you left the wedding shop, she's been working with the mayor's wife on her daughter's wedding."

Tandy twisted her lips. Could the mayor be in on this? Probably not. But someone had threatened Marissa to protect Cash, and who would do that apart from the man's girlfriend?

Marissa stood. "What about the fraud of claiming to be Randon's twin sister?"

Moria crossed her arms. "I really am Randon's twin. No fraud there."

Griffin rubbed his jaw. "I'll be looking into the DNA testing later when I don't have attempted murder on my hands."

Moria lifted her chin. "Don't worry. You won't find anything. I didn't scam anybody. Randon is my brother, and he co-signed on a loan for me."

Tandy narrowed her eyes. She had yet to see the evidence, and if the two crimes were connected, it didn't do anyone any good to let Moria go. Simply the fact that she was dating the guy who'd stolen Randon's computer was a stronger connection than anyone else had.

Marissa stepped forward with a grunt—probably from the pain of still wearing her strappy heels, but she covered the sound nicely by pointing her whole arm dramatically. "If you weren't guilty of fraud, then why don't you hang out with your twin? Why has nobody seen you together since you opened your wedding shop."

Moria tossed her hair, just as dramatically. If she was anybody's twin, it should have been Marissa's. "Because I found out about the ransomware he'd designed and told him it was going to get him into trouble. He doesn't like it when people tell him what to do, so he stopped talking to me."

She sounded so convincing. It was true about Randon being a bit hardheaded, but it still all seemed too coincidental. Tandy crossed her arms. "How can you be okay with your boyfriend trying to end Randon's life?"

Moria sniffed before turning away and gliding toward the door. "Cash didn't do it. He's been framed."

"Right." Tandy called after her. "What are the chances of there being another evil twin in town?"

Moria pushed through the doors without looking back.

Marissa, on the other hand, turned approving eyes on her. "That was a good one, Tandy."

Tandy rubbed her face. It had felt good in the moment, but it didn't do any good. Rather than being closer to their goal of getting Marissa out of danger by putting another attempted murderer in jail, the first murderer's arrest was being questioned.

What if it wasn't Cash at all? Moria had wanted him out of jail, but she claimed it was because he wasn't guilty. And she hadn't put the note on Marissa's door.

If Cash wasn't the killer, the real killer was on the loose. Though he wouldn't make threats against Marissa for testifying against Cash since he'd set Cash up in the first place. Or maybe he knew Marissa would take that threat to the police, which would make Cash look even guiltier.

Or Cash was the guilty party, and he had someone other than Moria on the outside. "Did you check her alibi for the attack on Randon at the hospital?" she asked Griffin.

He turned and took a seat at his desk. "Yes, Tandy. She was meeting the owner of Valley Vineyards at their location miles away."

Well, she'd tried. Tandy picked up the little black backpack she used as a purse and slung it over a shoulder. Now that they'd hit a dead end, they could turn around and go a different direction. She'd be heading back to the coffee shop to perfect her iced s'mores coffee recipe. "Sorry for wasting your time, Griffin. It seemed plausible."

Griffin hit a few keys on his keyboard. "Sit down, girls."

Tandy scrunched her eyebrows then glanced at Marissa to see if the other woman knew what else was going on. Marissa didn't notice because she'd gone back to spying on the deputy.

Her obsession with him was even creepier than his beady eyes. Though the obsession could be coming from her subconscious. Might Marissa have gotten her bald dudes mixed up, and Deputy Romero was the real culprit? Tandy shivered.

"Marissa." Griffin waited for her to sit and face him. "Are you still willing to testify against Cash?"

She peeked over her shoulder once more. "Yes."

"Good." He went back to his computer. "Then we are going to have to keep you safe until the trial."

She gave him her full attention. "Safe?"

Tandy blinked as well. Did Griffin really think she was in danger? He'd accused her of crying wolf earlier. It was good he was taking her seriously now, but how serious was it?

"I..." Marissa stammered. "I can have Ranger stay with me again. Or do you think I should go over to Connor's parents' farmhouse instead?"

Griffin leveled his eyes on her. "Not unless you want to put his family in danger too."

"No." She reached for Tandy. Gripped her arm with fingernails as sharp as the look the sheriff was giving them. "Of course not. What...? Where...?" Her eyes filled with unshed tears. "Why...?"

Tandy peeled Marissa's fingernails off then gripped her hand in a way that could still be reassuring without the added side-effect of pain. She knew this would be especially important when she asked the question Marissa was afraid to. "What is the option you recommend?"

Griffin rubbed his face. "Marissa, I have a safehouse prepared for you."

Chapter Ten

Marissa wanted to scream like Kevin on *Home Alone*. She covered her mouth instead. "You expect me to leave town as I'm planning my wedding? I don't have a dress anymore. I don't even have a wedding planner. I have to do it all myself. How can I possibly do it from a safehouse?"

Griffin rubbed his temples. "How can you possibly attend your wedding if you're dead?"

He might as well have aimed his gun at her. Not being able to plan the perfect wedding was going to kill her.

Tandy squeezed her hand. "I can help out, Marissa."

The suggestion was worse than death. "So you can get your black bridesmaid dress?"

Tandy's lips curved up on one side. "Tempting, but no. I'll be good. I won't even pick up cowgirl boots for you."

"I hate this." Marissa dropped against her stiff seat back and stared at the ceiling. "I know you wouldn't do anything purposeful to ruin my wedding, Tandy, but you're so…"

Tandy's grip on her hand loosened.

Gah. With everything else going wrong in her life, Marissa didn't want to lose her best friend. She sat up and gripped tighter. "I mean, we have different styles."

Tandy didn't tighten her grip or let go. She was a hung jury.

Marissa made her final appeal. "You'd hate it if I planned your wedding."

Tandy shrugged at that, the muscle in front of her ear relaxing as she unclenched her jaw. "That's true. You'd dress me like a ballerina."

Marissa could picture it. A full tulle skirt. A bun that wasn't messy for a change. She gripped Tandy's hand with both of hers. "You'd be so pretty."

"I'd wear my motorcycle boots and black choker."

There went that image. Marissa's shoulders slumped. "Moria *did* call you an urban pirate."

Tandy's lips pursed thoughtfully. "I kinda like that."

"Ladies." Griffin scratched his head. "I'm sure the wedding stuff will get figured out. Right now we need to focus on the safehouse."

Marissa would rather talk about weddings. Her wedding. Her plans for a future that never involved a safehouse. "How long will I be there?"

Griffin picked up a pen to fiddle with. "Probably until I can arrest whoever stuck that note to your front door."

Probably? "What if you don't? Or what if you arrest them but they are part of a bigger network of criminals?"

Griffin snapped his pen lid on and off a few times before making eye contact. "If we had to, we could put you in the witness protection program with a new identity. Connor could join you, of course."

Marissa's stomach sunk from the ride on this roller coaster that was her life. If it came to that, Connor would join her, but she didn't want him to have to. Neither of them had ever lived anywhere else. She had her new shop. He had his construction business. They both had families. She didn't mind leaving her parents behind, but his mom and dad were the best. Though leaving the goats behind could be a good thing.

Tandy spoke for her. "Are you serious?"

Griffin sighed and put the pen down to type in the computer. "That's worst-case scenario. I've heard rumors of a secret witness protection town in the mountains somewhere with no roads in and no roads out. I think it would be a great place to live."

Marissa smacked the desk. "Griffin! I wear high heels. I don't want to live in the mountains."

Tandy tilted her head. "There's always cowboy boots."

Marissa bulged her eyes at the friend who should be standing up for her here no matter their difference in footwear.

Tandy let go of her hand to smack the desk, as well. "But you're not going to live in the mountains because Griffin is going to solve this case."

Griffin scratched his head.

"Or I will," Tandy finished.

Marissa nodded in appreciation as if that sealed the deal. "Thank you."

Griffin shot Tandy a withering glance before focusing on Marissa. "In the meantime, I have a safehouse set up. I'll personally escort you to get your things then say goodbye to Connor before taking you out there."

"Goodbye?" Marissa sank into her seat again. She'd been so upset about not being able to plan her wedding that she didn't stop to think about what life would be like without Connor. He was her rock. He kept her grounded.

Tandy rubbed her arm. "Not forever."

Marissa's chin quivered. She felt like crying, but without Connor, whose shoulder would she cry on? Certainly not Griffin's. "Will I be able to talk to him on the phone?"

Griffin nodded. "When I'm there to set up a secure line."

"See?" Tandy said, as if a secure line made everything better. "Then we can talk too. And I'll run all the wedding planning stuff past you."

If nothing else, this change of events would up Marissa's

prayer life. Probably Tandy's too with as much as she would be juggling. "You're going to plan my wedding, solve this mystery, and run the shop all by yourself?"

Tandy grimaced. "Not *all* by myself. I have Greg."

Marissa bit her lip. Should she mention how busy Greg already was with his law practice? "I know he'd do anything for you, even dress up like Abe Lincoln on a hot day, but..."

"I know." Tandy twisted her lips in thought. Then her blue eyes caught Marissa's and clouded with concern. "I'll figure out something. Don't worry about me. I just want you to be safe."

Marissa's heart squeezed tight. Was her life worth keeping safe if she was leaving it all behind?

Griffin stood. "Let's go, Marissa. The sooner I get you situated in our standard safehouse, the sooner I can get back to work on the case."

Her heart pitter-pattered like she was afraid, but if she was going to a safehouse, what did she have to fear? She stood and Tandy stood with her, demonstrating she wasn't alone.

That's what she was afraid of. Losing this kind of connection.

Her life was about to change. Not in the loud, crazy way she'd feared when Cash had chased her to the roof or when she'd found blood spattered throughout her house. But in this anticlimactic way that was as serene as it was surreal.

Would she ever see Tandy again?

She reached for a hug.

Tandy stiffened for a moment like she usually did before melting into Marissa's arms like chocolate on the tongue. "I don't like admitting how much I'm going to miss you."

"Then don't." Marissa wiped at a rogue tear behind Tandy's head before pulling away so that she could pretend to be as tough. "I'll be back soon. Just keep in mind that if you mess up my wedding, I'm going to make you wear pink."

Tandy took a minute to clear her throat before looking up and narrowing her eyes. "And I thought Moria was the heartless blonde."

Marissa mustered a weepy smile at Tandy's attempt at making her feel better. It was good to have friends like Tandy. Even if she wasn't sure they'd ever see each other again.

A weight formed in the pit of Tandy's stomach as she watched through the window. Marissa climbed into Griffin's cop car. Tandy needed to go finish preparing the Red, White, and Brew booth for the weekend's carnival, but the heaviness inside wouldn't let her get to work until she knew Marissa was really safe. Though the only way Marissa wouldn't be safe was if her instinct about Deputy Romero was accurate.

Tandy glanced over her shoulder. It was weird how quiet the guy was, but how could she judge when she'd never tried to talk to him before?

"Hey," she said before she changed her mind.

Kristin, the secretary wearing a headband with two red stars attached like antennas, looked up, sending the stars bouncing. "Is there something I can help you with, Tandy?"

Maybe the deputy didn't talk because Kristin spoke enough for both of them.

Tandy waved Kristin away. "I'd actually like to speak with Deputy Romero about my friend."

The deputy looked up, beady eyes neither friendly nor welcoming. It didn't bother Tandy as much as it had Marissa though. Back in her days at the newspaper in Cincinnati, she'd hated being interrupted at her desk. But that was before she bought a coffee shop and only got paid when people showed up.

Kristin smiled at her boss, obviously unfazed by his demeanor. "Do you have time to answer questions, Adrian?"

The deputy waved Tandy over without a word. Like sign language. Crazy that her new deaf friend spoke more than this guy.

She took a seat at the side of his desk and glanced down at the paperwork there to see exactly what she was interrupting. He scooped it into a pile and flipped it over on the far corner before she could make out anything other than the word "forensics" at the top. Were he not an officer of the law, working confidential cases, it might be considered suspicious behavior.

"Were you able to find any fingerprints at Marissa's house or on the note on her door?" she asked.

He flicked his eyes toward the paperwork as if confirming she couldn't see through it. "Yours were there."

She tucked in her chin in surprise. Did he suspect her? She'd been through that with Griffin once before, and it wasn't fun. "Well, yeah. I'm at Marissa's all the time. Did you find anything suspicious?"

"Not yet." His gaze bored into her. Unrelenting.

If he was suspicious of her, then she'd be suspicious of him. She checked his neck for any remains from a tattoo he might have drawn on to implicate Cash. Nothing. But if he had wanted to implicate Cash, then he would have had to know the guy first. Could they have been in the military together? They both had buzzed heads. "What did you do before you moved here?" she asked casually.

His eyes almost disappeared when he narrowed them. "Marines."

Aha! So he could have known Cash. But he didn't have the green eyes Marissa remembered. "Your eyes look like they are bothering you. Do you wear contacts?"

"My eyes are fine. Thank you for your concern."

Such evasive maneuvers. What was he hiding? If he'd attacked Randon and set Cash up as Moria claimed, then he was a killer on the loose with access to Marissa's whereabouts.

But why would he want to hurt her? Cash was currently the one under investigation, and Marissa was testifying against him. The note on her door had been trying to get her *not* to testify.

It would be counterproductive for the deputy to both pose as Cash then threaten the life of anyone who implicated the other man. Plus, there was the fact that the deputy had been guarding Randon at the hospital and Randon was still alive.

Or was he? Her heart revved like a car engine. "Why aren't you at the hospital protecting Randon anymore?"

He stared, his expression unflinching.

Did he have no soul? If Randon died on his watch then —

"The hospital brought in their own security."

Tandy closed her eyes and exhaled. "Oh, good."

Nobody had died on this case. That boded well for Marissa, right? If someone had really wanted to kill her, they wouldn't have left a warning note.

The deputy cleared his throat. "The hospital brought in security because they know I'm busy with the investigation as well as crowd control for the festival. We would all be better off if you could be so respectful."

Tandy blinked a few times then gave her thinnest smile. Marissa may see the deputy as creepy, but she saw him as a jerk.

"Since this crime is still unsolved…" She let the reminder of his current failure sink in as she pushed to her feet. "You certainly do have more work to do."

He turned to position his fingers on his keyboard, ignoring her, and she kinda wished he was guilty of a crime. Any crime.

But despite his resemblance and possible connection to Cash, she didn't think Marissa had anything to worry about with him. There didn't seem to be a motive. As for Marissa's creepy vibe, it could have simply come from Marissa never having been ignored by a man before.

Tandy stopped at Kristin's desk to finish putting her soul at ease. "Do you know where Griffin is taking Marissa?" she asked.

Kristin shook her head, sending her headband stars flailing for help. "The safehouse is owned by the county and its location is only shared on a need-to-know basis. Cash's accomplice could torture me for the information, and I'd never be able to tell."

Tandy's eyebrows arched at the extreme image. "How…comforting."

"Isn't it?"

Tandy hooked a thumb over her shoulder and lowered her voice. "What about the deputy? Could he be tortured for the information?"

Kristin propped an elbow on her desk and leaned her chin on her fist to study her coworker on the other side of the room. "I doubt it. Even if he knew, he never talks. Not everyone can be as heroic as Connor Thomas."

Tandy pursed her lips at the awkward turn in their conversation. Did she mean Greg? Because that was Tandy's boyfriend. Memories of Kristin's mistletoe headband from Christmas danced in Tandy's head. Maybe she'd tried to get somewhere with the deputy and had struck out. She was probably just lonely. "Does Romero have access to the safehouse location."

Kristin shrugged. "He doesn't know anything. The only way anybody would ever find out where Marissa is hiding is if they were a hacker and could break into Griffin's computer."

Tandy looked away. The only hacker she knew was in a coma from the attempted murder by the same person who had threatened Marissa's life.

"What do you mean your life has been threatened?" Connor yelled down to Marissa from the mayor's roof.

Connor's construction crew looked on, turning off power tools, probably to be able to hear as well. She had, after all, shown up with the sheriff.

This was not the ideal setting for what Marissa had hoped would be a private conversation. With as long as it had taken her to pack up all her stuff, Connor should have been off work. But he'd gone into overtime since the mayor's daughter's wedding reception was supposed to be held on this property in a week.

"Could you please come down here?" she called up. She wasn't going to climb any ladders in her new gold flip-flops. Even for a goodbye kiss.

Connor nodded, hooked his hammer in his tool belt, then motioned to a couple men to keep working before lowering a leg over the side of the house and descending the ladder with the speed of a fireman. He hopped to the ground and looked her up and down, concern creasing his sweaty brow. "Are you okay?"

He meant physically, which she was, but inside she crumbled like the topping on one of Billie's apple pies. She had to be honest with him. "No." Her bottom lip quivered.

"Oh, hon." He wrapped his strong hands around her upper arms. "What's going on?" He looked past her to Griffin, blame darkening his eyes.

"I'm taking her to a safehouse because someone doesn't want her to testify against Cash."

She didn't even get a chance to see Connor's face or add to the explanation before she was against his damp shirt. He usually smelled like pine, but today the scent was mixed with a musk that would need to be showered away. Not her favorite scent, but it could be a long time before she smelled it again. She wrapped her arms around his solid back and breathed deep.

"Who threatened her?" Connor asked over her head.

"There was an anonymous note on her door. We're investigating," Griffin said.

"Not good enough." Connor pulled away and cupped her face this time. "When is the trial? How long will you be gone?"

His concern wrapped around her heart like a warm blanket. She covered his hands with hers and looked into his eyes. "Cash's trial date isn't until September, but hopefully the accomplice is found before then."

His wild eyes reminded her of a caged lion. "I will find whoever threatened you. They won't get away with this."

She wanted to believe him, but she also needed a plan B in place before she left. She needed to know he was in this with her, so she'd feel less alone after she left. "What if they do get away with it? What if I have to go into the witness protection program? Will you go with me?"

He stilled.

She curled her toes.

This was a big ask. He'd be giving up everything for her. If he wouldn't go, she'd stay. She'd risk her life for him.

"Yes," he said.

Before she could breathe a sigh of relief, his mouth found hers and kissed away her fears.

Chapter Eleven

TANDY WOULD BE SURPRISED IF SHE made it home before midnight. She usually cleaned up the shop while Marissa baked, but now she had to do both. Not to mention the special pastries Marissa had planned for the festivities. The rice crispy treats dipped halfway in white chocolate then sprinkled with blue and white edible glitter were easy, compared to the blueberry tartlets with the star cutouts in the pastry and the red, white, and blue macaroons.

Who was Tandy kidding? She'd be there all night. Greg would have joined her if he wasn't at his office designing coffee coupons, printing tea house flyers, and running background checks on both Moria Evans and Adrian Romero.

She brushed flour off her hands. "Might as well make another espresso, huh, Cocoa?"

Cocoa yipped, which was his normal response, but then he jumped up and ran circles around his gated corner.

"Potty break?" she asked him.

He yipped again.

Poor guy. She hadn't been able to take him on a walk since the parade. Maybe she shouldn't with a possible killer on the loose.

She grabbed his leash and looked through the windows at the dimming light with apprehension. Movement caught her eye, and she tensed, ready to grab a rolling pin to use as a weapon.

Zam strolled down the street with Sheila, completely unaware Tandy was ready to bash his skull in. Maybe he should be careful too. With his hearing loss, he wouldn't be able to hear a killer sneaking up on him.

Tandy scanned the area to make sure both he and she were safe before stooping to hook Cocoa's collar with the leash and lead him outside. He caught her eye through the glass door and gave her a nod as she pushed it open. Perfect timing, though with the way Cocoa charged toward Sheila, this had been her pup's plan all along.

Zam slowed. "You have flour on your face." He brushed his own cheek to demonstrate.

"Oops. Thanks." She lifted an elbow to wipe it off with her shoulder sleeve. If she didn't get it all, oh well. She still had a long way to go.

Zam pointed to the shop. "You working late to practice the napkin trick I taught you?"

She wished. Might as well tell him what was really going on. If he didn't hear it from her, he'd be sure to learn it from the town gossips within the next twenty-four hours. "Marissa had to leave for a safehouse because someone doesn't want her to testify against Cash."

Zam's mouth opened the same way it had when he'd spelled out WOW with his hands. Only this time he had no words.

She looked down at Cocoa who danced around like he needed a jog to get all his energy out. How was she going to do everything she had to do over the next month or two?

She looked back up so Zam could read her lips. "I'm trying to get all her baking done and thinking I might have to start selling Costco muffins until she returns. People like Costco muffins, right?"

"No," he said.

She rolled her eyes. "You're a lot of help."

He reached for Cocoa's leash. "I can be."

Oh no. She hadn't meant to be rude or to even ask for assistance. Maybe she should call it a day and get some sleep. She pulled the leash her way. "I didn't mean…"

Zam didn't let go. "Tandy, let me help. I'm walking my dog anyway. And since I sold my bar, I don't have anything else to do at night."

His wide eyes spoke of sincerity. And Cocoa would appreciate it.

"Only if you're sure." She didn't like needing help from anyone.

"I'm sure." He took the leash. "But if there are other things you want me to do at your shop when I get back, you'll have to hire me."

Tandy tried to read his expression as he walked away. Was he sincere about that offer, as well? Because she could use another employee. And with his experience, he would be a good one.

She debated the pros and cons as she finished rolling out the dough for tarts. If only the guy could bake, because her stars looked more like Patrick the Starfish from the Sponge Bob cartoon.

The bell over the door chimed.

Zam nodded as he entered then opened the corner gate for the dogs and hung up both their leashes. Was he planning to stay?

She waited until he faced her again to ask, "What are you doing?"

He picked up a chair and flipped it over to set on top of a table. "Mopping."

She wanted to argue that the floor wasn't that dirty, but with her baking, there was flour everywhere. Granted, Marissa wouldn't be here to slip in it tomorrow, but there was no guarantee the shop wouldn't have any clumsy customers.

"You're hired."

Zam grinned. "I know."

The door flung open behind him, banging against the doorjamb loud enough to block out the sound of the bells. Tandy wielded her rolling pin.

Connor stormed in, jaw set, hands in fists. If she didn't know him so well, she'd be a little scared. However, she did know him, but not well enough to ever have seen this side of him before.

Zam lifted the mop as his weapon.

Connor glared at the man. "You replaced Marissa already?"

Oh boy. "Marissa is irreplaceable, Connor. Though I can make you some of her chamomile tea to help you calm down."

He turned his gaze on her. A warning not to offer him more tea. "I don't want to calm down. I want to find whoever is threatening my bride."

Tandy held up her hands to show she was on his side. "So do I."

Connor faced off with Zam. "Is it you?"

Zam looked at Tandy with wide eyes then stuffed the mop back in the big yellow water bucket on wheels as if to say he was out of there. She didn't blame him. And she also didn't want to lose his help.

"Connor, this is Zam who won the dog show. Remember?"

Zam held out a hand to shake, despite the unwelcoming flash in the other man's eyes.

Connor tilted his chin away but kept eye contact with Zam, also radiating mistrust.

Tandy didn't need to deal with any more drama. "Zam took Cocoa on a walk for me, and he's offered to help around here since I'm short-staffed. It's a good thing."

Zam stuffed his extended hand in his pocket. "I'm sorry, dude. I'm only trying to help."

"We need more help than a janitor. Where's Greg? I need him to run a background check on the wedding planner, that deputy Marissa thinks is creepy, and… and…" Connor turned so his back was to Zam so he could point across his chest without the motion being seen and talk without the man reading his lips. "Him."

Zam's eyes hardened like he knew what Connor was saying anyway, which wasn't surprising as Connor really hadn't been that covert. Apparently, with Marissa gone, her fiancé had taken over her theatrics.

Tandy smiled an apology. "Zam, if I'm going to hire you, I really should run a background check and do a drug test anyway. Nothing personal."

Connor kept his back to Zam. "Maybe not for you."

Tandy shook her head in disapproval.

Zam picked up the mop again. "I've been a business owner. I understand. And, speaking as a business owner, you should start locking your doors after hours."

Connor shot a scowl over his shoulder.

Tandy huffed. "Connor, Greg is already looking into Moria and Deputy Romero. We're going to find whoever put that note on Marissa's door. It's been an exhausting day. Why don't you go home and get some rest?"

Connor stalked to a bar stool, sat facing Zam, and crossed his arms like Tandy's bodyguard.

Zam stuck the mop in the bucket for the second time. "Let me know when you get my background check, Tandy. Until then, your bouncer here can mop the floor."

Tandy watched him retrieve Sheila with the urge to cry in the cookie dough. "Thanks for your help, Zam," she called after him even though he couldn't hear.

Cocoa yipped, his little paws against the gate holding him upright. He was sad to see them go too.

Connor followed Zam to the door and flipped the lock closed. "I'm sure Greg will thank me later."

Tandy was too tired to argue. She also didn't want to upset Connor if there was a chance he might help clean.

"I've heard mopping is a great way to vent frustration," she said a fraction of a second before turning on her mixer so she couldn't hear his response.

Marissa could just imagine what a great time her friends were having without her. She'd put all the work into planning special red, white, and blue goodies, and Tandy got to make them, while she sat alone on a back patio in the dark. The safehouse was so far from town that there wasn't even enough light to see the outlines of the trees in the woods.

Griffin planned to stay the first night to make sure Marissa was safe, but he'd fallen asleep on the couch in front of the television, and he snored. So she'd escaped onto the back patio where the only sound was the chirping of crickets and the occasional hoot of an owl. If this was her life for the next two months, she was going to go crazy. She might get to return home after the trial, but then Connor would be marrying an insane woman.

If Tandy was able to get her wedding planned.

Marissa had a special email address set up where they could communicate, but it still wouldn't be the same as taste-testing the wedding cake herself.

Well, that was the one good thing. Since she wasn't baking for the shop, she wouldn't be eating as much sugar.

She'd also have plenty of time to do workout videos. She'd be so fit when she returned that Connor wouldn't even recognize her.

It would be a tradeoff. Fit body, mentally unfit mind.

She smiled at the memory of Connor's goodbye kiss. The man was willing to give up his life for her. Could she ask for anything more?

Well, yeah. For him *not* to have to give it up.

Griffin needed to catch whoever it was that posted the note on her door. Had he even questioned her neighbors yet? Surely Opal had seen something.

A spot on Marissa's bicep zapped with the sting of a mosquito. She slapped at the pest. Then she hugged her arms, but either the night chill was overcoming the summer heat, or she was shivering from anxiety. *See?* She was going crazy already.

She pushed to her feet. Griffin's snoring may keep her awake, but at least she'd be warm in her bed. She slid the door open and considered slamming it to wake Griffin from his snoring, but it probably wouldn't stop him for long. Instead she gently closed and locked the door, sure to draw the blinds. Just in case any fishermen happened to recognize her and mention to their buddies exactly where she was located, and their conversation was overheard by whoever it was that wanted Cash out of jail.

The idea sounded so preposterous that her hideout seemed like a joke. An overreaction. A waste of her life.

Marissa pulled the hairband from her ponytail and massaged her scalp as she trudged toward the hallway. What was her hair going to look like after two months without seeing a stylist? Was she going to have to face the jury like that, or would she get a chance to go to the spa on the way to court?

Something hard jabbed into her hip. The table. Something else smashed against the top of her foot then clattered to the floor.

She looked down to find the cell phone she knocked over. Griffin's, since she wasn't allowed to bring hers.

She rubbed her hip that was sure to bruise then bent to pick up Griffin's phone. She set it farther back on the table this time so there wouldn't be another accident.

It buzzed under her touch.

She jumped and snatched her hand to her chest. Goodness, she was edgy. She willed her heart rate to slow and sent the offensive device a mock scowl.

The name DEPUTY ROMERO glowed in blue letters from the screen. A text.

She glanced over her shoulder at Griffin. Should she wake him? Could this be important? Or might it possibly incriminate the deputy, but Griffin wouldn't even notice because he didn't suspect Romero.

Griffin's chest rose and fell with a terrible shudder. He was out.

Marissa would check the message for him and make sure it wasn't anything he needed to be woken up for. That's what she would tell him anyway.

Tipping forward to get a better look, Marissa tapped the screen. A keypad with nine numbers popped up. Drat. Even though she'd babysat Little Lukey Griffin as a kid, she didn't know Big Griffin well enough now to figure out his password. She'd have to wake him.

Reaching to pick up the phone, her hand bumped a pile of Griffin's other possessions. His badge spun then clinked against the table. It landed in such a way that his badge number stared her straight in the face.

Divine providence? Probably not. More like the curiosity that killed the cat. But what if it was the very information in the deputy's text that saved her life. She could at least try the badge number as Griffin's password.

Biting her lip, she checked over her shoulder one more time to make sure the coast was clear. Griffin continued snoring loud enough to drown out the sound of even an oncoming tornado. She was good.

She tapped the digits into the screen. A giant Superman logo appeared. Seemed like an appropriate wallpaper choice for the wannabe superhero. But who was Lex Luther?

Marissa clicked on the messaging app. The deputy's name popped up at the top of a list. She took a deep breath and selected it.

"Finished questioning witness's neighborhood. Nobody saw anything, including the nosy old lady who plays the organ at church. Could witness have faked the note like she did when she blamed the dog's blood on an intruder?"

Marissa gasped. What a creep.

First of all, she had trouble believing Romero questioned her neighbors since he hardly ever spoke. Secondly, faking the note would mean she sentenced herself to exile during the most important time in her life.

Nobody would ever believe that. Griffin would most certainly never believe that. He was there when she kissed Connor goodbye.

But why would the deputy want to discredit her? She'd feared that maybe he'd been the one to try to kill Randon and pin it on Cash. But what if they were in this together? What if they'd both been snipers in the military? Cash took the contract killer route, Romero took a job with law enforcement.

Then when his buddy got caught, he was there trying to finish the job as well as save him.

Marissa's mind whirled with different scenarios. Perhaps the deputy hadn't been able to finish off Randon because Susan had been by his side ever since the last attempt. But Randon was still in danger. And, therefore, so was she.

Chapter Twelve

Tandy yawned and stared at her pathetic attempt at patriotic macaroons in the silver morning light. She'd given up on baking at one in the morning and gone home, but six hours later she was back and even groggier than before.

As for the cookies, they were lumpy and uneven. Cream oozed out the sides. Should she even put them in the display case? Maybe if they tasted good.

She lifted one and nibbled on the sugary fluff. Not bad. Except for the way the filling ran down her fingers. She popped the rest of the cookie in her mouth so she was free to lick her sticky skin.

The bell over the door rang. Sheila entered, followed by Zam.

"You must have had a rough night if you're eating cookies for breakfast," he said.

Cocoa woofed.

Tandy would be happy to see him if she wasn't embarrassed about how Connor had treated him. Connor hadn't actually gone home last night. He'd fallen asleep upstairs in the tea loft because it reminded him of Marissa. She'd have to wake him soon so he could go clean up before work.

"Hi, Zam," she said quietly, preferring to wait to wake Connor when there wasn't anyone in her shop that he could accuse of threatening to kill his fiancée. The sooner she got Zam's background check the better. Though, if she remembered correctly, Zam wasn't his first name. "Are you still wanting to work here?"

"I want to help you, and I can do that whether or not you hire me." He set a large white paper bag with handles on her counter. "Here."

What could he have brought that would possibly help her? Caffeine. A macaroon-fixing magic wand. A time machine so she could sleep for another four hours. "What is it?"

"Open it."

Why did he want to help her so badly?

She gave him a funny grin but crossed to the counter and pulled the edge down to peek inside. A carton of store-bought cupcakes. They had star spangled wrappers, but they still weren't any better than Costco muffins. Sadly, they beat her macaroons and would go in the display case. It was better than she'd done.

She tried not to let her tone go too flat as she thanked him, though it wasn't like he'd hear it.

He led Sheila to the puppy corner and returned with a smirk. "You don't seem thrilled with my gift, but maybe I can change your mind."

With the pizazz of a circus performer, he whisked out the carton along with a bag of clear plastic goblets, M&Ms in the colors of the American flag, and star sprinkles. Juggling and tossing the goblet, he filled it with the chocolate candies, stuck the cupcake on top, and finished with a dash of colorful sprinkles over the whipped cream frosting.

He presented it like Indiana Jones holding out the Holy Grail. "It's all about plating."

Tandy accepted the treat and turned it around in her hands to admire. She'd never seen such adorable food. Not that she'd tell Marissa. "If only you'd brought this over before I spent the night slaving away."

Zam rubbed his head. "I didn't think you wanted me around last night."

The bell rang, and she looked up. Zam followed the direction of her gaze. A large group of elderly people she'd never seen before poured in, wearing patriotic gear. Tourists who got bussed in for the town's festivities.

"I definitely want you around right now. I'll take orders if you want to pour."

Zam saluted and marched behind the counter.

Tandy ran the cash register but could barely keep up with him. Mugs clinked around her. Drinks were delivered with froth in the shape of American flags or with stars sprinkled on in cinnamon. And Zam even had a way to pour in syrup from high above, ending the pour the very moment he swept his arm across the area where he'd been pouring.

The customers smiled as they carried their drinks away.

Tandy pointed at the syrup bottle. "I want to learn to do that."

"The hinge cut? Only takes a little finesse."

The front bell rang again. Opal's scowl entered before she did.

"Yes. The hinge cut. But not until after I brew Opal's Earl Grey."

Zam nodded. They watched Opal take her tiny, fragile steps. It could be a while before Tandy got to learn to do the new trick. While waiting, she might as well practice her napkin trick.

She grabbed the folded square, flicked it into the air, caught it on her elbow, bounced it up again, caught it on the back of her hand, and flicked her wrist over to set it on the counter in front of Opal. Success. She sent Zam a triumphant grin before facing her customer.

"What can I get you today?" she asked even though the

answer never changed. The one time she'd assumed, Opal berated her for being so disrespectful.

Opal's thin lips pressed together. "You could start with a clean napkin."

Zam laughed.

Tandy turned to grab another napkin, sticking out her tongue at Zam when Opal couldn't see. She set it down primly in front of her most discerning patron. "Anything else?"

"Now that you've gotten that out of your system, I'll take an Earl Grey tea steeped for exactly two minutes."

"You got it." Tandy nodded at Zam to get started. Hopefully he'd realized not to try any of his tricks with this order.

Opal lowered her glasses to look at Tandy over the brim. "Young lady, I'm not finished."

And Tandy had been trying so hard not to assume. She motioned to Zam's cupcake display. "Could I get you something to eat with that?"

Opal glared at the patriotic dessert. "At this hour? Of course not. I have someone joining me."

"Oh." Who in town would be brave enough to drink tea with this lady? Was Tandy's ex-boyfriend back with his smile so Downy fresh that it even softened Opal's wrinkly heart? "Do you know what your friend would like to drink?"

"It's my grandson."

That made more sense.

"And he has a sweet tooth, so I'll take one of your s'mores mochas."

Tandy took Opal's credit card and checked to make sure Zam was on top of both drinks. Heaven forbid he leave the tea bag in too long while he was steaming the chocolate milk for Opal's grandson.

Of course, he was already pulling out the whipped cream, mini marshmallows, and chocolate bar shavings while the espresso brewed. He caught her eye with a smirk of amusement at Opal's indulgence in her grandson's sweet tooth, so she mimicked Opal's cupcake contempt without making a sound. "At this hour?" He could read her lips while Opal would never know she'd said a word.

She faced the cash register again. "That will be eight dollars and fifty cents."

"I gave you my card. Swipe already."

Tandy didn't trust herself to say anything else. Thankfully, Zam had the drinks on the bar before she finished the transaction.

The bell rang again. Tandy glanced up and immediately took back her negativity toward Opal. The woman was an angel compared to the deadbeat detective Joseph Cross had hired. How would she get rid of Trenton this time?

He headed her way. "Tandy."

She grunted in acknowledgement.

He turned his attention to Opal. "Grandma."

Tandy's jaw dropped as he bent to kiss the old woman's cheek. But it made sense in a weird sort of way. At least they both had each other and wouldn't be talking to her anymore.

Unfortunately, as the dreary duo ambled away, Connor clomped down the stairs in his work boots, rubbing the sleep out of his eyes. Was he going to want Zam's fingerprints next? Greg should get there soon with his background checks, and she'd request to have one run on her miraculous new employee. With their relationship being professional, she'd have to get his written consent.

Connor didn't even look at Zam. Instead he held up his

phone. "I got an email from Marissa."

Tandy eyed the disastrous macaroons to make sure they were out of his sight, so he didn't report back to her business partner. Marissa didn't need anything else to stress about.

"She said the deputy interrogated her neighbors about the note on her door, and they didn't see anything, so he suspects her of faking it."

Tandy hadn't thought anything would shock her more than seeing Trenton kiss Opal on the cheek. But Marissa faking the note? "Why would she do that?"

Connor glowered, and not only from not being a morning person. "She wouldn't. It's preposterous."

Tandy shook her head. She'd been with Marissa when they'd first found the note. Before that, Marissa had been at the wedding planner's shop. "Somebody had to have seen something. I mean, Opal could run the neighborhood watch all by herself if she wanted to."

Zam pointed across the coffee shop. "That Opal."

Connor turned. "I'll go ask her some more…"

Zam grabbed the back of his shirt and held him in place. Connor shrugged away. "Hey, man."

Zam didn't look at him. Just held up a hand to stop him. "Wait. She's telling Trenton about her neighbor Marissa."

Tandy strained to hear the conversation over the Yankee Doodle playlist she'd put together. Nothing. And she definitely couldn't make out any words from watching their lips. If she'd had to guess, Opal had said, *Something, something, Scooby-Doo.*

"Don't stare," Zam admonished.

Connor spun to face her, so she spun to face the opposite wall, as well.

Zam lifted his eyebrows at her behavior before focusing

back on Opal and her grandson at the far end of a round table. "It would be more normal for you to pretend to be in conversation with each other rather than synchronized spinning."

"Right." She faced Connor again, smiled, and nodded.

Connor's pained expression told her he wasn't going to play along.

"Okay," Zam translated. "Opal didn't tell the police what she saw because she thought it might be a clue for Trenton."

Connor's eyes grew stormier, if that was possible. "Are you kidding me?"

Tandy stepped around the counter so she could anchor Connor in place. "What did Trenton say?"

"He wants to know what the person looked like who stuck the note to Marissa's door."

Tandy went from smiling and nodding to scowling and shaking her head. The private detective could get in serious trouble for this if he didn't go to the police. Though Tandy would. Deputy Romero needed to know there was somebody really out there threatening Marissa's life.

"Opal saw a woman," Zam said slowly like a kindergartner learning how to read.

Tandy gasped. "Then it has to be Moria. Do you think the mayor's wife would cover for her? Or maybe she was mistaken."

Connor's eyes slid sideways toward Zam in speculation. "Anything else?"

"Opal doesn't approve of Marissa's wedding dress not being full-length."

Connor blinked and looked at Tandy. "How short is it?"

Tandy waved away the question. It didn't even matter anymore since Marissa was getting a new dress. "It was tea-length because Marissa's mom didn't want her to trip on the train."

His head cocked in confusion. "But she's planning to wear heels?"

"I think I can talk her into cowboy boots."

Connor nodded in appreciation. "Did Trenton say anything else?" he asked Zam.

Tandy stilled to wait for the answer, not even turning when the bell rang over the door.

Zam dropped his forearms on the counter and leaned on them casually, looking the least conspicuous out of the three of them. "They're still talking about the way Officer Griffin dive-rolled around Marissa's house when she made the mistake of reporting an intruder."

Tandy bit back a smile.

Connor's lips twitched.

Files smacked down on the counter between them, jolting Tandy from surveillance mode.

"Hey." Greg looked back and forth between Connor and Tandy. "Staring competition?"

Yes. Because they had nothing better to do. She turned her head slightly toward her boyfriend and instinctively covered her mouth in case there were other people in the world who could read lips. Specifically, Opal. She was full of surprises today. "Zam's reading Opal's lips. She lied to the police."

Greg shoved his hands in the pockets of his khaki suit, looking decidedly more J. Crew than when in his Abraham Lincoln costume, but his pinched expression made him appear less comfortable. "She lied? That's obstruction of justice."

"Yeah, we'll have to tell Griffin. Opal saw a woman

leaving the note on Marissa's door. The only person I can think who'd do that would be Moria Evans. Did you find anything on her?"

Greg nodded toward the files. "Nothing criminal, but she does have some financial issues. It's no wonder she needed Randon to co-sign for her loan."

Tandy pulled her phone from the back pocket of her ripped jeans. "I'll tell Marissa."

The bell over the door rang again. She looked up. More tourists. This couple dressed to match. Him in stars, her in stripes.

"I got it." Zam stood tall behind the counter. "You email Marissa."

Tandy smiled. What would she do without him? "Thanks." She tapped on her phone to open her email app.

Connor turned his back to Zam and crossed his arms. "You're telling Marissa that Opal saw a woman leave a note on her door?"

Her email opened. A message from Marissa waited there. Probably the same thing she'd sent Connor. "Yep."

Connor glanced over his shoulder. "What if Zam is lying? What if he put the note there, and he's claiming Opal said it was a woman to throw us off his scent?"

Tandy's vision blurred as she considered the possibility. "Why would he have to say anything at all? He knew Romero already suspected Marissa of lying."

Greg looked past them to the corner where Opal sat. "It's easy enough to find out."

Connor rubbed his jaw. "You think Opal will tell us the truth when she lied to the police?"

"Maybe Opal did it."

Tandy rolled her eyes. This was getting ridiculous. She

ignored the conspiracy theories to read Marissa's email.

Moria has your dress ready for your fitting.

Really? Connor got an email about investigating, and she only got an email about wedding planning? Well, maybe she could do both at once.

"Guys." She held up her phone. "How about I go try on my dress at As You Wish Weddings and question Moria in the process?"

Chapter Thirteen

GREG PREPPED TANDY ON QUESTIONS TO ask as he drove her to her dress fitting. She'd scheduled it on his lunch because he didn't want her to go alone. And because she appreciated his expertise.

"Be simple and precise. One question at a time. Start general and work your way to the specifics. Listen for anything that might discredit her testimony."

Tandy nodded. It was a good thing he'd be there listening to Moria too. Though knowing he'd also be listening to her was a little nerve wracking. "Can't you ask the questions?"

Greg pulled to the curb in front of the storefront. "She already knows Marissa suspects her. So she's definitely going to put her guard up if I go in as a lawyer."

Tandy looked him up and down. Wearing a suit in the small town was a dead giveaway. "You should probably take off your jacket."

"I'd be glad to." He popped open his door and stepped into the blazing noon sun.

Tandy would never make a good lawyer. Not because she couldn't ask questions but because she couldn't wear a suit in summer. Even the back of the concert tee she wore had slashes in it for ventilation. Greg somehow seemed to remain cool as he walked around the gold Mercedes to join her on the sidewalk.

He hung his jacket on a hanger he just happened to carry in his car and hooked it on a hook inside the door to the backseat. But his tie was still a dead giveaway.

She tugged on it and stepped closer. "You gotta lose this."

He watched her loosen the knot at his neck with unabashed enjoyment.

She smiled up into his watching eyes. "You think Moria will buy us as a couple?"

"We are a couple."

"I know. But look at us. I'm in Converse. You're in…" She looked down at the shiny brown leather. "Penny loafers?"

He popped up his collar so she could remove the tie. "They're not penny loafers. They're called formal loafers."

She lifted the tie over his head, careful not to mess up the sleek, black style. As much as she despised his shoe selection, she was very aware what a catch he was. "There's a place for a penny," she pointed out.

He lifted the tie from her hands and looped it over the hook of the hanger. "I would never put a penny in them. Not only because the slits are sewn shut but because my girlfriend would make fun of me mercilessly."

"She sounds cool. I think I'd like her."

Greg closed the car door then grinned as he looped an arm around her waist to escort her inside like a gentleman. "She has her moments."

Tandy snuggled closer despite the way sweat slicked her skin. Those beads of sweat would only help cool her off once they opened the ornately carved door and stepped inside with the air conditioning. They weren't going to keep her from enjoying a rare moment with her man. Though if Zam stayed on to help at the coffee shop, they might be able to do lunch dates more often.

Greg grabbed the brass handle and pulled. Icy air poured

out along with a clean, floral scent that reminded Tandy of the summer days when Grandma hung laundry out to dry by her flower garden. Stepping inside would have been inviting if not for the deputy who regarded them with suspicious, beady eyes.

Shouldn't she and Greg be the suspicious ones? They'd had reason to do a background check on the very two people who were meeting right in front of them. Not that they'd turned up anything on Romero. He'd served in the military until moving here. That was honorable—but still.

Romero turned to face them. "You shouldn't be here."

Tandy arched a brow. Did the deputy somehow know they'd run a background check and were here to follow up with questions?

He lifted his scruffy chin. "Are you here to harass Miss Evans?"

He knew.

"It's all right, Adrian." Moria motioned Greg and Tandy inside. "I ordered Marissa's maid of honor dress before she fired me. Would be nice to get paid a little for all the work I did."

Romero glanced from Moria to Greg and narrowed his eyes. He finally stepped to the side.

Greg slid his palm to the small of Tandy's back and ushered her forward.

Romero lifted a hand in farewell to the wedding planner. "I'll be outside if you need me."

Why would Moria need him? Romero was getting creepier and creepier. And now Tandy was really thankful Greg insisted on coming.

The door swung shut. Tandy looked around, even more uncomfortable than she normally would have been in the fancy space with its chandeliers and gilded mirrors and brocade tuffets. Not that she knew what a tuffet was, but if anybody sat on a tuffet besides Miss Muffet, it would be Moria.

Greg motioned toward the door with his thumb. "Have you known him long?"

"I don't know him that well." Moria busied herself clearing garments from the one curtained fitting room. "My adopted brother served in the military with him. Jamie died in a helicopter crash overseas, while Adrian survived. We started writing each other for support. He said he needed to get out of the military but didn't know what to do, so I told him about the opening here."

Tandy widened her eyes at Greg. This answer was pretty specific. Where to go from here?

Also, did they need to go anywhere? Two men had moved to Grace Springs for Moria. One was in a coma, the other able to protect her from investigation. Then there was her military boyfriend who'd been arrested for the attack on Randon.

Pieces fell into place. The boyfriend found out Moria would inherit money if Randon died. The boyfriend tried to kill him but told her he was being framed. In his defense, she put the threatening note on Marissa's door. She didn't really have an alibi with the mayor, but the deputy made it up to protect her. He did want Cash to go to jail, but not at Moria's expense.

The only question was who still wanted Randon dead? Had Moria gone to the hospital and tried to smother him? Would Romero still defend her if she had?

Moria disappeared into the back then returned with a dress bag.

"How nice the deputy supports you," Tandy offered to break the silence. "Though I'm curious about why you were worried about Cash's prosecutor finding out Randon's sister was dating him if law enforcement already knew."

Moria paused and titled her head. She didn't seem offended the way she had in the police station. Only curious. "Is that why Marissa thought I'd stuck the note on her door? She suspected I'm Cash's accomplice?"

How was this news? "Why else?"

The woman's dark eyes widened with innocence. "I assumed she thought I was after her because she fired me."

If Tandy was being honest, that changed everything. Though it made no sense. "Then who didn't you want to know you were related to Randon?"

"The media, of course." Moria sniffed and walked past her into the changing room to hang up the dress bag. "Randon seemed like a cool brother, but then I caught him with the ransomware file. I'm so glad I stayed away from him after that. It's probably why someone went after him. And when the media finds out about it, I don't want my dress shop linked to their news reports. It would be bad for business."

Tandy glanced at Greg. Should they believe her?

Even if Moria was telling the truth about her involvement, that didn't mean the others weren't guilty. Though with two men who looked alike both involved with the wedding planner, who'd really attacked Randon? The little revelation about Romero didn't make him seem any less creepy.

"Well." Moria motioned to the fitting room. "Size six, right?"

Six had been the right size until Tandy had opened a shop with Marissa where her standard breakfast was scones and clotted cream. Hopefully the dress fit.

She turned to pull the curtains closed and caught Greg

watching her with a tinge of pink in his clean-shaven cheeks. This whole afternoon she'd been focusing on investigating and not really thinking about where she was and who she was with. If their relationship kept going the direction it was headed, she might be eventually trying on a wedding dress in this very room for him. That is, if Moria didn't turn out to be a murderous wedding planner after all.

Her own cheeks heated as she pulled the curtains closed. She and Greg needed a real date soon. Not just a lunch date. And she'd even wear a dress for him.

She gripped the zipper of the garment bag.

Of course, she'd never wear a dress this fancy unless she had to. This dress was…

She pulled the zipper for the big reveal. Then she screamed.

Marissa was going to kill her.

Marissa checked her email for the 20th time. What was everybody doing? Connor had messaged earlier that morning that Greg had run background checks on the creepy deputy and the wedding planner but didn't find much. Marissa had returned an email, asking if they knew Moria's adopted name since there could be some other stuff on her there. No word.

As for Tandy, she hadn't responded about the dress fitting at all. Of course, she had a business to run by herself. But that was worth shutting down for her best friend's wedding. She could do the fitting during a slow time at the shop. Everybody would probably be at the park for the festival anyway, wouldn't they?

Their booth opened that weekend. Marissa needed to know how her treats were turning out. Macaroons were delicate. Tandy not so much. Would Tandy avoid responding to Marissa's messages if she ruined the macaroons?

She wrinkled her nose at the computer monitor and jabbed the mouse then poised her fingers over the keyboard to start a new message.

A ding interrupted Marissa's mental tantrum.

Her heart lurched in anticipation. How sad was it that email was now the highlight of her day?

Who cared? She had mail.

Tandy's email address appeared at the top of the screen. Should Marissa be happy that her friend wrote or sad that her fiancé hadn't? She'd simply be happy because this was all she had to be happy about in her life right now.

She bit her lip and clicked.

Tried on bridesmaid dress. Looked good. Except for the fact that it was black. Moria won't let me order another because you fired her. Sorry!!!

Marissa reread the short message. Was this a joke? Was she on Candid Camera? Was the whole thing a trick, including the attack on Randon? Were her friends trying to get her to relax about her wedding planning because she'd been so obnoxious? Because that was the only explanation for this.

Unless Tandy secretly hated her.

Or Moria…

Moria hated her. Moria did this. Sabotaged her wedding because Marissa had tried to get her arrested. That was bad business, and she'd be getting a very negative review.

Marissa jabbed at the computer mouse to find a review website, formulating the words in her mind. *Wedding planner sabotages client who fired her for being an accomplice to murder.* Nobody in their right mind would hire Moria after that.

She typed the words and poised her finger over the enter

button.

Moria would know the post came from her. Could Moria have planned this? Did she have computer hacking skills like her twin brother? Could she track down Marissa by her IP address? Griffin had warned her not to interact with anyone online unless through her secure new email. But he hadn't known the bad guys could lure her like this.

Ugh.

Erasing her message with angry jabs at the delete button, she determined to rise above revenge. She had to buy a new wedding dress. Why couldn't Tandy buy a new bridesmaid dress? But where was she going to order those now? How was she going to try them on?

Tandy was her only hope.

She placed her fingers on the smooth keys, finding the only raised bump underneath her forefingers and wrote the kindest message to Tandy that she could manage.

Tandy, you have to get this under control, or I'm going to risk my life to come out of hiding and plan my own wedding. Have you found a DJ? Where are we with catering? Why haven't I received pictures of cake options and a list of flavors? Am I going to have to bake my own? Because I could. I've got enough time on my hands. Which reminds me, I need to know how the macaroons came out. Please fill me in on every detail before I go mad. That shouldn't be too much to ask. Sincerely, You Know Who

Then she waited. Tandy had been at her computer or on her phone a few minutes ago. She should be able to respond immediately.

Nothing.

Marissa shoved herself away from the desk. Maybe she should do another exercise video. She'd rather go on a walk in the setting sun. Even if the mosquitoes bit. It wasn't like there was anybody around to see the red bumps on her skin.

She pulled back the curtain and peeked out the window into the blinding golden light. Griffin had said nobody followed them. And she hadn't called anyone or contacted anyone outside her email network. Nobody in the world but Griffin should know her location.

Just to be safe, she put on her sunglasses then rifled through the old farmhouse for a hat. A ball cap hung from a four-poster bed in the guest bedroom. It advertised the Rock and Roll Hall of Fame. A great disguise.

She pulled it on her head then turned to check her reflection in the mirror over the antique dresser, but before she even saw herself, her gaze locked onto an old felt fedora. What kind of person had worn that and hidden out here in the past? A gangster from the '40s? That would be an even better disguise.

Her eyes wandered to the closet. What other treasures would be hidden there? She moved to the solid wood door and twisted the brass knob. Inside, a long skinny closet led deeper into the house. She felt along the walls for a light switch. The worn wood paneling remained smooth underneath her touch. No switch.

She looked up to see if there was even a light above. Yes. A single bulb hung down with a string attached. She reached up and pulled, averting her eyes from the direct light. A rack of vintage styles turned from black and white to color before her eyes. A-lined dresses with puffed shoulders. Wide-leg, high waist pants. Knee-length skirts. Lots of colorful patterns with contrasting trim. Even cocktail dresses with spaghetti straps.

She ran her hands along the material. Excellent condition. When was the last time they'd been worn? Did anyone claim these now?

She dug deeper, sweeping a full polka dot skirt to the

side to see if there was more. Champagne white lace caught her eye. A longer, sleek dress shone brightly in the back, like the bare bulb had been perfectly placed to spotlight the wedding gown.

It was nothing fancy. Not like the dresses she'd tried on at As You Wish Weddings with their layers of taffeta and intricate beadwork. This was simple and sophisticated, its only adornment the wide V-neck and floaty, lace sleeves that would brush a bride's bicep.

Marissa stepped inside the closet and took a breath of musty hardwood then ran her hand over the fabric, its soft silk strands caressing her fingertips. Time had only aged the gown to perfection. She lifted the hanger from the rod to get a closer look, knocking into other hangers.

One banged against the far wall and the sound echoed as if the panel was hollow. Marissa gave it a second glance. A small knob stuck out from the paneling. Why would there be another door back here? Did they have safes when this house was built? Maybe it would be unlocked. She reached down for the handle and gave a curious twist.

A soft click then the door released, swinging away into darkness. She extended her arm into the opening. A thicker fabric blocked her reach. More clothing? She reached around to see if she could push it to one side and half expected the winter wonderland of Narnia to greet her. A shiver ran down her spine, but no fantasy world appeared. Only more hanging material.

She was in another closet. If she kept going, would there be another door, or was this second closet a secret? Would make sense for a safehouse, though this place had to have been built in the 1800s. What would a secret tunnel have been used for back then? The Underground Railroad?

Though Ohio had been a free state before the Civil War,

slave owners could pursue from Kentucky and take them home unless they escaped into Canada. She was near a river that could have aided in such escape. Might this house have been one of their stops?

She lifted the wedding dress higher, so its train didn't drag on the ground then pushed forward to a far wall. This one had molding around an actual door with a normal sized knob. She twisted and found herself in the front room. She'd found a secret passageway. And she never would have if not for this gown.

She lifted the dress to hang on a window casing. It wasn't full, but it flared at the bottom. This would be perfect with cowboy boots. Not that she was going to wear cowboy boots to her wedding, but it could be pretty cute.

Should she try the gown on? Why not? There wasn't anybody around to stop her or claim the clothing. Then her wedding dress shopping would be done.

Behind the dress and outside the window, the bottoms of fluffy clouds burned pink in a lavender sky. It had to be a sign. She may be alone out here, but God was still providing for her. Loving her. Chasing her fear away with his perfect love like Connor with his goodbye kiss.

Her heart swelled. She needed to get outside and appreciate the beauty. But where was her hat? She spun around to cross back through the closet, grabbing a trench coat on the way and the fedora on the dresser. Perfect.

Wasn't there a scripture verse about how she shouldn't worry about what she ate or drank or even what she wore because the flowers of the field didn't worry, and God dressed them better than King Solomon? Well, now God was dressing her in splendor. It had to be a miracle that these vintage clothes didn't have any holes in them.

She adjusted her sunglasses then rushed toward the front

door, stopping to peek out a window and make sure she was alone.

All clear.

With determination, she strode onto the wrap-around porch then down toward the open field opposite the woods. The grass smelled fresh, the dirt somehow clean. She raised her arms and spun. This was so much better than an email.

She lifted her face to let the last drop of setting sun warm her skin. Stillness surrounded her. Tranquility. Could this have been how slaves felt in this very spot when preparing to float the river into freedom?

Overhead, the first star attempted to glimmer in a turquoise sky. Soon there would be a blanket of stars. She'd enjoy them tonight instead of dreading the darkness.

She'd spend time with God and in prayer. Maybe all this happened so He could get her alone long enough to show her how much he loved her. How he needed to be her first love if she was going to keep this peace with her wherever she went.

She'd go dig out her Bible. Hopefully she remembered to pack it. She'd packed everything else.

Marissa turned and started back toward the farmhouse. A shed tucked underneath the eaves caught her attention. She'd seen it last night during her pity party, but at the time she figured it housed a lawn mower and potting supplies. But now that she knew God had hidden surprises here for her, she was curious if there were more.

She tromped through overgrown weeds to reach the rickety door. A latch held it shut with a spot for a padlock, but no lock filled the hole. She pried away the latch and swung the panel open to the protest of squeaky hinges.

Now that it was starting to get dark out, it didn't take long for her eyes to adjust. There in front of her sat an old four-wheeler. The kind Mom would never let her ride when

Dad went out with the neighbors. This made her want to ride it more. One day she'd get to ride a four-wheeler and play a tuba.

But for now, she wouldn't. She'd promised Griffin she'd stay here. Of course, it was nice to know she had options for escape if anything went wrong. Like if someone found her, or the river flooded, or Tandy forgot to put sugar in the berries when making tarts.

But until then, she'd stay put.

Chapter Fourteen

TANDY TOSSED ZAM A MUG THE next morning. The tall, skinny kind of mug with no handle so he could roll it down his arm before filling.

He dumped in two shots of espresso, spun, and set it in front of Tandy so she could practice pouring in the syrup with his flashy method.

She held the bottle completely upside down then cut it off by angling the bottle to forty-five degrees and sweeping her arm over the mug with flair. And she didn't even drip on herself this time. In celebration, she slid the mug down the counter for Zam to finish with his decorative foam pour—a puppy face. And it was only for her because she had to snap a lid on the top before their customer, Billie, picked it up.

She'd never been a morning person, but this was fun. Much better than reading Marissa's email the night before.

A loud screeching sound exploded around them. She jumped. Her patrons froze and stared.

The screech repeated itself. Was that a fire alarm?

Zam continued his juggling routine, unaware of the noise.

Billie plugged her ears. "I think that's the fire alarm," she yelled to be heard.

Zam couldn't hear but the flashing light on the smoke detector must have alerted him. He caught both cups and looked around. "What's going in?"

Billie pointed towards the entryway to the kitchen. Smoke poured out. As soon as Tandy saw it, she could smell its charcoal scent. *Oh no*! It must be the cake pops she was supposed to decorate red and blue and display in the shape of a flag.

Well, they were ruined now. And if she didn't act fast, the sprinklers would go off and ruin everything else.

Zam grabbed a fire extinguisher. "Get the customers out," he called, not even looking back for her response. "Prop open the roof door open to get the smoke out too."

Tandy watched him head toward the kitchen as she circled the counter. Billie still stood there with fingers in her ears, so Tandy grabbed the woman's coffee with one hand and her elbow with the other. "Everyone out," she called, though most people had already stood and were gathering their things.

Mayor Kensington beat her to the door and held it open for everyone to exit faster. "I called Troy down at the fire department."

Oh man. It wasn't like the fire department needed more to do during fire season. The Fourth of July was their Super Bowl, and here she was, distracting the players before their game like a sideline reporter wanting an interview.

"Thanks," she said anyway. At least everyone was safe. She ran up to the loft to prop open the door to let smoke out before heading toward the kitchen to do what she could before the firemen arrived.

Zam messed with the oven knobs to turn off the appliance, but orange flames continued to dance inside. She grabbed a tub of baking soda like her dad had used when putting out a stovetop fire when she was little and instinctively reached for the oven handle.

Zam held his hands up. "Don't—"

Too late. She'd already pulled. Flames roared as they escaped their cage. Waves of heat clawed her skin. Tandy fought to keep her stinging eyes open to see through the growing haze even as the charcoal taste of smoke snaked down her throat.

She should have let the fire die out on its own, rather than feed it oxygen. That must have been what Zam had been trying to tell her. She covered her mouth with one arm and shook baking soda toward the burning cake pops with the other.

Zam aimed the nozzle of the fire extinguisher and sprayed. White foam blanketed the cake pop pan along with the rest of the oven. No more tongues of fire threatened to lick off Tandy's skin, but black smoke scratched at her lungs.

"Thanks." She coughed and attempted to wave the air clear. But maybe she shouldn't have. Because now she could see the huge mess they'd made of Marissa's oven.

Even if the oven still worked, they'd still lost business for the morning, if not the whole day.

"You're welcome. But you should probably take the pans outside."

A siren sounded from the alley. The fire fighters. How embarrassing.

Tandy grabbed Marissa's striped pink oven mitts with the bows on the back and stuffed her hands inside. She'd just take the cake pop pans out and throw the burnt lumps of dessert and the charred black sticks in the dumpster. Baking was hard.

Zam caught her eye as she passed. "You're not supposed to put the sticks in the pops until after they're out of the oven."

She looked back down at her charbroiled treats. What had she been thinking? Marissa never would have done this.

Marissa's old boyfriend Troy strutted in, bright and authoritative in his yellow protective gear. He took one look at the pans in her hand and broke into a grin. "Marissa put cake pop sticks in the oven?"

"No." Tandy grimaced and pushed past. "I did."

Troy followed her out. "Well, I'm glad everyone's okay. Is Marissa sick?"

He hadn't heard? "She's staying in a safehouse until after she testifies against Cash Hudson."

Troy's laugh lines faded as his expression turned dim. "My wife will be glad to hear that."

Tandy blinked. "What?"

Troy waved Tandy's confusion away. "She'll be glad to know Marissa wasn't here during this call. She knows we used to date, and she has some jealousy issues."

"Oh," Tandy said. Though if Marissa had been there, the firemen never would have been called. She continued past him into the brick alley so his men could make sure the fire was completely out.

Eventually her feet began to throb, so she sat on a stack of wooden pallets Marissa had been saving for a decorative project. Zam joined her since they had nothing else to do.

She bit her lip.

Zam looked at her like he expected her to say something.

What she had to say, she wasn't worried about saying to the guy who just saved her shop from burning down. "I know Marissa has reason to fear for her life right now, but I'm afraid to email her about this."

Zam's face pinched together as if to say she had reason to worry. "Then tell her God provided time for you to go taste test cakes for her wedding." His eyebrows arched like the top of a light bulb that just flashed on in his brain. "My baker friend who made the cupcakes is looking for new business. I bet she could see you today."

It wasn't a bad idea, but Tandy couldn't keep from

sulking. "I bet *she's* never started a fire when baking cake pops."

"You're an original."

Talk about spinning the truth. But it was very kind of Zam to try to cheer her up. "If you can set up the cake tasting, I'll see if Connor's free."

She sent a text to Connor then stared at her phone. She should write her business partner now. "Marissa freaked out when I told her about the black bridesmaid dress. When I tell her we have to get the oven cleaned and repaired she's going to suspect me of being the one out to destroy her life. Maybe I won't tell her."

Zam turned sideways on the pallet so he could face her and read her lips better. "When we met, you mentioned that you are also a Christian. Doesn't the Bible say something about lying?"

Tandy guffawed. A sermon was the last thing she expected to come from the mouth of this former bartender. "I know Marissa will find out eventually. I simply don't want to add to her stress right now. And, you know, I'm a little scared of how she's going to react."

He pressed his mouth closed. "Hmm."

Tandy narrowed her eyes. "What do you mean, 'hmm'?"

Zam held out his hands. "I mean there's also a verse about how we're not supposed to fear what man does to us— only what God can do to the soul."

Tandy dropped her head back with a groan. Should she tell Zam that she'd faced off with killers before? She'd literally had her life threatened more than once. She could write books on overcoming the fear of man. "Marissa is a woman."

"I hear ya." Zam chuckled. "But part of becoming a Christian is the belief that God gave us commandments because He knows what's best for us. So I don't want you to make a poor choice out of fear."

Zam was right, but his message was as hard to swallow as one of her burnt cake pops would be. She studied him. The jagged edges of his skinny face. The hard lines of a wide forehead made even wider by a receding hairline. The long tuft of hair in the center of his scalp that gave the appearance he was trying to grow a mohawk rather than simply going bald. The haunted wisdom in his pale eyes. "Spoken like someone who's been the bad guy before."

Zam didn't flinch. "Haven't we all?"

Ouch. Tandy had never thought of herself as a bad guy. Even when she'd made big mistakes, she'd always assured herself she was doing what she had to do. But the truth was that in those moments she'd been ruled by fear. And she'd hurt people. From the scathing newspaper article she'd written that had ended her journalism career to the love-triangle she'd gotten herself into as recently as Valentine's. Not her finer moments.

"I've been learning the hard way that to overcome any fear, we need a bigger fear." Zam shrugged. "For example, a woman might be afraid of swimming, but if her baby falls into the pool, she's going to jump in to save the baby because she's more afraid of something happening to her child than something happening to her."

That made sense. Though it also made Tandy squirm in discomfort. "You're saying in order to make right choices, displeasing God needs to be my biggest fear."

Zam read her lips then looked her in the eye. "If the fear of the Lord was Randon's biggest fear, he never would have developed a ransomware virus. If the fear of the Lord was Cash's biggest fear, he never would have tried to kill Randon."

Tandy twisted her lips in thought and a little self-derision. "If the fear of the Lord is my biggest fear, then I won't hide the truth about the stove from Marissa for fear of her reaction."

Zam nodded.

Tandy had never really understood the fear of the Lord before, but this idea was freeing in a way. Because no matter what others did, she still had the power to make the right choice.

She took a deep breath. She'd write Marissa about the stove because it was the right thing to do. Not because it was going to be easy.

Marissa stared in horror at her email. Tandy had almost burned down their shop. And she'd thought her friend couldn't do any worse than a black bridesmaid dress.

Her amazing evening with the Lord did not make up for having the rest of her life destroyed. Seriously. If God loved her so much, she didn't get why He'd let her future go up in smoke.

Marissa ran her fingers into her hair and squeezed the roots away from her scalp. Was she supposed to sit around for the next couple of months while Tandy planned the biggest day of her life? And she wanted to do the cake tasting that day. She'd probably pick coffee and cream flavor. And make the frosting black. Everybody who ate it would look like they were missing teeth in her wedding photos. Which reminded Marissa, she still needed a photographer. What a nightmare.

She jabbed at the mouse to reply and give specific directions. Would Tandy get the message in time? Or would she put a deposit down on a disaster. It would be a deposit Marissa couldn't afford because they had to get their oven checked out and possibly repaired.

If only Marissa could run back to town for a day and get everything taken care of. Then she could actually enjoy her time of rest in the middle of nowhere.

Her eyes slid toward the window where she could see the shed. She *could* go back to town for a day.

Nobody would be looking for her because they didn't expect her to be there. And she had a disguise to keep her from being recognized. She'd simply start by checking on Tandy and Connor at the cake tasting. She knew where they'd be and when. If they messed up the cake selection, she'd have a little heart to heart with them.

Well, she hoped to have a heart to heart with Connor either way. Her heart thumped in anticipation of another goodbye kiss.

He wouldn't like that she'd come out of hiding, but he'd be happy to see her. Maybe she could even tell him her secret location so he would come for surprise visits.

No. She couldn't go that far.

She was still afraid of the killer, but she was more afraid of having her wedding ruined.

Zam's baker friend turned out to be one of his old employees, Bunny. She had to be at least in her seventies, dressed in leather like she belonged on a Harley, and with enough eye makeup to get mistaken for an '80s rock star. Tandy loved her. Especially with her newfound respect for anybody who could bake.

The name of the woman's shop fit too. Cake My Day. It

wasn't cutesy like one might expect in a small tourist town either. It had the traditional black and white tiled flooring, but the walls were black and there was only one chrome table where she and Connor sat at the back of the skinny storefront behind the shiny glass display case along the wall.

Bunny disappeared into a side room to retrieve their samples.

Connor groaned, leaning against his minimalist leather chair, and rubbing his belly. "Why did you have to schedule this tasting on the same day as the Americana Festival hotdog eating contest?"

Tandy stared at the man. First of all, she was new to these festivals and didn't know such a contest existed. Second, she never would have expected Connor to participate. Didn't you need a big belly to hold all that food? Third, how could he participate in such frivolity at a time like this? "How many did you eat?"

"Fourteen."

Ugh. One would make her sick. "Why?"

"The mayor wanted a challenger. Said it would be good publicity for my business since I'm remodeling his house."

"Did you win?"

"No."

"Of course, Grace Springs would have a mayor who was also a hot dog eating champion." Tandy looked from Connor toward the kitchen where Bunny's fluffy gray ponytail bounced against her patched vest. "It makes me appreciate Bunny all the more."

"About that." Connor leaned forward as if wanting to converse quietly, but he groaned, clutched his stomach, and leaned away again. His eyes flicked Bunny's way instead. Making sure she was still out of hearing range? "I'm not sure this baker would be Marissa's first choice. Maybe we can use my stomachache as an excuse to leave. Then we can hire someone from a nearby town or something."

Tandy closed her eyes and took a deep breath of the vanilla air. She didn't want to be planning Marissa's wedding at all, but working with someone as real as Bunny was would help her get through it. She opened her eyes and frowned. "Did you look in the display case? She does good work."

Connor glanced at the bright lighting on all the layers of fondant, combed icing, and piped flowers. The sparkling sweetness took Tandy back to her childhood of memories of sneaking onto the kitchen counter in order to stick her finger in the sugar bowl.

The front door swung open and a customer dressed like Inspector Gadget stepped in front of the display to admire the handiwork. Tandy might think the outfit strange if not for all the crazy costumes their townsfolk liked to wear. As far as she knew, there was some scavenger hunt going on for the Americana Festival that required entrants to dress like their favorite detectives.

"They're beautiful," Connor conceded. "I'm just afraid this baker is going to deliver the cake to my farm on the back of a motorcycle or something."

Tandy tried to imagine such a feat. Maybe the motorcycle had a refrigerated trailer on the back. Or a sidecar with a cakebox shaped seatbelt. "Nothing wrong with that."

Connor opened his mouth to argue.

Bunny's biker boots clomped their way. Tandy admired their buckles and made a mental note to ask where the baker got them.

"All right, cutie-pies. I brought you some classics such as vanilla and chocolate, but I also want you to taste my tortes. They don't use flour, which gives them a smooth, silky texture. I also have some memorable flavors for summer like berry and citrus."

Tandy's stomach growled. She hadn't had a good piece of cake since Marissa left her to do the baking. "Let's try them all before we make any decisions," she suggested to Connor.

He looked at her like she'd sent him a ransom note for Ranger.

Bunny dropped into a seat between them. "When's your big day, kiddos?"

Connor set about to explain their situation while Tandy eyed the variety of lush layers, trying to decide which to start with. She picked up a fork and reached for the closest little square plate. That was the polite thing to do, right?

Mmm… The creamy texture melted on her tongue. Light and delicate and not too sweet. "Is this cheesecake?" The brilliance of such a selection blew her mind. "Connor, you have to try this."

Connor grunted and fiddled with his fork.

Bunny looked back and forth between them. "You know, I had a friend in witness protection once. Her dad testified against the leader of a biker gang."

"Really?" Bunny got more and more interesting. "Is that green one pistachio?"

"Key lime. With cinnamon graham cracker crumbles to imitate pie crust."

Tandy took a sip of the coffee she'd brought to cleanse her palate. "A vacation for my mouth. Hand it over."

Bunny passed her the shiny plate.

Connor didn't even look at the dessert but continued to stare at Bunny. "Is the gang leader still in prison?"

"That is a good question, baby cakes."

Tang exploded on Tandy's tongue. Surprising, yet mixed with the subtlety of sugar and cinnamon for the perfect combination of cool and refreshing. "Oh, Connor. You have to get this one. And then take Marissa to Key West for your Honeymoon."

Connor wiped his forehead. "I'm gonna take your word for it. I don't have the appetite for anything right now."

Oh yeah, the hot dog competition. He probably had the meat sweats. If hot dogs could be considered meat.

Bunny handed him a bottle of water. "Are you all right, sugar?" She may look like a tough biker chick, but she sounded like a southern belle.

"Yeah." Connor shifted and adjusted his belt. "I just ate more hot dogs than I should have in a hot dog eating competition."

Something clattered from the front of the room. Tandy glanced over her shoulder to see the customer playing Cloak and Dagger with a napkin holder she'd overturned. Reminded her of Marissa's clumsiness.

Tandy turned back toward the cake selection. She was here for Marissa, but so far it was a job she enjoyed. "Is that raspberry filling I see?"

"Raspberry on white chocolate cake. It will make you feel rich."

Tandy wouldn't mind feeling rich. "I could use some money. Though maybe instead of repairing our oven, I should serve your desserts in my shop. Those cupcakes Zam brought in when I ruined the macaroons were a little piece of heaven."

More clattering. Tandy glanced over her shoulder to find the lady in the fedora bent over to pick up business cards and their holder off the floor. Whoever she was, she had the look of a spy but obviously not the stealth.

"Excuse me," said Bunny. Probably also concerned. She stood and headed toward the counter. "Can I help you, sweet pea?"

Tandy returned to her tray of enjoyments. "Are you sure you want me to pick, Connor?"

"As long as there's no ketchup or mustard involved, I approve."

Using the side of her fork, she cut off a piece that looked to be fudge but scooping it into her mouth revealed a nutty flavor. Like peanut butter cups or Nutella. "Add some coffee flavor to this and you've got a hazelnut mocha."

"I knew it!" The voice sounded like Marissa.

Had Tandy accidentally butt-dialed the bride and put her on speaker phone? She looked toward her rear pocket even though Marissa wasn't supposed to have access to her cell phone even if Tandy had accidentally called her.

Cowboy boots stomped toward them.

Tandy looked up in time to see the Carmen Sandiego whip off her hat and sunglasses. Long blonde hair cascaded down to frame a pair of seething brown eyes.

Chapter Fifteen

"MARISSA." CONNOR JUMPED TO HIS FEET as if he hadn't been in a hot dog eating contest earlier and bounded to her other side to block her from view of the window. "Put your hat back on before someone sees you. What are you doing here?"

Being discovered was the least of her worries.

Tandy gulped down the bite in her mouth like she was trying to swallow her guilt. "I highly recommend the hazelnut mocha cake, though I ate it all, so hopefully Bunny has another piece for you to try."

Bunny placed her hands on tiny, frail hips. "Hazelnut mocha? I didn't make a hazelnut mocha."

Marissa flipped her hat on with one hand and pointed at Tandy with the other. She never thought she'd be on the same side as a baking biker, but here she was. "EX-actly. You're adding coffee to my cake, and you probably special ordered the black bridesmaid dress, didn't you?"

Tandy blinked. "Uh…no."

Bunny tilted her head. "You're the bride who's also supposed to be in a safehouse? Oh, muffin. The government doesn't protect you anymore once you come out of hiding."

Marissa dropped her hand. They didn't? "Well, they don't know I'm gone. And I'll ride my four-wheeler back before they find out. I *had* to set these two straight."

Tandy's eyebrows dropped. "You have a four-wheeler?"

Connor tucked Marissa's hair inside the back of her coat. "Did you wear a helmet?"

"Yes. And yes." She wasn't an idiot. "But I'm not here to

talk about that. I'm here to discuss wedding planning. If you don't want me coming out of hiding to fix things anymore, stop messing them up."

Tandy's eyes rounded as if finally realizing what she'd said before Marissa took her disguise off. "I was only kidding when I said we shouldn't buy a new oven. Bunny's cakes are remarkable, but your crumpets are... are..."

"Crumpety," Connor finished for her.

Marissa turned her displeasure his direction.

He held up his hands. "You're mad at Tandy, remember? I'm trying to help."

"Thanks, Connor." Tandy deadpanned. "That was so helpful."

Marissa crossed her arms, still focused on her fiancé. "About as helpful as showing up for a wedding cake tasting too full from a hot dog eating contest to taste anything."

Connor held his stomach. "You have no idea how miserable I feel about the hot dogs right now." He stuffed his hands in his pockets, expression stern. "But Marissa, planning this wedding is not as important as your life. If you want to plan it yourself, then maybe we should postpone."

What? She exhaled her anger, and a new feeling took its place. Despair.

Bunny clomped into the kitchen. Tandy busied herself with the rest of the cake.

Marissa stared into Connor's steely eyes. They'd been here before. On the homestretch to their wedding day only for a roadblock to send her off course. And then the whole fiasco when he'd tried to propose a second time. Were they ever going to get to the altar?

She held a hand to her heart. "The wedding is what's keeping me going. It's what I have to look forward to."

He reached for her hands. Rubbed them with his manly

callouses for a moment before making eye contact again. "We're getting married, Marissa. You can look forward to that. As for the wedding, you don't know that it won't be done under assumed names once we join WitSec."

Bunny glanced at them through the window to the kitchen. Though "Bunny" probably wasn't her real name.

Marissa pictured the secret mountain town Griffin had referenced. She mentally scrolled through her favorite movie characters to figure out what she'd want to be called should she have to change her name. Should she go traditional or ridiculous? Scarlet or Rapunzel?

Then she pictured leaving her life behind, and her stomach dropped. What fun would it be to introduce herself as Rapunzel if Tandy wasn't there to laugh about it?

Is that how Connor felt? His family was so much closer than Marissa's had ever been. Not to mention his dog. She didn't like the idea of Ranger splattering more blood in her new home, but Connor was the only owner he'd ever known. Would Connor have to give him up for her?

Maybe the hot dog contest was his way of coping. He was going to cram in as much enjoyment as he could from his last Americana Festival. He was eating his feelings.

"I'm planning to marry you here." She bit her lip. "This is our home."

He stepped forward and wrapped his arms around her back, warm and strong. The way her body relaxed against him made her realize how tense she'd been.

"Your arms are my home," he said.

Her heart melted like ice with sun tea poured over it. No way she could be mad at him after that line. But it was going to make it even harder for her to leave him again.

They'd only been apart for a couple days, and she was going nuts. How was she going to survive months of this?

"I changed my mind," Tandy called, still facing away from them. "This banana cake with caramel sauce is to die for." She dropped her fork with a clink and twisted to face them, eyes wide. "Not literally."

Marissa wrinkled her nose. Of course Tandy had to go there.

Connor kissed the top of Marissa's head. "We're all worried about you, Marissa. Please, please, please go back to your safehouse and stay there until Griffin catches whoever threatened you."

Marissa wrapped her arms around his neck and leaned into his solid chest. He smelled of pine wood and forever. "I'll promise to go and stay if you promise to keep planning the wedding with Tandy. As long as I can walk down the aisle to you when this is all over, it will be worth it."

Connor leaned back and lifted her chin. "What if Tandy accidentally books a DJ who only plays rap?"

Marissa cringed. But there were worse things. "Then we'll get jiggy with it."

"What if it rains?"

Marissa shrugged. "We'll hold the ceremony in your barn, and I'll definitely wear these cowboy boots that I found at the safehouse."

Connor glanced at her feet in thought. "What if the photographer's camera breaks?"

A corner of Marissa's mouth curved up. If she simply expected everything in her life to go wrong, she'd never be disappointed. Because it usually did. "Then I'll pull out my camera and take a selfie when you kiss me."

Connor grinned and leaned down to brush his lips over hers.

All too soon, he pulled away. "As much as I want you to stay and practice our first kiss as man and wife, I want you to get back to the safehouse even more."

She nodded. He was right. Though she felt safer than ever, having resolved their differences.

Tandy licked her fork. "We can box up some cake samples for you to take back with you. Then you can make your selection."

Marissa tapped the glass of the case next to her. She might as well take advantage of her trip. "I want that three-tiered square cake with the light frosting and the raffia ribbon. We can add sunflowers as decoration."

"Good choice, pumpkin." Bunny grabbed a binder to make a note.

"You could make each layer a different flavor," Tandy suggested. "Including my mocha layer and this London Fog cake with the lavender Earl Grey infused buttercream."

Marissa's tongue watered. "That sounds good. As long as the Earl Gray layer is bigger."

Tandy picked up another sample. "Are you trying to ruin your own wedding now?" A sly smile escorted the teasing words.

Marissa narrowed her eyes in a playful warning.

Connor shook his head. "Now that you've got that out of the way, I'm going out first and make sure the coast is clear for you to sneak back to your ATV. Don't look at or talk to anyone and email me as soon as you arrive safely."

Marissa nodded. She'd parked in the woods around the corner of the hospital, and she should be able to find her way back without a compass or GPS. Getting here had been straight forward. She'd only had to follow the river.

Connor hugged her tightly once more. "You shouldn't be discovered with everyone down at the park for the festival, but put your sunglasses back on to be sure."

Marissa let him go and slid the shades up her nose as

directed.

Connor nodded then strode out the door like a man on a mission.

Tandy's Converse tapped across the floor and Marissa found herself in another embrace. "I never thought I'd miss you so much."

"From the looks of it, you mostly miss my baking," Marissa joked around the lump in her throat.

She hugged her friend closer. It wasn't long ago that she and Tandy had been rivals, vying for the same storefront and looking for things to hate about each other. Now Marissa could show up, guns blazing, and Tandy would just love her more for it.

Tandy clicked her tongue. "If you were here to bake, I'd never fit into my black bridesmaid dress by your wedding."

Marissa shook her head in mock admonition. "Are you trying to get me to stay?"

Tandy squeezed her upper arms before striding to the window. "I wish you could, but I'll be your lookout instead."

Bunny waved from the kitchen. "It was nice to meet you, Marissa. I know what you're going through, and I promise not to say a word."

Marissa smiled ruefully at her agreement to trust a grizzled old biker with her wedding cake. Mom would be incensed. But in spite of sincerely doubting she and Bunny's friend had anything in common when it came to going into hiding, it was obvious the woman was as passionate about baking as Marissa was about tea. "Thank you, Bunny. I'm glad I got to meet you too."

"Connor is motioning that it's all clear," Tandy called from the front of the store.

Marissa's heart rate picked up. As much as she'd needed to connect with Connor and Tandy today, coming into town hadn't been smart. She bit her lip and looked up and down the road to double check before heading back out into the moist heat that slicked her skin underneath the coat.

The place was a ghost town, but were someone to see her, they'd do a double take at her excessive layers. Nobody else dressed like this in the heat. What she'd considered to be a disguise might actually make her stand out more. Too late now.

She click-clacked down the empty street, not even pausing when blowing a kiss to Connor before rounding the corner of the hospital building.

Something smacked into her body, knocking her hat back and her glasses sideways.

"Oof." She reached to readjust before even recognizing Trenton, the private investigator Joseph Cross had hired.

"Excuse me," the man said, straightening his bright red bow tie. Of all the people she could run into, he would probably be the least likely to question her ensemble. If one could wear a bow tie in July, why not a fedora?

He also didn't seem to have a very good memory with as many times as he liked to repeat his questions. He'd forget bumping into her as soon as she left. As long as she got away before he started quizzing her.

"No, excuse *me*." She circled him and continued click-clacking down the street, only glancing back discreetly when looking both ways before crossing the road.

Trenton was already gone.

Tandy waited for Connor to return. "Marissa got away okay?"

Connor grimaced. "She ran into that detective Joseph

Cross hired, but the guy didn't seem to recognize her. He got in his car and drove off."

Tandy's eyebrows zipped upward. "Trenton? Opal's grandson?"

Connor's gaze zeroed in on her. "Yes. Have you spoken with Griffin yet about what Opal told him? Or...what Zam says Opal told him?"

Tandy pressed her lips together. She didn't want to get in the middle of the whole Connor and Zam thing. Connor was obviously stressed because his fiancée's life was being threatened, and if the culprit didn't get caught, he might have to go into hiding with her.

"Not yet," she admitted. "I've been too busy running a business all by myself and planning a wedding that is not my own."

"Well, now that you've got wedding stuff squared away and your oven needs professional care, you've got plenty of time."

"Sad but true." She wanted to punch him in his overstuffed gut for that remark, but she let it go. She'd already caused Marissa enough trouble without sending her future groom to the emergency room.

She also let him go home to lie down instead of accompanying her to see the sheriff. The only good thing about Connor's hot dog eating contest was that he knew Griffin was doing security at the mission trip fund-raising BBQ in the park.

She found the sheriff leaning one hand against a tree, looking as green as the key lime cake. "Don't tell me you were in the hot dog eating contest too."

Griffin took a moment to focus on her. "I wish. Would have been another opportunity to beat Connor at something."

Tandy frowned then looked around at the thinning

crowd and kids laying on blankets rather than climbing the jungle gym. "Why didn't you? What's wrong?"

He took off his Smokey the Bear hat to wipe his brow. "I don't know. Ever since lunch, I feel low energy and nauseous."

Lunch? As in the BBQ being sponsored by the church's youth group? "Did everything taste okay?"

Griffin clutched his belly. "I would have preferred steak, but yeah."

Tandy scanned the nearby picnic tables where flies buzzed over leftovers. Charbroiled hotdogs, watermelon, corn on the cob, chips, and potato salad. She narrowed her eyes at the tubs of potato salad. Did it have eggs in it? Or mayo? Those could go bad in the heat. "You ate the potato salad?"

"Potato salad is my favorite."

Oh man. Just when Tandy thought things couldn't get worse, their sheriff contracted food poisoning. "Well, in case you're about to get sick, we'd better talk right now."

Griffin's head wobbled a little as he eyed her. "As long as we can sit down." He pushed off the tree to shuffle toward a bench.

Tandy shook her head as she watched. If the sheriff went down, they'd have to rely on a deputy who had close ties with a suspect's girlfriend.

Griffin sank onto the bench. "I heard you had a fire this morning."

She joined him, plopping onto the hard, wooden slats. "Unfortunately. After the smoke airs out, I can open again, but we won't have any pastries until I can get the oven checked."

"Are you here because you suspect foul play?"

Tandy rolled her eyes. "I wish."

Griffin shifted with a grunt. Either he was trying to get comfortable or her response disturbed him.

"I mean, I wish I hadn't been the one stupid enough to put sticks in the cake pops before baking them."

The sheriff shot her a withering look before closing his eyes. "Even I know that."

Tandy bit back a retort. The guy obviously felt lousy. "Anyway… Before I tried to burn the shop down, my new barista saw a conversation between Opal and her grandson."

"He saw it?" Griffin opened his eyes long enough for another one of his looks. "How do you *see* a conversation?"

Tandy wished she didn't have to *see* the way Griffin was looking at her. "He's deaf. He reads lips."

"Ah. Of course." Griffin closed his eyes again. "Note that I'm already skeptical but do go on."

"Noted." Should she be more skeptical of Zam? The only way to find out was to have Griffin investigate his claims. "You should question Opal again. Apparently, she saw a woman go up to Marissa's door around the time when the note would have been stuck there. She didn't tell your deputy because she wanted to save the information for her grandson to use in his investigation for Joseph Cross."

Griffin groaned. "Well that complicates things."

Tandy nodded though she wasn't sure which part he considered the most complicated. The part about how Opal lied, the part about how Trenton was her grandson, or the part about the perp who left the note was female? That ruled out both the deputy and Zam. Not that she honestly considered Zam a suspect.

"I'll have Romero question Opal again."

Tandy pursed her lips. "About that."

Griffin opened his eyes though they didn't hold the same amount of zing this time. They didn't hold much of anything.

"What?" he asked, his voice lacking zing, as well.

"Did you know your deputy moved here because of Moria Evans?"

Griffin took a deep breath and exhaled slowly. "I knew he moved here to support the sister of a buddy who died when they were deployed. I didn't know it was Moria."

"Yeah." Tandy studied his pale, chubby cheeks which were normally a ruddy hue. Perhaps she should be more concerned about the sheriff than about the deputy.

"I suppose that since Opal says the note on Marissa's door was left by a woman…and the deputy might have been biased in his questioning of Moria…you want me to go talk to her myself." He made the connection, though in a slow and stilted manner that wasn't his usual M.O.

"I would, except you don't appear to be in any condition to question anyone." She lifted the back of her hand to Griffin's scalding forehead. Yikes. If he were one of Marissa's teapots, he'd be whistling. "I'm taking you to the emergency room, Sheriff."

Could his illness be from something other than the potato salad? The timing in the case seemed to be more than coincidental. Could what she'd feared to be food poisoning be a different type of poison?

Chapter Sixteen

MARISSA PULLED THE HELMET OFF HER head and shook out her hair before climbing off the four-wheeler. The ride had been fun at first, but then the bumpiness became jarring. Both her rear and her jaw ached from all the hard landings. Though she never thought she'd feel this way, she was glad to be back at the safehouse.

She rushed inside to remove the trench coat that made her feel like one of Tandy's ill-fated cake pop sticks. Yeah, Tandy had destroyed their expensive oven, but life could be worse. Marissa was alive. She had a wedding cake ordered. She had a man who loved her enough that he was willing to give up his identity to start a new one with her if necessary.

It was nice to have her worries with Connor and Tandy resolved, but now what?

Marissa hung up the trench coat in the closet then paused to stare at the wedding dress she'd left hanging on the window casing. It was as simple and beautiful as she remembered. So beautiful she hadn't wanted to destroy the magic of it by trying it on, but if it wasn't going to fit, she needed to know.

In that case, she'd pick out a dress online with her exact measurements, have it delivered to Tandy, then get Griffin to bring it out the next time he came to check on her. But with the way her wedding plans had gone so far, she couldn't help thinking that something bad would happen if she was forced to rely on such a process. Finding a dress waiting for her in the closet like this held so much more promise. She wanted to believe it was a gift from God.

In one movement, she whisked the hanger off the window and whirled to change in the bedroom where there was one of those free-standing full-length mirrors that made everything feel more romantic. Marissa kicked off the cowboy boots, removed her outer clothing, then gingerly coerced the antique zipper down the back of the dress.

Though the zipper moved stiffly, the lace slid through her fingers like it might melt at her touch. She stepped into the center and slid the under layer of silk up her body. The sheer sleeves fit over her shoulders like custom curtains and the wide V-neck exposed her collarbones in a graceful way. In fact, she'd never felt more graceful.

The trick was to reach behind her to tug the zipper up and see if the cut still caressed her curves. The low V cut of the back made reaching the top of the zipper even easier than expected.

She dropped her hands to her sides and stared at her reflection in the mirror. Stared at the gown that seemed to be designed just for her. Who else could have worn this dress? What was their story? Was it a sad one, and that was why it got left behind?

More curiously, if finding a wedding dress could really be this simple, then why was the rest of her life so hard?

She swished side to side, watching the lace graze against the lining. She turned to look over her shoulder at her back then fanned the oval train of lace around her for the kind of view wedding guests would get. Three pearl buttons glinted against her waistline. Could that be for cinching up the train during the reception?

The lace was woven together widely enough that a button could be popped through anywhere she wanted to bustle it up. She hitched the skirt in a way that lace floated in a double layer to her ankles, which would be perfect for dancing.

Memories of her mom's apprehension rose to the surface of her enthusiasm. Would Marissa trip over the skirt? Would her heels catch in the hem? She certainly wasn't going to wear those strappy gold sandals she'd tried out the other day.

Her gaze landed on the cowboy boots she'd used for her ride to town. They were simple and brown. She could always buy something more ornate later. White boots or boots with fancy white stitching or even those turquoise boots that said "I do" on the front. For now, she could put on the plain ones to see how the dress looked with boots.

She sat on the edge of the bed, reveling in how comfortable the dress was when sitting. Usually sitting in dresses made her feel she was wearing a girdle and about to pass out like Elizabeth Swan in *Pirates of the Caribbean*. Which might be partly to blame for Marissa's dive off the stage at the Miss Ohio pageant, but with this ensemble, she would be perfectly safe.

She stood and looked down at her feet. Only the pointy toes peeked out. Not bad. She looked in the mirror and lifted her skirt a little to see what she would look like to others when she walked. When paired with the dress, the cowboy boots went from simple to simply elegant.

Now for the final test. She flicked on the old radio in the corner and turned the dial through static until classical music floated around her. This would have been the kind of music the original bride who wore this dress danced to. A string quartet perhaps.

Marissa curtsied like the ballerina she never was then lifted her hands up to pretend she was hanging onto Connor's shoulders. He'd tried to teach her swing dancing a couple of times, but she'd always ended up flat on her back somehow, so they'd do a basic waltz for their wedding dance.

Step, side, close. Step, side, close.

She practiced around the bedroom, wishing Connor could practice with her. When he led, she didn't have to think of the choreography so much.

Step, side, close. Step, side, close.

Her boots clacked with each move, rewinding her thoughts to her dance lessons at The Buffalo Club. She could almost smell the tobacco smoke from the honky-tonk environment.

While she'd stepped on Connor's toes and whirled until she was dizzy during dance lessons, people around her had line danced to the music. It had looked so much less complicated. Maybe she could do that. It would be fun during a reception at the farm. Like a big ol' barn dance.

She stomped back to the radio and twisted the dial again until banjos and harmonicas joined together with the twang of a western singer. Maybe she should get into country music. It certainly depicted the kind of luck she'd had in life.

If only she could remember the moves to the Electric Slide. Hadn't it started with a grapevine?

She moved right then left. Now what?

Four steps backwards if she remembered correctly. She glanced over her shoulder to make sure she wasn't going to bump into anything.

There was nothing on the floor in her way, but something out of place made her look again as she backed up.

Four, three, two…

Black smoke rose past the window.

She froze and sniffed. That wasn't cigarette smoke she'd thought she smelled earlier. It was more like a campfire.

She rushed to the window and looked down into an orange glow. Flames used the long grass as kindling and licked the glass panels like roasted marshmallows. Her safehouse was not safe anymore. Had nobody inspected the fire alarms? Just because the sheriff didn't get along well with the fire department, that was no excuse. Griffin didn't get along well with many people. As for her, she had to get out.

Marissa hoisted her skirt and spun to race toward the door. More dark smoke slipped underneath the door jam. She watched the billows lift toward the exposed ceiling beams, creating a haze as if her contacts were dirty. The campfire smell threatened to choke her.

Panic curled around her heart like a fist, and she couldn't tell if it wanted to hold her in place or was preparing to shoot her forward in a slingshot of adrenaline. Her brain scrambled from memories of dance lessons to fire safety day in elementary school.

Side, step, close became *stop, drop, and roll*. Except that was only if she was on fire, right?

She frantically looked down her body at the gorgeous dress still fully intact. Was silk flammable? Hopefully not. What else had she learned?

Get low and stay low. She dropped to her hands and knees.

Cover your nose. She grabbed the shirt she'd taken off to tie around her face like a mask. The mask made her suck harder at the air like she was suffocating, but at least she wasn't breathing as many toxins. She coughed and wiped at the beads of sweat dripping along her temples.

Call 9-1-1. If only Griffin hadn't taken her phone away. She could contact them through her computer though. If she could get to it.

Test doorknobs before opening. She tapped the brass knob. The tip of her finger lit up with pain.

She was trapped. Her only choices were to rush through a burning house or open the window and jumping directly into the flames. Only this morning she'd thought her worst option was joining the witness protection program. Now she'd be happy to live that long.

She crawled back and forth between her two options, her reality ready to snuff her life out like a candle. She lifted her head to peek out the window in hopelessness. There was no possible way to survive this. She was about to meet her maker.

How ironic that those same fields that now raged with fire were the exact spot where she'd worshipped God's glory the night before. Where he reminded her of how He'd dressed her like He dressed the wildflowers. She'd felt so loved at the time…

Her heartbeat tripped. Her eyes widened. Watered. And she wasn't sure if the tears were from the thick air that burned like a summer sidewalk or if she was overcome with gratefulness for God's love.

Because not only did He dress her like a flower last night, He'd shown her a secret passage that could help her escape.

Tandy pulled to the curb in front of the hospital. Griffin protested for the whole ride and even now insisted that she take him home. But he'd also rolled down the window and was hanging out of it like Cocoa wished she would let him do. That was after he'd turned her air conditioning up to full blast then turned it off because he got cold.

"I'm going to get you a wheelchair." She turned off the ignition, hopped out, and raced around the car to grab one of the wheelchairs inside the entryway doors.

"No," he said when she opened his car door, but not with either his usual authority or stubbornness. A two-year-old would put up more of a fight. The only problem was that two-year-olds didn't weigh this much.

She swung his feet out the door, looped his arm around her neck, and rocked him forward in hopes that his legs would support his weight. Instead he slid sideways, but at least he landed halfway in the chair.

"Tandy, I'm the sheriff, and I told you no..." he drawled like a Texas Ranger.

Tandy stood. "I'll let you get up and walk home if you want."

"No." He curled forward clutching his belly. "I told you...take me home."

The hospital doors slid open. A nurse in American flag scrubs strolled out. Probably the same one who'd once saved Tandy's life, though with the shock her body had been in at the time, Tandy couldn't tell for sure.

"Hello, Sheriff," greeted the nurse. "Did you eat barbecue in the park this afternoon?"

Tandy arched an eyebrow. First of all, this lady seemed pretty casual about the town sheriff being so sick he couldn't even sit upright in a wheelchair. Secondly, she'd known exactly why he was in such a condition.

"Yes," Tandy answered for him. "How'd you know?"

The nurse stepped behind Griffin, hooked his armpits to hoist him deeper into the seat, then unlocked the wheels to roll him inside the ER. "We've had a few patients with salmonella. None this bad though. How much potato salad did he have?"

Tandy grimaced. "I'm not sure, but he said it was his fave."

Griffin grunted. "I'm never eating potato salad again."

"Well, Sheriff, I'm thinking we better get you to a bathroom. Then we'll give you an IV to replenish your fluids." She turned the wheelchair and looked over her shoulder at Tandy. "If you want to park, he'll be free for you to take him home in a couple of hours."

A couple of hours? Tandy had enough to do without adding babysitting the sheriff to her list. She rubbed her face. "Okay." Might as well check on Randon while she was here. See how Susan was doing.

She parked and filled out admission paperwork for Griffin. She hated paperwork. Griffin would owe her for this. All she'd ask for was that he'd question Moria a second time. Because what other female had any motive to threaten Marissa's life?

Tandy stared at the insurance section of Griffin's paperwork. Should she see if the nurses wanted her to dig through Griffin's wallet for an insurance card? She wasn't family or anything. She hadn't even been his babysitter growing up the way Marissa had.

She stood and carried the clipboard to the receptionist. The oversized white man reached for the paperwork without looking up from his baseball game playing silently on a tablet.

Tandy didn't release it when he tugged. "It's not complete yet. Should I see if I can get the sheriff's insurance info from him?"

"Yeah-yeah." He pushed a button and metal double doors swung inward. "Room two."

Tandy looked at the open doors. With a receptionist like this, anybody could get in to try to kill Randon without being recognized.

"Uh..." She didn't move. "Do you still have Randon Evans in ICU?"

He looked up then, wide blue eyes that made him more mischievous than mean-spirited. "We do. Why? Do you know him?"

How much should she say? If she wanted a chance to see him and talk to Susan, might as well tell all. "My best friend witnessed his attack and is currently in a safehouse because someone doesn't want her to testify against his attacker. If Randon came out of a coma, he could also be a witness, and then some of the pressure would be off her."

"Seriously?" The receptionist leaned forward on his elbows, and Tandy couldn't help wondering if maybe this guy was the reason their town had such a bad gossip problem. Chad Chadwick, according to his name badge. Probably not the best person to have working in a hospital with the healthcare privacy act, not to mention a patient in a coma who someone wanted dead.

"Seriously." Tandy tilted her head, hoping Chad Chadwick's loose lips would benefit her. "I'm wondering how he's doing. Any better?"

Chad looked around as if making sure nobody else was listening.

Tandy turned her ear toward him and held her breath, so she wouldn't miss a word. He apparently knew something. Too bad the sheriff was currently incapable of making an arrest.

"I heard..." he whispered.

Goosebumps popped up on Tandy's skin.

"There's a private investigator who thinks Randon's responsible for the ransomware virus going around."

Tandy dropped back onto her heels, the tingle at the base of her neck dissipating. "Ya don't say?"

"Seriously." The man sipped his soda through a straw until gurgling sounded at the bottom.

Tandy motioned to the wide doorway, still open and waiting for her to enter. "So you're keeping him extra safe by not letting in any suspicious characters who are only here for revenge."

Chad Chadwick nodded again solemnly before his gaze caught on the open doorway and he jabbed a button to close it. "Exactly," he said, resuming his somber expression as if he hadn't been caught leaving the entrance unattended. "There's already been one attempt on his life here, and the hospital board approved paying to post our own security guard at his door. You know, to make up for the previous security breach."

"Hmm." Chad Chadwick wasn't a suspect, but he was dangerous. "How is Susan doing?"

"Oh, that poor girl. She eats day and night to cope with the stress. Pizza. Chinese. Vending machine. But she doesn't leave his side." He cupped a hand around his mouth. "She should at least do some jumping jacks or squats, if you ask me."

Tandy refrained from letting her eyes rove over his size with that statement. "Has Pastor Dave been in to offer his support?"

"Oh, yes. There's been a few prayer vigils out here in the lobby too."

Guilt pricked Tandy's conscience. Guilt that she was surprised enough people cared about Randon to pray over him and guilt that she hadn't been one of them. She'd make up for that now.

"Though if you ask me," Chad Chadwick continued like someone had actually asked him a question, "Randon kind of had it coming, and Susan could do much better. She's already been through enough with her uncle being murdered earlier this year. Did you know about that?"

"Yes." Tandy knew way too much about that. "Thank you for sharing. I'll let you get back to your baseball game now. Is it okay if I visit with Susan after I get the sheriff's insurance info?"

"Sure. No prob. Room five." He smacked the button and turned back to his game.

Wow. Tandy would have to mention him to the sheriff. Honestly, Randon wasn't much of a threat while in a coma, but if he started to come to, Cash's partner-in-crime might try to take him out again.

Tandy didn't have to go far to get to room two. It was the second door on the left, but the bed was empty. Had Chad Chadwick messed up, or had the sheriff taken off? He couldn't have gotten far.

Violent retching made Tandy jump. She glanced at a door to a small closet looking space. If Griffin was throwing up inside, she hoped that door led to a bathroom.

Hmm. Should she wait for him to finish or go visit Susan first?

Griffin's pants and shirt rested over the back of a chair. The nurse must have made him change into one of those embarrassing flappy gowns. If Tandy was to see him dressed that way, she wasn't sure which of them would be more embarrassed. He might appreciate it if she retrieved his wallet from his pants and found his insurance card herself.

She leaned toward the bathroom door and raised her voice. "Griffin, I'm going to look in your pants for your wallet so I can fill out the insurance paperwork for your admission."

He heaved in response.

Okay then.

She slid her hand into his pocket and pulled out a thin, smooth, rectangle. His phone.

She set it down on the chair to check his other pocket when a picture of Marissa filled the screen. Tandy did a double take. It was a video chat. She wouldn't have thought that was allowed from Marissa's safehouse.

She yelled toward the door, "Marissa is calling you. Can I answer?"

More gagging sounds. Followed by splashing. Eww.

Tandy frowned at the phone. Surely, she wouldn't be endangering Marissa's life by answering. Griffin probably had this phone app set up in case of emergency. In which case, Tandy better answer.

She tapped the button. It took a moment for Marissa's picture to appear. And when it did, it was kind of blurry. But it was the way Marissa was panting that got Tandy's attention. Was she running?

"Marissa?"

The blonde's eyes turned toward the screen and widened. "Tandy! Where's Griffin?"

"He's puking his guts out. Are you okay?"

"No."

Marissa's image disappeared. A thud followed. Then nothing.

Tandy gripped the phone tighter and stared at the screen for signs of life. Marissa had been running, and now she wasn't responding. "Marissa?"

All Tandy could make out was long thin strands of something light green. Like Marissa's phone screen had landed in a wheat field, although something flickered in the background. Something orange. Accompanied by a popping and crackling sound.

Her heart plummeted. Because she had a recent experience with the only flickering orange thing that would smoke, crackle, and send Marissa running. "Marissa?"

Please respond. Please.

Tandy juggled Griffin's phone to pull her own out and call the fire department. Though would they know where to go if only Griffin knew how to get to the safehouse?

"Marissa, are you there?" Prayers jumbled through Tandy's mind. "Marissa?"

"Oof." Marissa's long blonde hair swung in front of the screen. Half her face followed. "Sorry, I tripped."

She tripped? Tandy would strangle her later for causing such a scare. "Where are you? Is that a fire I see?"

"Yes." The image on screen jostled. Marissa's breathing rasped. "The safehouse is burning down. I'm running across a field with my laptop. Thankfully I have a hotspot for it, but the field is catching on fire too, and I need Griffin to send the firemen. I don't know how to tell them to get here."

Tandy looked toward the bathroom. "I'll find out and call Troy. Then I'll come get you because it sounds like someone is actually trying to kill you this time."

Chapter Seventeen

Marissa ran through the field, calves aching, heart pounding, throat scratching with every gulp of char-broiled air. Sparks of fire whirled around like fireflies. The fire hadn't caught up with her yet, but any one of these sparks could light up the dress she wore or the grass in front of her. That was how fires jumped roads.

She clutched her laptop under her arm, half tempted to drop it so she could escape faster. Even if she didn't mean to drop it, sweat on her skin made the device hard to hang on to. But video chat was her only means of communication. She'd need it if Tandy couldn't find her.

They'd agreed Tandy would pick her up on a familiar road at the river bend, but if the fire wasn't under control at that point, Marissa would have to travel farther while waiting for her friend.

Sirens wailed in the distance.

Relief flooded through her. Even if the emergency workers weren't aware she was here, it was good to know she wasn't alone.

Marissa continued her sprint toward the river, looking back to see the big red trucks roll up to the house. It wasn't likely anything she'd brought with her would survive the flames. Hopefully the fire marshal would figure out what had started the fire. She didn't want to think someone had deliberately tried to kill her the way Tandy suggested.

The rock under her right boot slipped. Again. She pushed her weight into it to propel herself forward. She'd landed hard when tripping before, but this time her ankle cranked sideways, igniting a whole new fire. This one burned inside her skin, just as intense. Her shin and calf lit up, as well.

Marissa crumpled to the ground, happy to sink into the cool dirt and take the weight off her throbbing leg. She dropped onto her side, clutched the knee to her chest, and pinched her eyes shut in hopes of blocking out the pain. It stabbed relentlessly.

She sucked in shallow breaths with a Lamaze like effort at controlling the ache. It only intensified. She rolled back and forth then slapped a palm against the prickly grass in order to feel anything other than the wrenching of her ankle.

Now what? Had God rescued her from burning inside the house only to let her get stuck in a grass fire?

No. She'd crawl if she had to. Roll even. The river wasn't too far away. She could roll down the embankment if needed. The cool waves might even bring relief to the blaze inside her foot.

Gritting her teeth, she forced herself onto hands and knees. Pain shot through her entire side. Even her stomach roiled in protest. Dare she try to put any weight on the injured leg?

"I got ya." Strong arms reached around her, and before she knew it, she was lifted off the ground.

She hooked her hands onto broad shoulders covered in a slick yellow coat and peered through a clear face shield at her senior high prom date.

Troy's green eyes underneath his thick eyebrows peered back. "Marissa? Aren't you supposed to be in a safehouse?" He scanned the area, his gaze stopping at the house fire. Obviously not safe anymore. He made eye contact again, and one of his thick eyebrows lowered. "Are you alone? Why are you wearing a wedding dress?"

Marissa didn't have the energy to answer. She adjusted her bad ankle over her good one so it didn't strain other muscles with the way it hung. It still hurt, but she didn't have the pit of dread churning inside anymore at the thought of how she might further injure it in order to get herself to safety.

He looked around. "I hope no pictures of this make it into the newspaper."

A tear rolled down Marissa's cheek, leaving behind a wet trail for the wind to cool. She couldn't be sure if she was crying from pain or relief. Probably a mixture of both, but it had nothing to do with newspapers.

"I'm sorry. I didn't mean anything by that," he said when she didn't respond. "I'm glad you're okay. We're going to get you to the hospital."

She looked past him toward the fire engines. No ambulance had arrived yet. She'd rather go with Tandy anyway. Tandy wouldn't ask as many questions.

She pointed the opposite direction. Toward the river bend. "Can you help me over there instead? I have Tandy picking me up. She can take me to the hospital."

Troy glanced the direction she pointed. A black Bug sat on the gravel road by a tree. He sighed and started walking. Behind him, his crew held a hose, shooting a large arc of water into the flames. The air hissed and sizzled. Smoke poured into the sky like an upside-down espresso.

"You ladies are sure keeping me busy today. You know Tandy tried to start a fire today too, right?"

"I know." Marissa focused back on the Bug. The door swung open and Tandy rushed toward them. "But I didn't start this fire."

Maybe it was still her fault, since she'd ridden the four-wheeler into town and been seen by Opal's grandson.

Connor stormed into Marissa's emergency room, stony eyes daring anyone to stop him. Tandy doubted that Chad Chadwick would even try. The male receptionist would probably be more likely to follow him back in hope of overhearing gossip.

Connor brushed past her to wrap Marissa in his arms. And Tandy had thought being with them during their lover's spat at the cake shop had been awkward.

She side-stepped towards the door. Might as well go see Randon and Susan since she hadn't made it on her earlier visit. At least she knew Marissa was going to be okay despite the walking boot she'd have to wear for a month in order to let her sprained ankle heal. And at least the bride-to-be had changed out of the antique wedding dress she'd worn on her escape from the fire. Leave it to Marissa to make a dramatic situation even more dramatic.

Tandy checked on her friend once more to make sure she wouldn't be missed.

Marissa pulled away from the hug. "You think Trenton did this?"

Connor nodded grimly.

Tandy paused. It was good to know he now suspected someone other than her new employee, Zam.

Marissa gave Connor her puppy dog eyes. Her go-to for getting out of trouble with both Connor and Tandy. "If so, I feel horrible for coming out of hiding. Because then it would be my fault he found the safehouse. My fault he burned up all those beautiful old clothes."

Connor tilted his head. "Who cares about clothes in a fire? You're wearing an ugly old hospital gown, and you've never been more beautiful."

Ah. That was sweet. Tandy resumed her side-stepping.

Connor let go of Marissa and spun around to face her. "Where's Griffin? He needs to track down Trenton."

Tandy pointed towards the wall. "He's in the next room."

Connor strode toward the door. "Checking on Randon and Susan?"

"No, puking his guts out."

Connor stopped. Held his arms wide, his eyes even wider. "He's sick?"

Tandy shrugged. It was practically a crime scene reunion right there at the hospital. "Yep."

"Of all the times to get sick."

"Hey," Marissa admonished. "You had your own stomachache last time I saw you. And that wasn't the best timing either."

Connor pressed his lips together as if knowing that to defend himself would be to start another argument. "True."

Tandy tilted her head with compassion filling her heart—for both Connor and Griffin. Nobody wanted to get sick. "The BBQ potato salad sat out too long in the sun. It had eggs and mayo in it."

Marissa scrunched her nose. "Gross. Poor little Lukey Griffin."

Connor breezed past. "Well, I'm still going to talk to him."

"I think he's connected to an IV and can't go anywhere," Tandy called after him.

Connor didn't slow.

Oh well. Tandy bugged her eyes at Marissa. She could follow or keep Marissa company. With someone trying to kill her friend, she should probably stay and play bodyguard. Though where would Marissa go when discharged from the hospital?

"Now what?" Tandy asked.

"I don't know." Marissa wrinkled her nose. "The safehouse is destroyed. Griffin can't protect me. And it's not like I could run away from any more danger." She pointed at her huge boot. "Though you wanna hear something crazy? I'm not scared."

Tandy blinked. She wasn't the one whose life was in danger, yet she was terrified. "Why not? You think Trenton set the fire, Griffin will send the deputy to arrest him, and all this will be over?"

Marissa's forehead wrinkled in thought. "I don't know. But I know God is keeping me safe."

Tandy studied the woman who really should be dead. "That is pretty amazing about the secret passageway."

Marissa nodded. "When God gave me the wedding dress..." She pointed to the bathroom door where they'd hung the gown out of Connor's sight for superstitious reasons. "He reminded me of the verse where it says He dresses the flowers of the field more beautiful than King Solomon and they never had to worry about where their clothes would come from."

An interesting verse coming from a clotheshorse like Marissa. Though maybe that's what gave it so much meaning.

Marissa held up a finger. "If you really read that passage, it's about fear. It starts out talking about how we aren't to fear man who can only kill the body but to fear God who has the power to destroy both body and soul in hell."

That was exactly what Zam had been saying.

"But that's where it goes into the verse about how we

shouldn't fear God because God loves us."

"Hmm." Tandy would have to think about that a little longer. Because Zam hadn't mentioned that part.

"Don't you see?" Marissa beamed. "We have nothing to fear besides God, but He loves us so much that there's no need to fear Him."

Tandy stilled. She'd never heard her friend talk this way before. Yeah, pastors said stuff like this, but only from their nice safe pulpits. Marissa had barely survived what was most likely attempted murder. She was living the idea of God's perfect love casting out fear. It was crazy to see. Like the apostle Stephen forgiving the very people who were stoning him as he died.

"You still need to be careful," Tandy warned. Marissa's fearlessness actually made her a little more fearful. And how did the fear of the Lord play into all this not-being-afraid stuff?

Marissa sank deeper into her pillow and smiled at the ceiling. "Remember when the Israelites accused God of rescuing them out of Egypt only for them to die in the desert?"

Tandy arched her eyebrows. She probably would have been one of those Israelites. "Yeah."

"Well, He didn't. And He won't."

A nice sentiment. But Tandy still wasn't going to leave her post.

Connor charged back in, followed by the sheriff dressed in a pale blue hospital gown and rolling a metal stand for his IV.

The sheriff's skin glistened with sweat even while he shivered. "Connor, you need to wait for Deputy Romero to investigate." What would normally sound like an order, came out like a plea.

"Right." Connor roamed the room as if looking for something. "Like we waited for Romero to investigate the attempt on Randon's life?"

Griffin sank into the chair Tandy had vacated. "We are following up on some leads. There's a process."

"Great. Keep following your leads. Meanwhile, I'm going to talk to Joseph Cross about his P.I." Connor clapped his hands together and looked at Marissa. "Where are your clothes, hon?"

Marissa turned wide eyes Tandy's way. Tandy rolled her eyes. How did she end up in the middle again?

"She can't wear that outfit anymore," Tandy offered.

Connor sniffed. "Yeah, I guess the trench coat and hat were a little much. Though they didn't keep Trenton from recognizing you when you snuck into town."

Griffin rocked forward in his seat. He gripped his forehead. "Please tell me I'm hallucinating and did not hear you correctly. Marissa, you did not sneak into town today, did you?"

"Uh…" Marissa scrunched her nose. "Kinda."

"Why?" Griffin flailed his hands, one knocking into the IV stand. The long metal pole crashed sideways onto the linoleum floor, tugging on the tubing taped to his arm.

Susan stood in the doorway looking down at it. Her rose pink hair slid away from her face when she lifted her chin. Concern flashed in her dark eyes. She had enough to be concerned about without having to worry about the sheriff's food poisoning or Marissa's fearless escapades. "What's going on?" she asked.

The room grew quiet as they all stared at the dark circles under Susan's eyes, her ashen pallor, and the puffy redness around her nose ring as if she'd been blowing her nose a lot. Even her wrinkled clothes hung loosely on her shriveled frame despite the pizza slice held in her hand as evidence of her appetite. Tandy's heart constricted. She hadn't gotten off to the right start with Susan earlier that year when she'd suspected the younger woman of killing her uncle, and it made her feel worse now.

"Susan, I've been meaning to come see how you're doing," she offered.

Susan met Tandy's eyes, hers as fearful as Marissa's had been confident. "I'm doing okay. Randon had movement in his right thumb this morning. I think he knows I'm here for him."

But did Susan know God was there for her? Hopefully Pastor Dave had shared as much. Or maybe Marissa would in her newfound boldness.

Tandy nodded and helped Griffin right his IV stand.

Susan's gaze landed on Marissa in bed. "Did you trip?"

Marissa twisted her lips at the phrase. "Yes," she answered, both honestly and ironically.

"She got attacked," Connor corrected.

Susan rocked backward. Like Rocky Balboa with one too many blows. "Is Cash Hudson out of prison?"

"No," they all said, almost in unison.

Tandy checked with Griffin to confirm. She'd know if Cash got out, right? Greg would know. And he'd tell her.

Susan gripped the door. "You scared me." If that scared her, Tandy sincerely hoped she wouldn't ask any more questions and find out what was really going on. She must not have known about the threatening note or Marissa's stint in a safehouse or anything other than the fact that Randon moved his thumb that morning, and she'd be better off if they kept it that way.

"There was a fire, and Connor thinks it was arson," Tandy gave the simplified explanation.

"Oh…" The young woman's gaze dropped to Griffin. "Were you attacked too?"

The corner of Connor's mouth lifted as they all waited for the sheriff to respond.

"Worse." Griffin grunted. "Salmonella in the potato salad."

Susan studied him as if unsure whether to believe him or not. "Are you still looking for an accomplice?"

The Sheriff leaned forward, arms resting on legs, head hanging as if too heavy. "The deputy will be running the investigation until I'm back at a hundred percent."

Tandy glanced at Marissa to see how she would take that news as she'd been creeped out by him earlier. She didn't so much as flinch, so either she'd turned all suspicions onto Trenton, or she really had some kind of newfound peace.

Connor, on the other hand, stood up. "I'll also be investigating. As soon as we get a new outfit for Marissa to wear, we're heading to Cross Enterprises to find out more about this detective he hired."

Susan studied Marissa again. "Are you up for that?"

Marissa's head rolled to one side. She smiled softly. "Sure."

Connor rubbed his chin. "She's on some pretty strong painkiller right now, but I'll get her home before they wear off."

Tandy lifted her chin in understanding. Marissa wasn't truly fearless. She was doped up. That made more sense. "I can take her home," she offered. "It's not like I can open for business until tomorrow anyway."

"Oh no." Connor crossed his arms. "She's not leaving my sight. I'm going to talk to Joseph Cross, so she's going with me."

Tandy smirked at the idea of Connor having to deal with Marissa when her drugs wore off. She'd be a good friend and help him out. Plus, she wanted to hear what Joseph had to say. "I'm coming too."

Chapter Eighteen

A DULL THROB DREW MARISSA'S GAZE down to her ankle. Though it felt like the flesh was being mangled, her foot looked perfectly safe inside a huge black boot currently propped up in the backseat of Connor's pickup. And she'd thought wearing cowboy boots had been a stretch, though she still had a cowboy boot on her good foot. It sat on the floorboards next to a pair of crutches she was going to have to use for the next few weeks. She'd rather pick them up and swing them at things like a baseball bat.

She grimaced as her gaze followed her bare legs up to denim shorts cut off so high that the pockets stuck out below the jagged hem. Then there was a giant skull printed on the front of a black tank top she knew for certain she hadn't picked out.

"Tandy, did you dress me?" she asked her best friend who rode shotgun next to Connor.

Tandy grinned over her shoulder. "I did, but those are Susan's clothes."

What was the verse Marissa had been quoting about how God dressed the flowers? Today she felt like a weed. "You didn't dye my hair pink and pierce my nose while you were at it, did you?"

"Of course not."

Connor caught her eye in the rearview mirror. "You look adorable, hon."

Marissa blinked slowly. If he liked this look, he should have proposed to Bunny. "I'm an urban pirate."

"Hey." Tandy chuckled. "That's a compliment. Except my biker boots would really go better with your walking cast than those cowboy boots do. I could let you borrow them."

Tandy thought she was being funny, but Marissa did not have the patience for humor. "I would rather die."

"Whoa. Okay. Though I hope you don't." Tandy shot Connor a look before facing forward.

Marissa turned sideways to watch out the passenger side window as the green cornfields flew by. Connor's parents would turn them into a maze for Halloween. She'd run through a field like that earlier, and it was a miracle she'd only sprained her ankle. While Randon had to stay behind at the hospital, she got to leave within hours of arriving. She should be grateful. But the pounding in her ankle reverberated through her whole body, and she had to let that tension out somehow.

Maybe she *should* have stayed in the hospital. She'd felt better when lying in their bed.

Connor's grey eyes flicked toward the rearview mirror again, searching for eye contact. "Are you comfortable back there?"

"I want to punch things."

Tandy covered her mouth, but Marissa knew she was grinning underneath.

"I really am becoming you, aren't I, Tandy? Did you sprain your ankle once and never return to normal?"

"Hey," Connor chided.

Tandy waved him down. "She can have more pain killer in an hour. I'll handle her until then."

Handle her? They should be feeling sorry for her. Trying to comfort her. Not "handle" her.

Marissa was the one who handled everyone else. She was the sweet and pretty one. At least she used to be. Now she didn't even know what she looked like. She had to be a mess after escaping a burning building and visiting the hospital. Were there twigs and ash in her hair? Scratches on her face?

How was she ever going to get ready for a wedding now? She couldn't do workout videos to lose weight. She couldn't tan with the boot on her leg. She couldn't even work to make money to pay for the wedding that was now fully her responsibility.

Tears blurred her vision. She looked out the rear window and blinked them away. "How am I going to serve tea?" Her voice cracked a little, but she'd blame it on all the smoke she'd inhaled.

Tandy's tone turned somber. "I have someone who can fill in for you until you come back."

The deaf guy who would make a great circus clown? That was her replacement?

Marissa's nose tingled with the threat of turning runny. She sniffed back her emotions. "What does Zam know about high tea?"

"Probably nothing."

But people loved him anyway. He put on a great show. Her customers might not even miss Marissa's knowledge and class. They certainly wouldn't miss her clumsiness.

She glared at the boot. Honestly, how had she ever made it this long in life without hurting herself when she fell?

Connor flipped on the blinker. "Did Greg ever run the background check on him?"

Marissa frowned in the rearview mirror at her fiancé. Was Connor suspicious of Zam? She hadn't heard about this.

"No." Tandy twisted her hair up into a messy bun. "I would have had him fill out the form this morning, but we were a little distracted."

Connor turned onto the side road, leading through a

grove of trees toward headquarters for Cross Enterprises by Joseph Cross's docks. The man owned everything from a shipping business to steamboats to a swanky retirement center. Having his computer files held ransom would really be a big blow. Marissa wondered how much he'd paid to have the files restored.

An uncomfortable thought wiggled its way into her subconscious. "If Mr. Cross's private investigator is the one who set the safehouse on fire, could Cross have hired him to do that?"

Connor took a deep breath and pulled into a parking spot by a fancy looking warehouse with two stories of glass offices above the first floor of loading docks and storage areas. Through an open garage door, Marissa could see one end of the steamboat float that had been in the parade the day Randon was attacked.

Connor shifted into park and turned off the ignition before twisting her way. "I've been afraid to ask such a question."

Tandy quirked her lips. "I hadn't thought of that. But what if Cross hired both the hitman and the investigator to throw suspicion off himself."

Marissa leaned her head against the warm, smooth glass behind her and stared at the roof of the truck. Her brain was so foggy from painkiller, this hurt to think about. Or maybe it hurt because she knew how much Billie liked the guy. Mr. Cross had been a suspect in a different murder, but that was before Billie had started dating him.

She sighed. "Why else would Trenton come after me?"

Tandy scratched her head. "Maybe it wasn't Trenton who set the fire. Maybe he leaked to someone that he'd recognized you and which direction you'd headed on the four-wheeler."

Marissa thought back to their interactions. Both when she

bumped into him on the sidewalk and the repetitive interrogation session in her tea loft. "He's not exactly forthcoming with his knowledge."

"Or maybe he didn't answer any of your questions because he had nothing to say that wouldn't incriminate himself," Connor suggested. "Cross doesn't necessarily have to be involved. Maybe Trenton and Cash Hudson were cohorts without anyone else knowing."

"That's a possibility," agreed Tandy. "Except for the part about Trenton's grandma saying she saw a woman leave the note on Marissa's door."

Marissa sat up straighter. "It was a woman?"

Connor shrugged. "According to a lip reader. Even if Zam is innocent, he could have gotten his information wrong."

"Hmm." Tandy reached for her door handle. "I really want to believe Trenton did it so we can have him arrested and go back to our normal lives."

Marissa grimaced in preparation of lifting her foot. "I'm going to make sure whoever is responsible for ruining my wedding goes to jail."

Tandy hung back as Connor helped Marissa maneuver up the ramp built for those who couldn't take the stairs. Though her friend looked cool in her edgy clothing, Tandy did not envy her position. If Trenton turned out to be innocent, and there was still a killer on the loose, where swas Marissa going to stay that night? She would endanger anyone who stayed with her.

Tandy wouldn't worry about it right now. They were here to question Joseph Cross about Trenton, and she needed to be on her A game.

After what seemed like forever, they reached the front doors. Tandy held the door open for Marissa and Connor to enter in front of her.

The icy air conditioning greeted them like aloe vera on a sunburn. Soothing. However, the rest of the atmosphere was not.

A sleek white reception desk remained empty, while groups of employees congregated as you would expect them to do around a water cooler, and others charged with purpose over the striped carpet.

Tandy looked around for anyone who might notice them standing there while Marissa swung on her crutches to a funky white chair in the shape of a leaf. Funny how Billie and her love of all things antique would fall for a business owner who seemed to prefer modern furnishings. If the two ever married, it would be interesting to see how they decorated.

Joseph Cross stormed down white stairs that were connected to the far wall but seemed to float in thin air. He was dressed for business in one of his three-piece suits but sported a golden tan that contrasted so starkly against his trim silver beard that it screamed vacation. A herd of employees, including security guards followed, making notes in their phones and nodding as he spoke. The only one who mattered was Trenton in his polka dot bow tie and matching suspenders.

Tandy would have to get Joseph Cross alone.

Cross barked orders. "I want everyone to submit a list of any missing items by closing time. I want all data backed up by our mainframe, and everyone to change their computer passwords."

She arched her eyebrows at Marissa. Apparently Cross had problems of his own. Maybe they were caused by Trenton too.

Connor stepped forward. "Excuse me, Cross. Could we speak with you privately for a moment?"

Joseph paused long enough to look between the three of them. He did a double take at Marissa's getup. Tandy would have laughed if the situation wasn't so serious. "This isn't the best time, kids."

Connor rolled his neck like he was popping it and getting ready for a fight. Tandy understood that he felt protective of Marissa, but nobody won a fight with Cross. Especially when security guards were involved.

She stepped in. "Is something wrong?"

Cross made it to the ground floor and continued past them through the lobby. "We had a break-in. And the sheriff won't answer his phone."

Tandy clicked her tongue. "He's in the hospital with food poisoning. Is there something we can do for you?"

Joseph pivoted to face her. "Food poisoning? Are you sure it wasn't intentional?"

Tandy blinked. "He's not the only one who is sick, so I don't think so."

Connor crossed his arms. "Why do you think he'd be poisoned? What's going on?"

Joseph motioned for Trenton. "Why don't you tell them? Earn some of that money I'm paying you."

Trenton shrugged his brawny shoulders, looking much like Tandy remembered the high school wrestling coach except for the outfit. The bowtie could be a disguise. He might simply be an average thug underneath.

"There was a break-in. Nobody knew about it until the morning shipment arrived. One of the garage doors was unlocked."

Tandy's spine shot straight. A break-in right after a ransomware virus seemed a little too close for coincidence.

"What was taken?"

Joseph snapped and pointed for a couple of his employees to get into action before he responded. "That's what we are trying to figure out."

Marissa spoke up from her spot behind them. "If nothing is missing, then how do you know there was a break-in? Maybe someone simply forgot to lock up."

Joseph glanced at her like she was an inconvenience. "That's what I'd hoped, but security footage has been wiped out for the time between one and three in the morning."

Tandy gasped. "The same way it was wiped out at the hospital when Randon was attacked."

Connor shook his head. "Mr. Cross, I think it's even more important that we have a private word with you now."

Joseph huffed then tilted his head toward what looked like a conference room with white desk chairs that had to be more comfortable than the one Marissa was currently occupying. "I'll give you five minutes."

He turned to lead the way, and Trenton followed as if assuming he would be included.

Connor stepped in front of him. "I mean we need to talk to Mr. Cross alone."

Joseph paused to assess Connor's stance. He must have seen whatever he needed to see because he waved Trenton away with the back of his hand. Then he led the rest of them into a glass room with greenery covering windows for a treehouse feel. "It's fine. I'll be out in a minute."

Connor stood at the door, waiting to let Tandy enter first. She joined Cross in the room and watched as Marissa swung herself their way on crutches. With as long as it took her, she'd probably never won any three-legged races during elementary school field day.

Trenton watched as well. He could very well know how

Marissa had been injured.

Tandy shifted uncomfortably at the thought. Marissa's crutch smacked the doorframe, and Tandy jumped. She took a deep breath to soothe her own nerves as Connor caught Marissa with an arm around her waist. He supported her until she was safely inside then swung the door shut behind them.

Cross tapped a pen on the table. "Why is it so important that we meet privately? What do you know that my investigator doesn't?"

Connor rested a hand on his fiancée's shoulder. "We think your investigator could be involved."

"What?" Cross turned to stare through the window at Trenton. The man stayed right where he was but straightened his tie. "Why would you think that?"

Tandy narrowed her eyes at their suspect. He'd have to be pretty sneaky to fool Cross.

Marissa slumped into a chair. "I received a threatening note. Someone doesn't want me testifying against Cash Hudson. The Sheriff put me in a safehouse to protect me, but it got burned down today."

Joseph eyed her leg. "I'm sorry to hear that. Did you injure yourself getting away?"

"Yes." Marissa's lashes lowered to hood her eyes. "But it could have been worse."

Tandy's stomach dropped at the thought. Some things were a lot worse to think about than a damaged oven.

The businessman's chest rose and fell. "I'm glad you survived. Now why do you think this has anything to do with Trenton?"

Tandy shrugged. "He's the only one who ran into Marissa in disguise at noon today. He's the only one who could have followed her back to the safehouse."

Joseph checked his watch. "Noon, you say? Then it couldn't have been Trenton. I called him as soon as we found out about the break-in. He was at the hospital, questioning Susan at noon, and it only took him a few minutes to get here. He's been here ever since."

Tandy sank into the seat next to Marissa's foot. Trenton had an alibi. So where did that leave them? "There could be a third person involved."

Joseph stuck the pen in his breast pocket. "You kids are looking the wrong direction."

Connor stared through the glass at the man he now had to cross off their suspect list. "I don't know where to look then. This was the only thing that made sense."

Tandy grimaced at Marissa. So much for getting a good night's sleep that night.

Joseph rubbed his whiskers. "If you believe all these crimes are connected, find what connects them."

Marissa looked up. Her eyes widened. "Computers."

Tandy tilted her head as if that would help her see the connection Marissa made. "How so?"

Marissa held up a finger. "Randon is suspected of the ransomware virus. He's a suspect because he's a computer genius. But whoever tried to kill him at the hospital was also able to hack into the security computers to destroy evidence. And same thing here today."

Tandy leaned forward against the table. "You're right. I wonder why they'd want to break in here. Do you think they left evidence behind from their cyber-attack and had to return to destroy it?"

Connor slapped his hands together. "That's what you should have your investigator looking for, Cross."

Joseph motioned for Trenton to join them. "I will, but since we never found the evidence the perps supposedly left behind, we'll never know if it went missing after this break-in."

Tandy quirked her lips. The criminal was ahead of them at every turn.

"You guys." Marissa's hushed voice drew their attention faster than a scream would have. "If our criminal is a hacker, then it's possible he hacked into the police computer and found the files on my safehouse."

Chills prickled up Tandy's arm. If the hacker could get into police files, then nothing was safe.

Chapter Nineteen

MARISSA FOUGHT THE SLEEP THAT ATTEMPTED to wash over her on the warm, lolling truck ride back into town. Drowsiness was apparently a side effect of her pain killers. Though the darn things eased the ache in her ankle as well as her armpits, which felt rubbed raw by her stupid crutches, they also made it hard to keep her eyes open.

If there was anything she needed to do, it was keep her eyes open. Especially since they were going to face off with the creepy deputy.

Okay, she wasn't really going to face off with him. She wasn't even going to accuse him of covering up for Moria or for framing Cash the way she wanted to. They were going to the police station under the guise of reporting the break in at Cross Enterprises and to warn the deputy that their computer system might be compromised.

The truck rocked to a stop. They were there already? As much as she would have appreciated a nap, at least now they could get this over with and she could go to bed early. Where she'd sleep, she didn't know.

Connor popped the back door open and she almost fell into his arms. "I got ya." He scooped her out by her tender underarms and helped her balance on one foot so she could drag out her crutches.

"What if I still have these at our wedding?" she asked.

He kept his hands at her waist until she was steady then kissed her on the back of the neck for encouragement. "You could get one of those knee carts. I'm sure Tandy and Greg would love to decorate it with a 'Just Married' sign and streamers."

The image made her want to laugh and cry at the same time. Or could that be another side effect of the drugs? A constant state of PMS. Tandy rounded the truck with a grin. "I could attach paper coffee cups to the back of it instead of the traditional cans used when decorating the getaway car."

Marissa swung her crutches forward, ready to get the day over with. "That isn't how I imagined my wedding."

"I know, hon." Connor followed.

"It's going to work out." Tandy fell in step beside her.

Marissa harrumphed. "Says the woman who gets to wear her black bridesmaid dress and eat the mocha cake she wanted."

Tandy grinned. "See? It's working out splendidly."

Marissa couldn't prevent a small smile from playing on her lips. "Just wait until I'm your maid-of-honor."

Tandy's face pinched together in mock pain as she opened the door. "Ohh…"

"Yeah, you didn't think of that, did you?" Marissa swung through the entrance. "Two words: Barbie pink."

Speaking of Barbie pink, Kristin stood up from her desk wearing a black t-shirt with a pink version of the American flag on it. If that was patriotic, what did it say about their country? "Connor. What are you doing here?"

Marissa lowered into the nearest chair. It was hard and plastic, but more comfortable than whatever it was that Mr. Cross had at his office.

Connor motioned toward her. "I'm helping Marissa track down the person after her."

Kristin glanced at Marissa then did a double take. "What happened?"

Marissa grunted and tried to put her leg up. Did nobody

in Grace Springs own comfortable chairs. "I escaped a fire."

"That's a relief." Kristin motioned to her leg. "But are you going to wear a walking cast in your wedding? You might have to postpone, huh?"

"I should be healed by then." She looked past Kristin to see how Deputy Creepy McCreeperson would respond. He was the real reason they'd come.

Romero glanced up from his computer and leaned against the back of his chair like he found both her outfit and predicament entertaining.

Connor crossed his arms. "Deputy, we're here to talk to you about who might have been trying to kill Marissa. The only person who saw her come out in public was Joseph Cross's private investigator, but he's been busy at Cross Enterprises ever since Marissa bumped into him. He couldn't have followed her back to the safehouse and set the fire."

"Hmm." The deputy flicked her a look of condescension. "The sheriff asked me to secure a new safehouse for you, Miss Alexander, but if it's true that you came out from hiding, I don't think we really have any responsibility to spend more government funding on your protection."

Marissa gave him her best blank stare. "Like I'd ever entrust my life to the likes of you."

He rubbed his bald head. "What's that supposed to mean?"

Tandy stepped in front of Marissa, blocking her view. "She means your computer system might have been hacked."

"Really?"

Marissa couldn't see the deputy's expression, but he sounded as skeptical as the opposing party in a presidential debate.

"Really." Connor crossed his arms. "If the attack on Randon in the hospital is connected with the break-in at Cross

Enterprises—"

"Break-in? Nobody reported a break-in."

They had now.

"And..." Connor continued as if uninterrupted. "They both involved hacking into security systems. Then whoever the perp is, he probably had the skills to hack into your computer and find out where the safehouse was located."

Marissa leaned sideways to peek around Tandy's legs to find Romero in a staring contest with her fiancé. Go Connor.

The deputy turned toward his computer, pretending he hadn't lost the stare down. "Do you want me to find you a safehouse or not?" he asked as if he had better things to do.

"We want you to find whoever is trying to kill her," Connor shot back.

Romero rubbed his face. "Sure. Fine. If you think this fire is related to the break-in at Cross Enterprises, then tell me about that."

The front door swung open. Troy strode in. Marissa's heart leaped with hope despite how his backwards baseball cap and basketball shorts signaled him to be off duty. His pert little wife followed, toddler on her hip.

Marissa waved to the shy little girl before looking up at Troy. "Did you find what started the fire?"

"Yeah, that's actually why I'm here." He ignored her as he spoke to Connor, Tandy, then the deputy. "The fire was caused by illegal fireworks."

Marissa's lips parted. Fireworks? They did cause a lot of trouble this time of year. But did that mean the fire was an accident?

"Likely some kids fooling around who took off so as not to get in trouble." He shrugged a brawny shoulder before focusing on the ground in front of Marissa. "We'll keep looking, but I didn't want you to worry someone was after you if they weren't."

Marissa leaned her head against the wall. She'd almost died because kids were playing with fireworks?

She should be relieved, right? This was good news. Except for the fact that while they'd thought they were hot on the trail of a murderer, they were really chasing their own tails. Unless the killer only used fireworks to set the fire to make it look like an accident…

Connor clapped Troy on the back. "Thank you for letting us know."

"Yeah," Kristin chimed in as if she had some personal stake in this. "Unfortunately, that doesn't help Connor get any closer to finding the killer."

"You okay, Marissa?" asked Troy. "I stopped in at the hospital after we got the fire out to check on you. Griffin was there and said you only had a sprain."

His wife cleared her throat. She had to be incensed as well. The nerve of Troy calling Marissa's injury "only a sprain." And Griffin was "only" a little nauseous.

This wasn't Troy's fault though. She lifted her head to give him a brave smile. "I got another boot for my shoe collection."

"Atta girl."

Troy's wife grabbed his hand. "Come on, babe. Hailey has been waiting all day to go to the pool with you."

Marissa waved again at the cute toddler. Maybe one day she and Connor would have a daughter like that. You know, if she survived all the fireworks the following night. Because apparently the patriotic holiday was out to get her.

Tandy grimaced as Troy and his family walked out. As much as she was glad nobody had hacked into the police computer in order to kill her best friend, she really, *really* did not want to turn around and admit they were wrong to Deputy Know-It-All. He wasn't creepy the way Marissa had thought. He was an arrogant punk.

"Maybe you don't need to go back into a safehouse at all," she offered as a consolation prize.

"I don't know." Connor's jaw softened as his eyes caressed Marissa's face. "There's still the matter of the threatening note."

"Put on the door by a woman," Tandy added. Did that make it less threatening or not?

"A woman?" Kristin echoed.

"Yeah." Tandy turned to face the deputy, hand on hip. If Griffin had been too sick to confront the deputy about his relationship to Randon's sister, she would. "Interesting that the only female suspect is Moria Evans."

Romero shook his head. "Not again."

"Yes again." Tandy argued. "Because now we know that you moved here to be closer to Moria Evans. You could be biased when investigating her. Or..."

Romero lowered his chin. "Or?"

"Or you're covering for her!" Marissa cried.

Tandy had planned to stop with the insinuation, but Marissa's drugs must have affected her filter. Though she'd probably been looking for an opportunity to make such an accusation.

Romero's dark eyes smoldered. "If I had the power to

protect Moria from anything, I would have done it by now. Her adopted brother died in my arms after an IED explosion in Iran. Her twin turns his back on her when she calls him on his ransomware virus. Her loser boyfriend is in jail for going after her twin. Princess here…" he motioned toward Marissa, "…let her go from the wedding planner position she needed in order to pay her bills."

Marissa held a hand to her heart. Good night. She was going soft.

The deputy continued as if once he found his voice, he couldn't be quieted. Or maybe he just had something to say for a change. "Don't you think Moria's been through enough without you claiming she's a killer based on some random informant telling you a woman left the note on Marissa's door?" He turned the full heat of his glare on Tandy. "Where did you get that idea anyway?"

Tandy sized him up. Was he being sincere about Moria? And had Griffin really not told him to question Opal again? "Opal lied to you. Zam read her lips at the coffee shop when she was talking to her grandson, the private investigator Joseph Cross hired. She wanted him to solve the crime before the police department."

Romero crossed an ankle over one knee. "Zam read their lips?" His eyebrows arched like question marks. "Is this Phillip Zamorano who used to own the bar in town?"

Tandy glanced at Connor. He'd wanted her to check out Zam's background. Well, now that she knew his name, she could. "I don't know his first name."

Romero nodded. "Deaf guy with a dog named Sheila?"

Connor snickered. "Sheila."

Kristin grinned at him as if sharing an inside joke.

Tandy shook her head. This wasn't the time. "Yes," she

answered the deputy. Her pulse picked up speed as she forced herself to ask one of her own. One his mocking expression told her she wouldn't like the answer to. "How do you know him?"

Romero rubbed a hand over his mouth. "I broke up a bar fight between him and Randon a month ago. He blamed Randon for the ransomware virus that destroyed his records and ultimately made him lose his liquor license."

Chapter Twenty

"I SUSPECTED THAT GUY ALL ALONG!" Connor declared on the way out the door of the police station. They were meeting Greg for dinner at Mama's Kitchen, which was a good thing, as Marissa hadn't had the opportunity to pig out on wedding cake for lunch the way Tandy had.

Marissa hobbled along, happy about appeasing her rumbling stomach, but unsure how to take the news about Zam. She didn't know him, so the pieces didn't all fit together so easily for her.

Tandy wasn't as thrilled as Connor. "I thought Zam was a new Christian. I thought that's why he left the bar industry."

"He probably told you that to gain your trust." Connor held the door open for Marissa to climb into the rear of the cab. Though with as high as the truck was off the ground and as low as her energy had gone, she couldn't hoist herself all the way up.

He squatted, wrapped his arms around her thighs, and lifted her as if she didn't weigh a thing. It would have been romantic if not for the throb in her ankle and the giant boot she was afraid could accidentally kick him when he sat her down.

"Hon, you don't have to be a witness anymore. You don't have to worry about being forced to start a new life away from our home."

She held his shoulders to steady her from tipping over. "I don't?"

"No." He lowered her gently despite his boyish enthusiasm. "If Romero arrests Zam, he can testify against Cash Hudson for a lighter sentence. Or Cash can testify against Zam if Zam's the one who hired him as a contract killer in the first place." Connor looked up to where Tandy opened the front passenger door. "That's how it works, right? We should ask Greg at dinner." He closed Marissa's door to climb in his own.

Tandy plopped into the front seat across from him, and slammed her door shut. "I'm not ready to declare Zam guilty. He seemed so sincere about believing in the fear of the Lord." She sighed. "But I guess he could have been as sincere as Marissa claiming not to be afraid for her life anymore when she was doped up on pain killer."

"Hey." Marissa would have frowned if she had the energy for it. "I may have been doped up, but I was sincere."

Tandy twisted in her seat. "You're not afraid of what man can do to you?"

She'd quoted that verse, hadn't she? Well it was a good verse. "If I was afraid, you think I would have risked my life to leave the safehouse and check on your wedding planning?"

Connor snorted as he started the engine. "There's a fine line between fearless and senseless."

Senseless? Really? Marissa let it go. Wow, these drugs really did help her relax. "You know what? I knew what I was doing. God loved me so much that He gave me a wedding dress, and why would He do that if I wasn't going to get a chance to wear it?"

"Hmm." Tandy studied her, the wrinkle between her eyebrows signaling deep thought. She wasn't feeling as loved.

"I'm sorry, Tandy." Marissa reached up and squeezed her shoulder. "I know you enjoyed working with Zam.

Looking back, can you see suspicious behaviors you might have overlooked?"

Tandy jabbed a thumb at Connor. "I know Connor did."

He nodded. "Yeah, I was right about him putting words in Opal's mouth."

Marissa had missed so much of the investigation. "You mean the part where he said a woman left the note on my door? Obviously, he was trying to throw suspicion off himself. Though if Griffin hadn't gotten sick, he probably would have had the deputy question Opal again. Or even Trenton. If that was a lie, Zam couldn't keep it going."

As for causing Griffin's illness, Marissa couldn't be sure how Zam would have pulled that one off. Leave eggs in the sun for a day? Sneak into the church and add them to the potato salad? Let a bunch of other people also get sick in the process?

Tandy groaned. "Do you think Zam was only offering to help at Caffeine Conundrum in order to point us in the wrong direction?"

Connor shrugged and turned a corner. "Or he could have been spying on you. You're getting quite the reputation as a detective."

Tandy gazed out the window. "He did only show up after he found out our connection to Randon at the pet costume contest."

Connor slapped the steering wheel. "That's right."

Tandy looked down at her lap. "He also pretended not to know about Randon. Now that I think about it, he once said Randon's last name without me ever telling him what it was."

Their discussion helped put all the pieces in place. Zam hired Cash Hudson. Zam threatened Marissa so Cash wouldn't fear going to prison and turn him in as part of a plea bargain. Zam tried to finish the job on Randon and had been there when Tandy found out about it. So he'd befriended Tandy to keep anyone from suspecting him.

Tandy had been betrayed by someone she considered a friend.

Marissa wanted to show her she had real friends. She'd be that friend to Tandy even if it meant risking her life. She wanted Tandy to feel the kind of love she felt.

With determination she nodded toward the rearview mirror to look her fiancé in the eye. "Connor, if you're right that I won't need to be a witness anymore, then I'm going to go ahead and tell Griffin now. That way he won't have to waste any time trying to find me another safehouse, and I won't have to worry about someone trying to kill me to keep me quiet."

Connor pulled to the curb on Main Street and twisted to face her. "I support your decision one- hundred percent. Though maybe Tandy should stay with you until Zam's arrested." He pulled the keys from the ignition. "Is that all right with you, Tandy? I mean I'd let her keep Ranger again, but I don't know that she wants to."

Marissa nodded at her friend. "He has a point." Also, they'd never had a sleepover before.

Tandy's blue eyes zinged her way. "What if Zam's not guilty?"

Marissa waited for Connor to tug his door handle, hop out, and close the door before sharing her plan.

"We're going to find out for sure if Zam is guilty or not," she assured her friend. "Without me as a witness, the police can't keep Cash in jail. So as soon as he gets out tomorrow, we'll follow Zam to see if they meet up."

Tandy held her gaze, eyes darkening. "And if they don't?"

"Do you really believe they won't?"

Tandy faced forward. "At least I'll be able to believe it because I've seen it with my own eyes."

"Exactly."

When Tandy agreed to Marissa's crazy scheme, she hadn't realized how hard it would be to work with Zam the next day at the Red, White, and Brew booth. While she suspected him of attempted murder, among other things, *she* felt like a liar and backstabber.

He grinned at her. "Okay, I'm going to toss both these mugs over my head. I'll catch one behind my back, and you'll catch the other. Then I'll turn, reach around you, and flip my cup under your arm to catch it in my opposite hand."

He made it sound so simple, but she was kind of glad it wasn't. This way she could completely concentrate on the juggling routine rather than on her frayed nerves. "Right. Then we'll both flip our mugs in the air, spin, and catch them."

Zam sipped his iced coffee through a straw in one hand while he flipped the mug in his other. Without spilling a drop, he grabbed a second mug to juggle one handed. Though she thought that impressive, it was nothing to the way he lowered his drink to the counter and began juggling two mugs in the second hand as well.

A crowd of early birds formed around the coffee stand Connor had painted completely in chalkboard paint. Marissa had drawn chalk art on one side with their drink prices and patriotic designs then left the other side blank for patrons to draw on while waiting for their brew.

"Three...two...one..." Zam counted down before a mug flew through the air toward her head. Perhaps this was how he was going to take her out. It could at least give her a concussion.

Or not. She gripped the smooth porcelain and swung around as planned to prevent herself from sustaining injury. Then she got into the act, flipping and spinning before sticking her final pose to the sound of cheers and wolf-whistles.

Zam bowed. "Who will be our first customer today?" He scanned faces for a response. A couple of teens stepped forward.

Tandy returned to her regularly scheduled program—slinging drinks and taking payments. The crowd didn't let up and neither did the heat. It was only going to get busier as the day progressed. All leading up to the fireworks show their town was known for.

Greg stole her for lunch. "Are we trying donut burgers or gumbo tater tots or fried gummy bears? And more importantly, why is Zam still working with you?"

Tandy glanced over her shoulder at the guy filling a little paper cup with whipped cream for a customer's dog. "What am I supposed to tell him? That it's only a matter of time until Griffin is healthy enough to make an arrest?"

Greg tugged her behind a food truck to sit at a picnic table. He slapped a folder on the table in front of her. "Well, I did a background check, and it looks like this won't be the first time Zam gets arrested."

Tandy's heart plummeted. Memories of Zam's sermon on the fear of the Lord came flooding back. She'd told him he spoke like someone who had been the bad guy before. *Haven't we all?* he'd asked. She should have known then. Though her heart still didn't want to believe.

Twisting her lips to one side, she flipped the top of the folder open. Zam's DUIs started as a minor. Drug dealing.

Armed robbery. Larceny.

Greg pointed to addresses. "It looks like he lived in Cincinnati. Was probably part of a gang."

Tandy pictured a younger Zam. His likability would have made him good at selling drugs, though that probably only added to his problem. "He must have gotten clean at some point."

"Tandy." Greg tilted his head in compassion. "I know you. What's going on?"

Tandy closed the folder. "I'm from Cincinnati too, Greg."

"Hence the tough girl act."

She looked away. "When Mom left, my dad turned to alcohol. Sometimes he went on bender's for weeks. I had to take care of him."

He reached for her hand. Dear, sweet, perfect Greg. The guy who'd lived her summer vacation life year-round. How could he possibly understand?

If they were going to have a chance at a future, she'd have to be honest about her past. The same way she'd been honest with Marissa about setting the oven on fire. Now her beans were perfectly roasted and ready to spill.

Her heart shivered as she bared it. "If someone offered you a place to live but said there would be a time when they needed the favor returned, would you accept their offer?"

Greg's eyes twitched as if confused why this was even a question. "No."

She took a deep breath and met his gaze. "What if your only other option was to live on the streets?"

Greg's jaw slackened. He nodded in understanding. "You did some things you didn't want to do out of fear."

That same fear trickled down her spine, cold and consuming. "I did."

He squeezed her hand tighter. Hanging on like it was his

job to protect her now. Like he wished he could have protected her then. "You got out."

She did. She came here. To the town she'd visited before her bad memories were made. "I'm a success story. Success means leaving everyone else behind. No good leaders are left in the hood. Nobody with morals. Only the drug dealers and gang leaders and slum lords. Which leaves everyone else weak and defenseless." She lifted her gaze. "They take advantage of kids. They probably took advantage of Zam."

Greg released his tight grip to run his fingers along her arm. "This is a whole new world to me. I've never thought about life from this perspective."

Tandy bit the inside of her cheek. "I'm glad you haven't had to."

"I'm sorry you did." His eyes flashed with a silver flare of concern. "It's just that Zam's not there anymore. He got out too. And if he hired a hitman and threatened your best friend, then he's making those choices for himself."

Tandy's stomach churned. She'd also been judged when she first arrived in town. It seemed to be standard for small town folk. But she'd seen the best and worst of both worlds. "I don't want to assume he's a bad person because he made some mistakes in the past."

"I admire you for that."

His words eased the knot in her gut. He didn't judge her for what she'd been through; he respected her for what she'd come out of.

If only she'd known this kind of love back then. The kind that saw her at her worst and loved her anyway.

Yeah, Zam was right about how she didn't need to fear man, only God, but he'd missed this second important lesson. He'd missed what Marissa had learned at the safehouse. He'd missed the part about how perfect love casts out fear.

"Thank you." Her voice cracked.

Greg pulled her hands together then lowered his lips to brush over them. "I'm going to buy you that donut burger now. Then I'll go check on Griffin and see where he's at with an arrest warrant. I want justice for Zam either way, but since Cash was released this morning, my priority is to make sure you're safe."

Tandy understood his viewpoint, as well. But she was still torn. She wanted Zam to be a Cincinnati success story as much as she wanted Grace Springs to be safe again.

She wanted Cash to go to jail. She wanted Susan to stop eating like she was at the Americana Festival every day simply to cope with the possibility of more attempts on Randon's life. She especially wanted Marissa to be able to sleep in her own home. Because, good night, that woman had a bedtime routine that would have rivaled Queen Esther's twelve months of beauty treatments.

So she and Greg ate donut burgers together, then she went back to work while Greg joined Connor and Marissa in getting henna tattoos and playing carnival games. Greg returned to check on her from time to time, bearing hand-crafted jewelry and a balloon animal bouquet.

All the while, Zam poured drinks like a barista Olympian. Hope swelled in Tandy's chest that he wasn't going to get a call from Cash after all.

After dinner Marissa reappeared on her crutches. She sank into the folding chair Tandy had brought to the booth but hadn't had a chance to use. "The guys are watching a comedian, and it's standing room only. I need to sit."

Tandy poured strawberry basil iced tea into a glass mason jar and handed it to her.

Marissa sipped. "I have taught you well. If I'd known I was going to get this kind of treatment, I would have hobbled over here sooner."

Zam flipped a customer's change into the air before handing it over then spun to face his bosses. "Hey, Marissa. I'm sorry to hear about your ankle, but I'm also glad for the work. Are you safe here?"

Marissa sipped serenely while studying him. "What do you think?"

He grinned at Tandy. "Your partner is the only one I know who sets things on fire, so you are on very dangerous ground."

Tandy snorted. "Thanks."

Marissa motioned to the booth. "Things going well? Besides Tandy trying to burn down our shop?"

"Very well. Watch this." He stepped away, tossing a mug before Tandy was even ready.

She dodged and gripped it in time to prevent it from crashing to the ground then automatically went into her spin and flip. It became easier every time. Made her want to learn more tricks. Made her sad that the next time Zam got to perform this, he might be in prison. Though if he'd hired a hitman, she really shouldn't be sad for him.

But maybe he hadn't. He'd worked all day without distraction. Maybe Cash had already reunited with his real partner in crime.

A vibration whispered over the carnival music and carnie calls. Zam set his glass down and reached for his back pocket. He pulled out his phone and squinted at the screen.

Tandy's stomach cramped.

Marissa looked up at her. "Does he get many texts?"

Tandy wanted to hush her friend, but since Zam had turned his back to them, they were free to talk as loudly as they wanted without concern of being caught.

Tandy didn't want to talk about him at all. She wanted

him to teach her more juggling tricks. "No. But that doesn't mean anything."

Zam turned around to face them. "Since most people are going to head to see the fireworks soon, do you mind if I take off now?"

Tandy couldn't meet his eyes. The guy may be a lip reader, but surely he was also as attuned with expressions. And hers would undeniably read disappointment. She busied herself with mixing cold brew coffee with Mexican Coke over ice. "That's fine." He didn't move, so she stuck an American flag toothpick in a cherry and added it to the drink. "Happy Fourth."

He waited a moment longer before saluting. "Happy Fourth."

Tandy lifted the bittersweet mixture to her lips and chugged until her line of site was high enough to watch Zam's retreating back.

Marissa flipped their sign from "open" to "closed" and locked the cash box in a cabinet. "We're going to have to hurry to keep up."

Chapter Twenty-One

TANDY SPRINTED AHEAD TO KEEP WATCH on Zam in the dimming light. She'd hide herself around corners and wait for Marissa to join her. Thankfully he didn't seem to be in a hurry. Or was it unfortunate? Because with the way he kept looking around, he was obviously waiting for someone.

He paused outside a large trailer marked Mirror Maze.

Marissa announced her presence by bumping into Tandy. She slumped with her armpits on the padding of her crutches. "I hope that's where he's supposed to meet Cash because I don't think I can go much farther on these things."

Tandy did a double take. "You want him to meet Cash in the maze of mirrors? We could get lost in there."

Marissa's eyes widened. "It would also be a great way to spy without Zam seeing. And even if he did see us, it would only be a reflection. We'd have time to escape."

"I know you like your reflection, Marissa, but…"

Marissa slapped her arm. "He bought a ticket. Let's go."

Tandy spun around to watch. Sure enough, Zam scanned his surroundings then took a step through the entrance.

Marissa swung her crutches forward and took off with renewed vigor. "Do you think he was looking for Cash, or do you think Cash is already in there and he was checking to make sure he wasn't followed?"

Tandy shook her head at both the question and the situation then trotted to catch up. "It would actually be a good place to meet up in secret." Everybody else was headed to the high school football field to watch fireworks, and anybody who did see Zam and Cash together in the maze might be too busy trying to get out to even notice.

"Right." Marissa stopped at the entrance to reach into her pocket for tickets. "Have your camera ready to film him because I can't use my camera and crutches at the same time."

Tandy dug into her back pocket for her phone then swiped the screen to camera mode. Her heart jittered. Maybe she shouldn't have chugged that Coke with coffee. Caffeine and anxiety were not a good combination.

Marissa nodded for her to enter. "You enter first," she whispered. "I don't want to trip you with my crutches."

Tandy crouched down to keep out of Zam's line of sight. Though Marissa wouldn't really have that option with the crutches holding her upright. "I'm going in."

She took baby steps through the entrance. Techno music blared around her and neon lights kept changing the atmosphere of the maze. Red felt angry. Blue felt eerie. Green felt like a sci-fi movie.

She stopped at the first corner to peek around. A million Tandy's peered back.

Marissa tried to see over the top of her. "Did you spot him?" she whispered.

"No." Now where? It was like someone who looked exactly like her blocked her path in every direction. She reached out a hand toward the smooth glass and finally found an opening. "This way."

They made slow progress. Slower because Marissa hobbled behind her. Zam wouldn't have been this slow. Maybe he'd reached the exit already.

A thought struck her. She looked over her shoulder at Marissa. "What if he saw us following and only led us in here to lose us so he could go meet Cash somewhere else?"

A hand touched her from behind. She jumped and spun,

hands out like she was prepared to fight kung fu even though she still held a phone in her hand.

Marissa stood in front of her. Apparently, the Marissa she'd been talking to was only a reflection. The real Marissa eyed her hands. "Were you going to karate chop me or threaten to take a bad picture of me and post it on social media?"

Tandy's pulse settled back into a manageable elevated state. "Which would scare you more?" she challenged.

Marissa nodded at her phone. "The bad pic."

"I'll keep that in mind."

Marissa pointed forward, if indeed the direction Tandy had been facing would lead them forward and not into a mirror.

Tandy nodded and resumed her reach and creep technique. They'd have to turn another corner. This was taking forever. "I bet he's out by now."

Zam appeared, his face lit up green like an alien. "Who?" he asked.

A scream burst from Tandy's lips. She turned and ran directly into a warm body.

Zam gripped her shoulders, in front of her for real this time. She'd run from his reflection. How had she not considered this scenario when deciding to sleuth in a mirror maze?

His gaze pinched harder than his grip. "Why are you following me?"

"I...uh...wanted to practice more juggling. Catch!" She tossed her phone in the air.

Zam released his grip.

Tandy spun and charged directly into Marissa, smashing her against another mirror.

Marissa's head thunked into the glass. She grunted. "I

think I'd prefer the bad Instagram pic post to being trampled."

Tandy pushed against the mirror and scrambled to balance herself in order to help right Marissa's crutches. She'd have enough trouble escaping Zam through the maze by herself. She'd never be able to get them both out. She needed another plan.

Zam scratched his cheek while watching her from every angle. It was like she was surrounded. "Here." All the Zams held out the phone towards her.

She lifted her hands, ready to protect herself, then twisted around to see if she could figure out which image to be afraid of.

The cool rubber of her phone case brushed her arm. She whirled to face the man who held it.

He tilted his head and squinted. "Are you afraid of me?"

She ripped the phone from his grip. "My fear is in the Lord." Yeah. She threw that back in his face. How dare he quote scripture to her while plotting to kill her best friend.

He dropped his hands to his side. "Then what are you doing following me around?"

Marissa righted herself and faced the wrong Zam. "We know what you did."

Good night. Were they going to have it out right in the middle of a carnival attraction? Might as well get Marissa to address the real man.

Tandy tapped her friend's shoulder and pointed to where Zam stood. "I don't think he read your lips because you're facing the wrong direction."

Marissa took a moment to move her crutches and reposition herself. She finally looked him in the eye. "We know what you did."

Zam held out his hands. "What?"

Okay, this had gone on long enough. "We know about your bar fight with Randon."

Red light intensified Zam's profile. "You do?"

If things got out of control, it would be two against one. No Cash here to help in a fight. Yet.

"Yeah." Tandy crossed her arms. "You claimed you gave up the bar when you became a Christian, but really Randon made you lose your liquor license. Then you lied to me about not knowing who Randon was."

Zam stuck his hands in his pockets. "You're right about how I lost the bar. That was my low point. That's where I turned to Jesus."

Another lie. Tandy threw her head back and laughed. "If you truly believe your fear should be in the Lord, then why pretend you weren't angry at Randon? Why lie to me?"

"I didn't." Zam ran a hand over his thinning hair. "Randon wasn't behind the ransomware attacks. He told me he had proof."

Marissa shook her head. Zam had to be guilty. Otherwise she'd backed out of being a witness for no reason. Cash would be released from jail to meet up with his co-conspirator, and she was following the wrong person.

But no. She wasn't ready to give up. "If Randon didn't do it, then why did someone want him killed?"

Zam crossed his arms, looking more contemplative than guilty. "Because Randon figured out it was Cash who'd been using the ransomware virus."

Tandy turned wide eyes Marissa's way as if questioning whether they should believe the guy. She obviously wanted to.

Marissa scrunched her nose. Even if Zam was guilty, it might behoove them to play along until they got free of the maze and could call for help. At this point, Marissa was even willing to call Deputy Romero. Her ankle throbbed, and they were going to miss the fireworks if they didn't wrap this up soon. "You're saying Cash is the computer genius behind the hacking? Nobody hired him, he simply did it on his own?"

"Exactly." Peaceful blue light washed over Zam, trying to trick her mind. "That's why he took Randon's computer."

Tandy shifted her weight. "Where did the computer go? He must still have had an accomplice."

Marissa bit her lip. "His girlfriend had to be involved. I was right all along."

Tandy lifted her chin in understanding. "You're right. Because she claimed her falling out with Randon was over his ransom attacks."

Zam nodded, watching them put the pieces together. "Yes. I've been looking for her but haven't seen her anywhere. You'd think someone with pink hair would stand out in our small town."

Marissa's thoughts jolted to a stop.

The wrinkles in Tandy's forehead reflected around them, mirroring Marissa's confusion.

She spoke slowly as if easing on the gas to keep the wheels in her brain from spinning out. "Why do you think Cash's girlfriend has pink hair?"

Zam looked back and forth between them. "Because they came into my bar together a lot."

Marissa covered her mouth, allowing a crutch to clatter against a mirror. Tandy righted it for her.

"Zam." Tandy took a deep breath. "The woman you're talking about is dating Randon."

Marissa nodded. "She's been at the hospital with him

ever since he got attacked."

Zam looked from where he was reading her lips to study her eyes. "You mean she was at the hospital when there was a second attempt on Randon's life?"

Marissa gasped. Could it be?

Tandy snapped her fingers. "She was on the float in the parade that passed Cash at the same time Cash's t-shirt, gun, and Randon's computer disappeared."

Marissa's heart crashed into her chest. "She would have left it to come running back to the coffee shop to pretend to mourn over Randon..."

"So she would have had to break into Cross Enterprises to get it off the float."

Zam's gaze ping-ponged to keep up. "And if Cash is the computer genius we think he is, he could have given her directions on how to hack into the security system and destroy evidence."

Tandy closed her eyes, her temple twitching. "She would have had to sneak past the front desk at the hospital to do all that, but it wouldn't have been hard with the receptionist. Especially if she kept ordering food as an excuse to leave the room."

The truth of their situation gripped Marissa's gut like a fist. "When I left the safehouse, Susan could have seen me from the hospital window. She could have followed me back and set the fire with fireworks on purpose."

Tandy rubbed her face. "Then what was up with Randon's sister? Is she involved? Did she ever date Cash?"

Marissa blew out her breath. She really wanted to believe Moria did it, but she could have been as much a pawn as anyone. "Cash is from Cincinnati where Susan is from. What if they have a history together?"

Tandy's chin bobbed like she was following along.

"Susan's dad had a past of crime. It wouldn't be too far off to suspect that she'd run into some other shady characters."

"Randon wooed Susan right away. If she had a history with Cash, he might have been jealous and researched Randon to discover they could take advantage of his brains."

"Meanwhile, Cash dated Randon's sister to get her to finger him for the crime."

Zam nodded. "Randon is innocent. Cash and Susan used him and orchestrated this whole thing."

Tandy lifted her chin. "If this is all true, then who texted you? Who were you going to meet, and why did you trap us in here?"

Zam reached for his pocket.

Marissa jumped, gripping her crutches to use as a weapon. She may not be able to get away, but she could defend herself.

Zam held up one hand to calm their nerves and moved slower when retrieving his phone. He tapped the screen then held up his messaging app for them to read.

YOUR DOG IS GROOMED AND READY FOR PICKUP.

"I signed up for the Americana Fest discount. I wanted to get Sheila home before the fireworks started. Then I saw you two in the mirror outside the maze and stopped here to see what you were up to. You were never in any danger."

"But Randon is." Marissa leaned back against a slick wall in both relief and dread. The weight from all Zam's revelations was too much to bear on one leg.

Tandy grabbed her arm. "Come on. We need to get to the hospital before Cash does."

Marissa eyed Zam before shifting forward. Just in case he'd made all this up, she wanted to stay behind him. "You go first. I don't want to slow anyone down."

Zam's eyes narrowed like he knew she still suspected

him, but he stepped forward without argument.

Tandy leaned close to whisper to Marissa before following Zam. "I want to believe Zam, but I pressed record on my digital voice recorder before putting it in my pocket to be safe. If anything looks suspicious, cover your mouth so Zam can't read your lips then whatever you say will be recorded for later."

Marissa opened her mouth to say she approved the precaution, but Zam looked back so she pressed her lips together.

Zam dropped an eyebrow but kept leading them through the maze until they reached the dark night and gentle breeze. Marissa inhaled the sulfur scent of fireworks, glad to return to a public area. Not that anyone still hung around the carnival when the show was beginning. The first pop of an explosion could be felt though the air.

Zam must have felt it too. Or maybe he saw the bright lights raining down from above. Because he looked up, completely missing the click of a gun being cocked and Cash stepping out from the shadows of the trailer.

The man's green eyes zeroed in on Marissa for the first time since she'd seen him attack Randon. She couldn't run this time. Her heart lurched into her throat. If he hurt anyone else, it would be her fault.

Chapter Twenty-Two

Tandy gasped. "You jerk."

Cash extended the barrel of his gun toward Zam's back and stopped her with a warning glare. "One move, and he's gone."

Zam stood unaware, arms relaxed to his sides, face turned toward the fireworks beyond. He casually glanced over his shoulder to see if the girls were ready to go, caught sight of Cash and staggered sideways before catching his balance. His wild eyes bounced from face to face to read the situation.

Tandy squeezed her hands into fists but forced herself to wait for a better opportunity. Cash hadn't shot anyone yet. Maybe he wanted something from them. Maybe she should want something from him…something like a confession. She did, after all, have her phone recording this conversation.

"So it was you, Cash Hudson." She made sure to pronounce his name clearly. "You hacked Cross Enterprises, set it up to look like Randon was responsible, then you tried to kill him with the belief that investigators would assume the hit had been made for revenge."

"Stop talking." Cash scanned their surroundings.

So much for the confessional idea.

The few employees in the area had their faces turned toward the sky. Not only would they be unable to hear the conversation going on, but any gunshots fired would likely be mistaken for fireworks. If nothing else, Tandy could at least stall until the show ended. Then, hopefully, if Cash fired his gun, there would be witnesses. "What do you want?" she asked.

Cash tilted his head past the bright lights of the carnival toward the dark part of the park where Tandy had first met Zam at the pet contest. "We're all going to head toward the gazebo. Unless you don't mind your new friend here taking a bullet for you."

Marissa met her gaze, dark eyes steady. She wiggled her crutches as if pointing out that she had big wooden sticks in her hands. What was she going to do? Knock the gun out of Cash's hands? If so, they'd have a fighting chance. But Marissa wasn't known for eye/hand coordination. If she missed, they could all be killed. Best to wait for the overhead explosions to cease fire.

Tandy lowered her chin as if in submission and lead the way slowly through the openings between trailers.

"That 'a girl."

Marissa huffed and followed, her extra appendages helping to block the phone in Tandy's back pocket. To Tandy, the device felt huge and obvious, much like the tell-tale heart Edgar Allen Poe once wrote about. She had to play it extra cool not to give herself away.

She glanced over her shoulder to see Zam follow them into the shadows. He looked down only long enough to step over electrical cords, but his gaze zeroed in on her once again.

Cash nudged him with the gun to his back. A reminder not to try anything.

Tandy's stomach roiled. "How did you know where to find us," she asked. "How did you know we'd figured you out?"

"Keep going to the gazebo."

"Why, what's at the gazebo?"

"Shut up."

Tandy's steps grew heavier. Is this what it was like to be led to execution? Would she be better off fighting here even if there was nobody to help? It was dark except for the flashes from overhead. If Cash couldn't see as well, they might have a better chance to escape.

A dim blue light glowed ominously from inside the gazebo, but no gang of ghetto computer geeks awaited them. It was still the three of them against Cash. They could…

A dark shape passed in front of the light. There was someone else there.

"Susan?" Marissa had seen it too.

"I'm sorry," a little voice responded. "This was never my intention. I only wanted money to go to college."

"It's their own fault, Susan," Cash's voice growled from behind them. "If they'd minded their own business, it wouldn't have come to this."

"Minded our own business?" Marissa trilled. "You came into my shop and chased me with a gun. How is that possibly my fault?"

Susan's shadow morphed into the shape of a body as they continued their march forward. Though Tandy had been angry at Susan earlier that year when the pink-haired visitor had hired Greg to defend her dad in court, she hadn't expected the other woman to do something else where she'd need an attorney.

The younger woman wouldn't even meet Tandy's eyes now. She glanced halfway up a couple of times, but mainly kept her gaze focused on the open laptop sitting on the ground in the center of the octagon shaped platform. What did the laptop have to do with anything?

"Don't listen to her, Susan. You know I was only trying to get Randon's laptop since he'd put a virus in the code he designed. None of this had to happen."

Yes… Tandy was getting Cash's explanation on audio. She'd try to keep Susan talking. "Were you dating Randon for the code, Susan? Is this the code that Cash used to take control of company data in exchange for ransom?"

Susan glanced at Cash. "I liked Randon. I did."

"Oh my gosh, Susan," Cash snarled. "He betrayed you."

Tandy snorted. "Who betrayed who? Randon is the one in a hospital bed."

Zam's gaze still zinged around, but how much of this could he possibly be getting? It had to be hard to read lips at night. He was in the dark, literally. But she needed him if her plan was going to work.

Susan stood in front of the computer, wringing her hands. "I just want to go to college."

"You're going to college, Sue." Cash's impatience did not make it sound like he had any concern for her goals at all. "As soon as we're done here, you'll be able to go anywhere you want."

"What exactly are we doing?" Tandy wanted to know.

Cash motioned with his gun for Zam to move toward the computer. "Zam is going to log into Randon's computer and download a virus into the computer systems of five major airlines. If only one of them pays the ransom, Susan here will be so rich she doesn't need to go to college."

Tandy's heart clenched.

"But Cash…" Susan's voice whimpered. Had she known this part of the plan?

"What happens to those who don't pay the ransom?" Tandy asked to make sure the cute little twenty-something knew what she'd gotten herself into. "There are planes in the air right now. What happens to their computer systems?"

"It depends on whether they pay the ransom or not."

Susan gasped.

Tandy focused on her. On the fear Cash used against her. Tandy needed to create a bigger fear to get her on their side. "This isn't simply wanting to go to college anymore, Susan. This isn't protecting your boyfriend from prison by trying to suffocate Randon or pinning a threatening note to Marissa's door or setting a fire with fireworks. This is terrorism."

"No," Susan argued, though her voice faltered. "They'll pay. They won't even lose any money because they have insurance. Nobody will be hurt." The words came out like a tour guide spouting off a script.

"What about us?" Tandy asked. "You don't think we're going to be hurt?"

"Do what you're told, and you'll all be fine." Cash extended his arm fully toward Zam. "Sit down and enter the password I tell you."

Susan covered her mouth.

Zam continued to look around, unsure what was going on. Probably unsure that he'd even been issued an order.

"Hey dumdum, he can't hear you," Marissa pointed out. "And it's too dark to read lips."

"That's a lame excuse." Cash kicked the back of Zam's knees.

Zam buckled then regained his composure, turning to seethe at Cash.

Cash enunciated every word. "Sit down, or you'll die."

Marissa moaned. "You're setting him up, aren't you? You want the police to think he did all this."

Cash pointed at the computer screen again. "He *is* going to do all this."

Tandy strained to see Marissa's eyes in the dim light. "Then we'll be witnesses. And we know what Cash and Susan do to witnesses."

"You're going to kill us anyway?" Marissa screeched. She

turned on Susan. "After all I did to help you when you moved to town, you're going to kill us?"

"I don't want to." Susan shook her head. "Cash, I don't want to go to college that bad."

"Well, do you want to go to jail?"

Susan whimpered. "No…"

Tandy had the evidence she needed. Slowly, she reached for the phone in her back pocket. If she could send her recording to Griffin, he might be able to find them in time to prevent Cash from killing anyone. Heart thumping, she waited for Cash to look at Zam so she could hit send on the audio file.

"All you have to do, Susan, is be quiet so I can explain the password to this idiot. When the police find the computer with him, they'll suspect him of the girls' deaths. Your conscience will be clean."

The man had no conscience. Tandy shivered and hit send then clicked Griffin's contact info. Done. Susan's eyes met Tandy's for the first time, their whites flashing with terror in the pale blue light. The same terror sent ice through Tandy's veins. For Susan had seen what she'd done.

The girl watched her without moving. She was in a tough position. She had been since birth, having grown up in a home with a car thief for a dad. She'd been introduced to scum like Cash. She'd tried to find her identity with tattoos and piercings and pink hair, but she had a longing for something more. This guy had taken advantage of her. Did she know she could say no to sin at any time? She could choose the fear of the Lord at any time. She could not tell Cash what Tandy had just done.

Tandy gave a small lift of her chin. An invitation to have a truly clean conscience rather than trying to hide the truth from herself any longer. For that had to be what caused the dark circles under Susan's eyes and emptiness in their depths.

The girl's lips remained still. But the phone in Tandy's hand buzzed. If Griffin was calling, she needed to answer. Stealthily, she tilted her phone to see the screen. A giant red exclamation point proclaimed her file too big to be sent.

Now what? She was empty handed. Though not as empty handed as when she'd tossed her phone at Zam in an effort to escape. It hadn't worked then, but if the four of them worked together, they could use their strengths against him. Four including Susan, who had to be on their side since she hadn't told Cash about the text she'd sent.

"Cash." Tandy laced her tone with ridicule, so he wouldn't suspect he was being played. "If you want Zam to know what you're saying, you'll need to have Susan shine a light on your lips."

"Tandy," Marissa hissed. "Don't help him."

"I just don't want him to kick Zam again."

Zam stood still in the center. His gaze lifted to hers. She needed to hold that gaze. Keep his eyes on her.

Cash cursed. "Let's get this over with. Susan, do you have a flashlight app on your phone?"

Susan sniffed but reached for her cell and tapped the screen. A beam of light sliced across the wooden planks then traveled up Cash's body to his ugly sneer. "Zam, look at me," the man said.

Zam kept his eyes on Tandy's.

Tandy gripped her phone. It was risky, but she had to take the risk before thousands of plane computers went dark. She was afraid for her life, but she was more afraid for all the other lives that hinged on her actions. "Even if Zam enters your password and you kill us, Cash, you're still going to jail. Because I recorded everything you said."

She hit the arrow icon. The recording of Cash's voice

echoed through the darkness: "One move and he's gone."

Her own voice came out with more control than she felt. "I'm sending this to the sheriff."

Cash swung his gun her direction. Every nerve ending jittered. But she soothed them with the knowledge that she'd prepared for this moment.

The fireworks overhead fizzled away. The roar of a crowd erupted.

With a prayer to the only One Tandy had to fear, she tossed the phone in the air.

Marissa's mouth dropped open at Tandy's bold move. Why would she reveal her trump card that way? Cash could simply shoot them all and take the phone before police ever found it.

Except Zam caught it, flipped it, spun.

Cash's gun darted his way.

Zam whisked the phone back toward Tandy. She juggled like a clown, then tossed it to him again.

Cash's gun swung back and forth like a contestant at a carnival game. Except if he fired, there would be bloodshed that would be hard to explain in his setup of Zam.

"Blind him, Susan," Tandy yelled.

The beam of light spotlighted Cash's fierce glare, but only until it forced him to pinch his eyes shut.

That was the cue Marissa had been praying for. She dropped one crutch, lifted the other like a baseball bat, and swung for a home run.

Cash went down hard. His gun clattered away. He scrambled after it.

Marissa's heart jerked. God wouldn't bring her this far

only to let her and thousands of innocent plane passengers die. She couldn't believe it. But she'd used all the tricks up her sleeve. It wasn't like she could race across the gazebo with a sprained ankle. All she had left now was the power of prayer, and that was enough.

Zam's sneaker smashed onto Cash's extended hand. He bent forward, retrieved the gun, and stood tall to point it at Cash. "I used to dream about this moment," he said.

Marissa's stomach clenched. Was he going to take revenge into his own hands? He certainly had reason to. Cash had ruined Zam's business and tried to make him responsible for acts of terrorism.

Susan tripped backwards to the ground and crab walked until she hit the gazebo railing.

"Zam," Tandy said, though he wouldn't be able to hear.

He leveled the weapon on Cash. The man rolled away but hit the railing on the opposite side from Susan. He pushed to a seated position and gripped the posts behind him.

"The man whose business you destroyed wouldn't hesitate to pull this trigger." Zam's voice was hard. Cold. Controlled.

This must be why Connor had suspected him. Maybe Zam's God talk was an act after all. He had befriended Tandy in order to gain this very opportunity.

Tandy shook her head slowly, but she was behind him. Her motions still had no impact.

"Lucky for you, I'm not that man anymore."

Marissa's abs released. She tipped sideways on her good foot and caught herself on the railing in order to sink down to the ground where Susan cowered. She reached for Susan's trembling hand.

Zam continued. "As crazy as it sounds, I believe God

allowed you to destroy my company. I believe what you intended for evil, God has used for good. I know my battle was never against flesh and blood, and I will pray that is a lesson you learn for yourself while behind bars."

A sob shook Susan's body. Tears rained down and splashed warm against Marissa's skin. She reached over and hugged the young woman closer for comfort. The very woman who'd used fireworks to try to burn down her safehouse. The reason she was in a walking cast.

But would they have been able to win this battle if Marissa hadn't had her crutch with which to strike?

"I'm so sorry," Susan mourned. "I'm so sorry."

"Shut up, Susan," Cash hissed. "This was your idea. This is all on you. You're going to be the one who goes to prison."

Susan shook harder. She looked up at Marissa, her wet face shiny in the blue light. "Am I going to prison?"

"Yes," Marissa told her, compassion clenching her throat. Somehow more words came out. More words she hadn't planned to say. "But that doesn't mean your life is over. You still get to choose everyday how you'll live. You can still choose to turn your life around the way Zam did."

Susan buried her face in Marissa's shoulder, weeping like she would never stop. Marissa didn't know whether she was weeping for herself or in remorse for the sins she'd committed, but she had a feeling God wasn't finished with the woman.

"Tandy," Zam barked, gun still aimed at Cash to prevent his escape. "Call Deputy Romero."

Chapter Twenty-Three

TANDY STUFFED A WARM BITE OF crumpet into her mouth. It was a little rubbery and a little spongy but comforting in a weird sort of way. And the homemade blackberry jam gave it good flavor. Definitely not as bad as she'd expected.

She'd been so glad to have a new oven in the shop that she'd happily agreed to eat whatever Marissa baked. And Greg was so happy to have her safe and sound after he found out what Cash had done, that he'd only left her side so she could sleep.

He sat next to her in the shop at that moment, but after fireworks and police paperwork the night before, he'd invited both Connor and Marissa over to join them for a soak in his hot tub that overlooked the river. This was one of the joys of having a successful boyfriend, though knowing Cash was behind bars is what truly helped them relax.

Connor seemed to be just as relieved as Greg, following Marissa around on her new knee cart so he could carry trays to and from the oven and such.

Greg watched with an amused smile. "Connor makes really good crumpets."

"I heard that," Connor yelled from the kitchen. "If you like those, you'll love seeing me in my new apron."

Tandy chuckled.

Zam hadn't overheard Greg's comment but he smiled at her from behind the counter. He juggled mugs for Joseph and Billie as part of preparing their drinks, and Tandy had a feeling the townsfolk would never want to see him go.

Greg sipped his coffee. "I can't thank that guy enough."

Tandy scooted closer to snuggle against his side. "Who would have thought learning to juggle would save my life?"

"Only our loving Creator could have orchestrated such events."

Tandy was still in awe. "In God we trust."

Marissa rolled out of the kitchen on her knee cart and crashed into their display rack. Bags of coffee beans plunged to the floor. Connor followed behind to pick them up.

Tandy cringed. "I'm pretty sure giving Marissa a scooter was *not* a good idea."

"I'm already preparing to defend her against future lawsuits."

"Do the benefits of dating you never end?"

Greg kissed her nose.

Marissa rolled to a hard stop in front of them. "Ready to go visit Randon?"

Tandy took a deep breath. It had been days now since his attack. It didn't seem fair that they should make it out alive if he didn't. "Yes."

Greg stood and helped her to her feet then checked on Zam. "You got this?"

Zam waved them out. "I ran my own business for years. This is a piece of cake—the kind that doesn't start a fire in your oven."

Tandy followed Greg toward the door, but on her way, she faced Zam, opened her mouth in a wide O shape and holding up three fingers on each side of her face to look like Ws. WOW.

He winked like a wise old bartender turned barista should.

She was going to enjoy having someone to take over for her when she wanted to get away from time to time. Though visiting a patient in the ICU wasn't her idea of a getaway.

At the hospital, the receptionist buzzed them through without even looking up from his baseball game, and there was no security guard at the door to show their IDs anymore. They entered the room silently. Except for Marissa, of course, who crashed into a tray table.

Moria looked up from a seat in front of the bed, her sapphire eyes surrounded by puffy skin. Romero stood above her, a hand on her shoulder. He'd probably been thrilled to explain to her how her "boyfriend" had only used her as a cover for being in town. Whether Cash had told her the lies about Randon in order to get revenge on the guy for dating Susan or whether Cash had needed the rumors started to get away with the crime he'd planned, Tandy couldn't be sure.

Romero nodded a greeting, which was friendly for him. Perhaps he'd forgiven them for accusing him of murder since they were the ones who'd freed Moria to date again.

Tandy followed Greg around to the other side of Randon's bed. Connor and Marissa followed.

"Wouldn't he be surprised if he woke up right now?" Marissa asked.

Moria gave a small smile. "He woke up this morning."

Tandy's heart expanded in surprise. "Really?"

Greg wrapped an arm around her shoulders, joy written all over his handsome face. "He could have saved us a lot of trouble if he'd woken up a few days sooner. I'm going to have to have a talk with him when he wakes up again."

"Oh yeah?" A raspy voice whispered from the bed. Randon opened dark eyes underneath a white bandage circling his head. Tubes of oxygen still stuck out from his nose, but for the first time since Tandy had known him, he hadn't seemed too concerned with his appearance.

She clasped her hands together. She'd never imagined

she'd be so happy to hear the hipster millionaire speak. "Randon."

Marissa waved Greg off. She owed Randon big time. "Don't listen to him. The boys are upset they left us alone to get into trouble again. But if not for you, Randon, I wouldn't have been around to get into trouble. You saved my life."

"I wish I could claim to be a hero, but I can't." Randon focused droopy eyes on Marissa. "I'm responsible for Cash trying to hurt you."

Marissa blinked. She hadn't expected either Randon's confession or his humility. "What do you mean?"

"When Susan told me her ex used to hack into the Department of Transportation to help her dad steal cars to impress her, I told her that I'd once shut down the Ohio Power grid to win a bet. She wanted to know if I'd asked for a ransom, which I hadn't. That's when she said I probably wouldn't have been able to anyway. I designed the ransomware virus just to prove I could."

Marissa's lips parted. What a crazy way to try to get a girl. Though he probably knew that now.

"It wasn't until my bar fight with Zam that I realized my code had been used. I planted a bug in it to keep it from being used again. And that's when Cash came after me." He gave a sad smile then turned toward Greg. "I'm sure there will be legal repercussions, but I'm simply glad to be alive."

As long as Randon had learned from his mistakes, Marissa had compassion to offer. "I'm glad you're alive too."

"Um..." Moria spoke softly. "You're not the only one who believed the lies of the person you were dating."

All eyes turned her way.

"I'm really sorry I believed the worst about you, Randon." Her chin puckered and her eyes brimmed with tears. "I'd already lost so much time with my brother, I can't believe I willingly gave up more."

Randon's hand slid slowly across the top of his thin blanket. Moria's hand met his halfway and clasped it.

He shrugged then grimaced before looking up into her eyes. "I'm sorry I didn't listen to your warning. If I had, I would have avoided all this."

The unlikely pair didn't look anything alike, but they were twins in more ways than one. Hopefully they'd continue to call each other on their faults and grow together like only they could. Marissa's heart softened toward them both. Plus, she could really use a wedding coordinator.

"Hey, Moria." She quirked her lips to one side and waited for the woman who should have been her twin to look up. "I found a new wedding dress, but it's going to need some repair. I figured with the way you got the blood out of my last dress, you might be able to help with it. Is my wedding date still open on your calendar?"

Moria's eyes widened in surprise. She looked Marissa over from head to scooter, a small smile playing on her lips. "You're definitely going to need my help."

Marissa stood in front of the gilded oval mirror at As You Wish Weddings. The gown still fit beautifully, but there were some rips in the lace and scorch marks from ash. It obviously needed work, but she wasn't going to back down no matter what Moria said.

Tandy stood next to her for the fitting of her black dress, which turned out was the exact color Marissa had accidentally ordered. And it really wasn't that bad. Marissa could picture her maid-of-honor holding sunflowers and standing in front of a red barn. The image was so perfect that she didn't know what she'd complained about.

As for Moria, she circled Marissa, lips pursed in thought. She was probably trying to think of a tactful way to sell Marissa a new dress. She stepped back, dropped her arms, and shook her head. "It's you."

"Wh…what?" Marissa blinked. Did they actually agree on something?

Tandy grinned at Marissa's reflection in the mirror. "It's you," she repeated.

Moria motioned toward the mirror, as if that should say it all. "It's beautiful, and I can't think of another style that would complement you more."

Marissa lifted the hem off the ground, revealing her walking boot. "I might trip since it's not tea length."

Moria laughed. "I'm sure Connor will catch you."

"That's what he said." Marissa grinned. Maybe Moria wasn't that bad.

The bell on the door rang behind her.

Moria's smile slipped. "I want your big day to be perfect. That's why I invited your mom to join us. Every bride deserves to have her mother here for her."

Moria was pure evil.

Marissa bugged her eyes at Tandy for help.

Tandy shrugged, not shocked at all. She'd known about this? "I'm going to help Moria get some refreshments from the back," she said before disappearing.

Marissa closed her eyes. When she opened them, her mom's reflection appeared over her shoulder. Though it held a strange expression that she couldn't quite place.

Mom looked her daughter up and down. "Oh, Marissa.

You're exquisite."

Marissa cocked her head. She'd never heard those words from Mom before. And she especially hadn't expected them when she was wearing an old dress that needed a lot of cleaning.

Mom circled to her front and reached out to lift a floaty lace sleeve. "Where did you find your grandmother's dress?"

Marissa sucked in a breath, tightening the bodice across her chest. Why did Mom think this was Grandmother's dress? "I found the dress in the safehouse where I had to stay."

Mom's hands snapped back to cover her mouth. Her wide eyes studied Marissa's face in alarm. "You were in a safehouse?"

Why did Mom care now? "Yeah. I told you my life was threatened."

"I thought you were simply being dramatic." Mom shook her head. "I didn't realize your life was in danger. Did they catch the person after you?"

"Yeah." Marissa had figured her parents had at least read about it in the newspaper.

Mom lowered her hands to clasp over her heart. "What would have happened if they hadn't?"

Marissa glanced at her mom. Was this some kind of act so Mom could reclaim her role as mother of the bride? "I would have had to go into the witness protection program with Connor."

Mom's face crinkled despite all her many Botox sessions. "I would have lost you."

Marissa studied the strange expression and even stranger behavior. "You didn't seem to mind losing me the last time you walked out of here."

"I..." Mom motioned to Marissa. "I..." She covered her

mouth with her hands. "I was afraid of someone seeing me as less than the respectable woman I've worked so hard to become."

Marissa barely refrained from snorting. What was respectable about trying to control her only daughter with money?

"See..." Mom fingered her sleeve again. "My own mother went into the witness protection program before I was born. But it was because her dad was part of a biker gang. When he went to jail, he became an informant, and her life was threatened."

Numbness washed over Marissa. How was this information supposed to make her feel? Because it only felt unreal. Mom was supposedly all about proper breeding. "Your grandfather was in a biker gang?"

Mom looked down, nodding in shame. "Yes, though I never met him. I never met any family beyond my mother. I was a nobody." Her eyes lifted, brimming with years of pain and fear. "So I worked really hard to become a somebody. I competed in beauty pageants. I married into the Alexander family. And I'm so afraid I'm going to mess it up."

The protective shell around Marissa's heart melted away. Her mom had made poor choices out of fear. But now she had a greater fear. The fear of losing Marissa.

Perfect love casts out fear. Marissa had the chance to join God in loving her mother despite her selfishness and the heartache she'd caused. She reached for her mom's hand.

"Sometimes I'm afraid of messing up too," she said. "But then I mess up anyway, and the people who love me just keep loving me."

A smile cracked her mother's face, releasing tears to rain onto their clasped fingers, warm and wet. "Really?"

Marissa mentally scrolled through numerous examples.

Her eyes caught Tandy in the back room. "Yeah. For example, I accidentally ordered Tandy's dress in black then I blamed her for trying to sabotage my wedding."

Mom blinked rapidly, her lashes drying the tears like a fan. "Your maid of honor is wearing black?"

Marissa laughed. "Yeah." This would be a good test as to whether Mom really meant her apology or not.

"Oh, baby," Mom hugged her like she really was a child she wanted to protect. "I'll keep loving you in spite of that mistake if you can love me even though I haven't been here for you the way a mother should."

Marissa closed her eyes and held on. Love conquered fear once again. "My dress is the one that really matters. Do you think it actually belonged to Grandma?"

Mom slid back to look her up and down again, radiating a kind of beauty she'd never had before. "I've only ever seen it in photographs, but my mother said it was specially designed for her grandmother and passed down through generations. She lost it when she went into hiding. This has to be it."

Marissa turned to stand side by side with her mother and look into the mirror with even more awe. Somehow they both looked more beautiful than before.

Tandy strolled in and leaned against the glass counter. She popped a grape in her mouth. "Did I overhear that your great-grandfather was in a biker gang?"

Marissa sighed with contentment. This was a fact she'd never expected to find out about herself, yet it didn't affect her the way it once would have. Knowing she was loved unconditionally had that kind of effect. "Yes, but don't offer to let me borrow your biker boots to wear with this dress."

Tandy grinned. "You said it, not me."

Marissa shook her head. "Urban pirate."

"Hey." Tandy held out the edges of her skirt. "My dress is the color of coffee, which is perfect for a wedding."

Mom shuddered. She still had a ways to go, but at least they were going to go together.

Marissa lifted her chin to challenge her best friend. Her wedding was going to be perfect in spite of Tandy's dress. "How can you possibly think a coffee colored dress is perfect for my wedding?"

"Because." Tandy smirked. "Love is brewing."

Marissa wanted to hate it, but she couldn't. Not after the week they'd been through. Love covered a multitude of sins.

As Moria returned with a silver tea tray, Marissa plucked a porcelain cup and held it high. The wedding planner was proving to be useful at more than simply fixing the wedding gowns Marissa had ruined. She waited for the shop owner, her mother, and her maid of honor to all pick up their own teacups. One day soon, Tandy would be toasting her and Connor. For now, she wanted to savor the moment and the women who stood beside her through all life's difficulties.

"I'll drink to that."

Author Note

Dear Reader,

I hope the town of Grace Springs is starting to feel familiar to you the way it is to me. I love bringing together all the crazy characters for local events, and I especially enjoyed creating the Americana Fest as I got to write it during the month of July.

I had fun researching everything from pet costume contests to bartending tricks to ransomware. My husband, Jim, works in IT, so he helped me with the ransomware.

He also inspired the beginning scene where Marissa tracks the attempted killer from the top of the roof, relaying his location over the phone to Sheriff Griffin. Jim and his coworkers did this very thing when there was a bank robbery next to his office. They were able to watch from their window and direct law enforcement officers to where the suspect was hiding.

The other story of real-life inspiration comes from my brother-in-law's dog, Baby, who has experience with Happy Tail Syndrome. We returned to his house during a visit to find blood splattered everywhere, and my imagination ran wild. How could I NOT put it in a mystery novel?

As much fun as I had, I wanted my mystery to include a message as well. In my own life, I've been wrestling with understanding the idea of the fear of the Lord, so I looked at it from a writer's perspective. It's an author's job to give our main character a fear at the beginning of the book that they must overcome by the end of the story, and the way we do that is to give them a *bigger* fear. This idea affected me powerfully.

For example, Marissa is terrified of not having her mom's approval at the beginning of the story, but in the end, she overcomes by replacing that fear of displeasing her mother with the *bigger* fear of settling for an unhealthy relationship. And that's how I think the Author of Life designed for us to fear Him. All our other fears can be overcome when our greatest fear is separation from His presence.

Learning this lesson can benefit our lives, and it will definitely benefit our spunky heroines in the next book when Marissa's wedding takes them to Connor's family corn maze in the middle of what my daughter calls "spooky season."

If you want to join me in the creation of such mayhem, join my Facebook fan page, write a review on my books, and sign up for my newsletter at www.angelaruthstrong.com. You won't want to miss the party because, I'm tellin' ya, we party like librarians on coffee beans.

Overflowing,
Angela